Aloha
from...
Hawaiʻi

LEI
AND THE
FIRE GODDESS

BY MALIA MAUNAKEA

Penguin Workshop

PENGUIN WORKSHOP
An imprint of Penguin Random House LLC, New York

First published in the United States of America by Penguin Workshop, an imprint of
Penguin Random House LLC, New York, 2023

Text copyright © 2023 by Malia Maunakea
Illustrations copyright © 2023 by Penguin Random House LLC

Jacket and interior illustrations by Phung Nguyen Quang and Huynh Kim Lien
Chapter and postcard illustrations by Shar Tuiasoa

Visit us online at penguinrandomhouse.com.

Library of Congress Cataloging-in-Publication Data is available.

Manufactured in Canada

ISBN 9780593522035   10 9 8 7 6 5 4 FRI

Design by Mary Claire Cruz

This book is dedicated to anyone who:

☑ *Has*

☑ *Ever*

☑ *Questioned*

☑ *Which*

☑ *Box*

☑ *To*

☑ *Check*

☐ *Other (please specify)*

You don't have to prove anything.

You are enough.

Curses Aren't Real

Curses aren't real.

Anna repeated the mantra to herself as she spotted Tūtū on the far side of the Hilo airport terminal.

"Leilani!" her grandma called as she made her way down the escalator. The big, smiley wrinkles around her tūtū's eyes and mouth had multiplied since last summer.

Anna mustered up a weak grin, trying to hide her crankiness. She had asked her grandma not to call her by her middle name the last time she was here. But her grandma had just said, "Pah, you don't even know what Anna means, why would you want to be called that?" Then her best-friend-in-Hawai'i, Kaipo, had whispered, "I told you it wouldn't work." Anna groaned because she had to buy him a pack of dried cuttlefish for losing their bet.

She waved at her grandma but stood firmly planted atop the escalator, instead of rushing down like she normally did. She needed time to go over her plan—a plan she'd tried to come up with when she wasn't staring at a tiny movie screen on the two planes it took to get to Hawai'i from Colorado.

It was all part of the deal Tūtū struck with her parents when Anna was too young to have any say. Mom had a job offer that let her use her physics degree at a climate-research company in Boulder, and though they were reluctant to leave their home in the islands, they'd be able to afford a better quality of life in Colorado with the income Mom's new job promised. Tūtū was crushed that her only grandchild was being taken so far away, so she made her son and daughter-in-law swear to send Anna back to visit her for just shy of a month every year so she "wouldn't forget her history." Tūtū claimed to have tried to teach it to her son, Anna's dad, but for all his writing out of the family tree, he said he just couldn't remember their roots. So it was up to Anna to memorize the stories. To become the keeper of the moʻolelo.

She was twelve now and knew—KNEW!—Tūtū was gonna make a big deal about what that *meant* in their family. It was annoying, having these random extra responsibilities attached to an even randomer birthday. Thirteen? Sure. Finally becoming a teen was pretty massive. Or better yet, sixteen and having extra responsibilities that go along with being allowed to drive. But twelve? Random.

Even more annoying was how her parents had forced her to review the moʻolelo and history factoids since her birthday. Dad even had quizzed her in the car on the ride to the airport, saying hopefully the solid foundation would make it easier for her to absorb the new stories Tūtū had in store this summer. Whenever she brought up doing something else with Tūtū, he liked to remind her that she had it easy by repeating things like, "When I turned twelve, I was supposed to recite our family tree from the beginning. I only managed to remember back to the early eighteen hundreds, so she gave up on me. You're lucky you just need to learn the stories." He wasn't going to help her out of it. She needed to convince Tūtū on her own.

Anna scratched the webbing of her backpack strap as she waited her turn to step off the escalator. The long flight gave her brain plenty of time to replay on a loop what had happened with Ridley. The last month without her friend had been the absolute worst ever. It was like showing-up-with-her-shirt-tucked-into-her-underwear-level awful on a daily basis. The final nail in their friendship coffin had been the horrible volcano incident.

They were finishing their geology unit right before spring break, and her science teacher, Ms. Finwell, asked, "Can anyone tell me why the Hawaiian Islands are formed in a line?"

They barely ever talked about Hawai'i in her Boulder school, so Anna was pumped to share what she knew. Her hand flew up, words spilling out of her mouth before she was even called on.

"The fire goddess, Pele, used her 'ō'ō to dig down deep and find a new volcanic crater to call home," Anna proudly explained. "She's on Hawai'i Island now, and people make sure not to make her mad."

Snickers immediately erupted around her, and Hennley Schinecky coughed "freak" behind a perfectly manicured hand. Heat blossomed in Anna's cheeks, and she sank lower into her seat, regretting her outburst.

"Class." Ms. Finwell had clapped her hands together to get them to settle. "Okay, that could be a theory. Thank you, Anna." She nodded at Anna and offered a tight smile before looking around the room. "That doesn't really tell us why they're in a line, though."

Anna squeezed her eyes shut and wished she could disappear.

"Yes, Ridley?"

Ridley lowered her raised hand and sat up straighter. "The tectonic plate that the islands are on is moving slowly in a northwest direction over a hotspot. Magma comes out of that hotspot and forms the islands. That's why they are in a line, with the oldest being in the northwest and the youngest in the southeast."

"Precisely! Very good."

Anna peeked at Ridley in time to see her best-friend-on-the-continent's proud smile at Hennley's approving nod and hair toss. That was that. The deal was sealed.

Before lunch, Hennley's flock, with their perfectly matching sneakers and perfectly parted hair, swarmed Ridley. Anna'd been held up changing after PE and had no idea that she really should have skipped the paper-towel wipe down in favor of speed that day.

By the time Anna got to the cafeteria, Ridley was at Hennley's table, the one closest to the doors where everyone would see them. Anna stood there like the ultimate fool, blinking and holding her sack lunch, before ducking her head and hurrying past the loud laughter to the empty table near the stinky trash cans.

Their plan going into sixth grade had been "New School, New Cool." They were in middle school, and Ridley was determined to find the right group of girls for her and Anna to hang out with. Now the year was over, and it seemed like Ridley had succeeded. Anna had not.

Anna blinked hard, the sound of rain on the airport's metal roof bringing her back to the present, and she shivered, grateful to be in a hoodie and jeans. The painful memory of her mistake was slowly healing, but like a newly formed scab she couldn't stop herself from picking at. Why hadn't she just kept her big mouth shut? It was *science* class, not mythology. She should have focused on the facts. And the facts stated that curses, legends, and all of Tūtū's gods and goddesses weren't real. Maybe then she'd still have Ridley.

Ugh. This summer's trip had to be different.

Anna checked her phone. Two new messages had appeared in reply to her letting her parents know she'd landed.

> **MOM:** Be respectful and help with dishes!
> Love you, sweetie!

> **DAD:** 😄 🩶

Anna analyzed the text. Dad liked to communicate in memes and emojis. Unfortunately, it made it tough to understand him at times. This one probably meant he was celebrating that she landed in Hawai'i and loved her. Nothing new from Ridley, and she didn't click on her friend's name again. She had the last message Ridley had sent her memorized, burned into her brain.

> **ANNA:** Are you going to go to the BoardRider retreat this summer

> **RIDLEY:** Im going w H to Paris

That was it.

No crying emoji at missing the camp they'd been going to together for the past five years at the end of every summer. How was Ridley going to get in shape for the winter snowboarding season?

And who was Anna going to tell all about this trip during their end-less cross-training runs?

And, seriously, she didn't even act excited about a trip to Paris?!

No "OMG can u evn BELIEVE" that they could both squee and gush over.

No "I really like you more, but Mom is having me expand my horizons."

Nope. She was going to freaking Paris with freaking Hennley, and there was zero chance Anna and her Hawaiian stories could ever compete. Well, maybe not zero. But it'd take some major con-vincing of Tūtū to change her plans. Which was exactly what Anna was going to do.

Anna stuffed her phone into the side pocket of her backpack. She straightened her spine, squared her shoulders, and prepared to go head-to-head with her grandma to earn a summer that would make her the equivalent of Paris chic in the eyes of Ridley.

Anna stepped off the escalator and weaved between groups of people reuniting, her ears filled with cries of joy and happiness. Tūtū draped a sweetly scented pīkake lei over Anna's head so it hung around her shoulders.

"Welcome home," she said as they gave each other a kiss on the cheek and a huge hug, smashing the lei between them, Tūtū's Ha-waiian bracelets jangling in Anna's ear.

Anna closed her eyes and inhaled deeply, her mind skipping back along the memories of previous trips to Hawai'i Island over the years. The familiar scent wafted around her, and a real smile stretched her cheeks. It *was* good to be with her grandma again, even if this wasn't home.

"Where's Kaipo?" Anna asked, scanning the crowd for her friend's wavy black hair. What if he'd ditched her like Ridley did? What if he suddenly got cool, too, and didn't want to hang out anymore? She chewed her lip. She could hardly remember a summer here without him. Maybe it would have been a good idea to call him a couple of times over the year to stay in touch. But she'd never had to do that before, and he'd always been here every summer when she returned, ready to pick up where they left off.

"He wanted to wait in the car," Tūtū answered. Relief flooded Anna. "You know how he gets with crowds. Oh, he told me to give you these as soon as I saw you." Tūtū rummaged through her huge purse for a minute, then pulled out a bag of li hing mui gummi bears. "He knows how *you* get after the long flight."

"*Yesss*," Anna said. She immediately ripped the bag open and popped a yellow one in her mouth, savoring the salty-sweet combo. One of the best things about her visits back here was the food.

Thank goodness Kaipo was still her friend. He was her grandma's neighbor and Anna's constant companion on these trips home—a friendship born of convenience that grew into something solid. More recently, he always seemed to know what Anna needed, sometimes even before she did. Gummi bears, distractions from Tūtū, a listening ear, knowledge of the best trees to climb. All the necessary things. Where things back home seemed to change all the time with invisible rules Anna never really understood (why did Ridley suddenly care about having the same shoes as Hennley and her friends?), Kaipo was constant. Reliable. And he rarely wore shoes, so he'd ignore that cool-school-shoe rule, too. She didn't know what she'd do if she were stuck here all summer without him.

Tūtū guided them through the breezy, open-sided building over to the baggage claim. Some of Anna's dark waves escaped her ponytail and stuck to her neck in the oppressive humidity. It always took a little bit to get used to the feeling of practically drinking the thick air here at sea level compared to her mile-high home.

"Tell me everything, Leilani," Tūtū said. She was holding her elbow as if being physically connected would speed up the process of getting reacquainted after a year apart. "Whatchu been up to? So good to see you. You taller than me now!"

Anna's ears adjusted to her grandma's pidgin English. She took a deep breath. Time to jump in.

"I'm good!" she started, words flowing in a torrent. "It is so great to see you and be here again. Thanks for the lei." She paused to take a deep, appreciative inhale, enjoying this last bit of peace before coming at Tūtū's world like a wrecking ball. But maybe breaking things down meant making room for new traditions. Surely Tūtū would agree that new isn't always bad, right? Only one way to find out. Putting a lid on the jar of butterflies in her stomach, Anna pressed on. "So I was thinking, you know how we usually hang out around the house for most of the time? What if we went over to Kona and did some touristy things on the cheap? Like, checked out some of the cool resort pools or followed a snorkel tour at a discreet distance or something? Wouldn't that be fun? Kaipo could come, too. We could do something interesting for once." Oh shoot. That last sentence was too much. Anna slammed her lips together and hoped she didn't just blow it.

"You don't think things are interesting here?" Tūtū asked, glancing at Anna as the carousel of luggage chugged slowly around.

Anna kept her eyes trained on the bags, looking for her silver suit-case with the rainbow strap. "Pah. You should hear about Pele's lat-est curse. She went swallow one guy whole!" Then Tūtū changed directions with lightning speed. "Hoooeee, you're twelve now." *Called it on the age thing*, Anna thought, shoulders drooping. Tūtū continued, "You are old enough to start really memorizing our moʻolelo. All the parts of our family history. Even some parts I never tell you about yet. Needed you to be old enough. Things going get interesting for you."

"Well, they would if we could have a real vacation," Anna mut-tered. She didn't so much as blink at Tūtū's claim that the fire god-dess had cursed a guy. Anna was used to Tūtū's tales of Hawaiian gods and goddesses.

"Eh? Try talk louder, Leilani," Tūtū said.

"Never mind, Tūtū. But, you know, just because I'm twelve doesn't mean things are going to magically become interesting in Volcano." Tūtū might think being older meant being able to handle more stories, but what it *really* meant was having to juggle all the expectations of being who people wanted you to be and cramming the *you* that you really were deep down into a little box or risk losing your friend forever. Anna kicked a lava rock wall that framed a pretty planting display full of red and pink anthuriums.

Tūtū gave her elbow another squeeze. Whoops, too much thinking. She had to loosen up.

"Unless you guys finally got a movie theater or arcade or some-thing," Anna said with a smile at Tūtū, knowing that'd never hap-pen in the small village. "Go on, tell me about this latest curse. Pele doesn't usually swallow people, right?" Exhaustion from the flight seeped into her bones. *One story. I can get through ONE of her stories. Then maybe I can bring up Kona again. That's not rude, right? Dad would totally approve.*

Tūtū seemed to remember what she had been talking about and picked up where she left off before getting sidetracked by Anna's age.

"You know my neighbor down da road?" Tūtū glanced at Anna to make sure she was paying attention. Anna nodded and snapped the spare hair band on her wrist. Tūtū used the term "neighbor" loosely. Her home was tucked so deep in the rainforest that Anna had to walk for ten minutes to the next nearest house. "Well, he never showed Pele enough respect."

Anna hoped Tūtū still had a sense of humor. "Clearly he should have offered some shave ice to the snow goddess," she said as she swallowed back a smile.

Tūtū gasped. Her mouth fell open and closed, her eyes bulging. For once, she didn't have anything to say. She looked so horrified that Anna almost felt bad. Almost.

Anna was all innocence, looking at Tūtū with a straight face. Tūtū let out a strangled, "Pahhhh!" Anna dropped the act and broke into a huge, cheesy smile.

Tūtū froze for a heartbeat, eyes blinking, and cracked into cackling laughter. Anna joined in; her heart lightened at the familiar sound. "Kidding, kidding. Tell me, what did your neighbor do to tick off the *fire* goddess?" she asked as she spotted her suitcase make it around the bend.

"He knows what he did," Tūtū said, clicking her tongue in her tsk-tsk manner to show how very disappointed she was in him.

"Pele knew, too. And Pele sent a lava tube under his home and yard. When he went outside to garden, Pele opened up her tube and he fell in—*schoomp*—and got swallowed whole."

"Hmm, I doubt Pele had anything to do with it," Anna said as she heaved her suitcase off the moving belt and put it on the ground. "It was probably just an old lava tube that caved in when the guy pulled the wrong weed. I'd read an article online about a similar story in science class." She pictured a tangled web of roots holding together a thin layer of soil and lava, and the web being broken when one critical plant was removed.

Tūtū reacted as if someone had just told her Hawaiian wasn't a real language, smacking Anna gently on the arm and glaring.

"Eh! No talk like that!" Tūtū scolded. "You're on Pele's land now. No be disrespectful. What, you like see her curse our family next?"

"Sorry, sorry. Sheesh. Just another theory that popped into my head. Rockslides and forest fires happen practically every year in Colorado, and nobody blames it on angry gods and curses there."

Tūtū frowned at her. Anna knew that look. *Not even home yet, and she's already mad at me. Way to go, Anna. Dad's gonna be thrilled to get that update.* Disrespecting Tūtū was the ultimate no-no. It didn't matter what was going on back in Colorado; her parents made it clear that during her three weeks with Grandma, she had to do whatever Tūtū wanted to do.

Of course they sympathized with Anna when she told them about the science-class-Pele-volcano incident. They hugged her as she sniffled and tried not to cry. Told her that being Hawaiian is something to be proud of and that she'd get it when she was older. They took her bowling to get her mind off it, while going overboard telling her about embarrassing things that happened to them in school, too. But clearly they'd never been the *only* kid in class who believed totally different things, so they just didn't get the humiliation and why she was determined to do things differently this summer.

But they did reiterate that Tūtū was going to be in charge here and that her vacation might not live up to Anna's plans. That it was still important for her to learn this side of her culture. They also reminded her that the touristy things were expensive.

Anna let out a sigh, the brief good mood gone, hidden behind clouds with the sun. They were both silent as they walked out from under the airport roof. The downpour had slowed to a drizzle, and they hurried across the street to the parking lot, toward Tūtū's lime-green car with floral seat covers that she'd had as long as Anna could remember. The bright color made it easy to spot wherever it was parked, especially in a small, flat parking lot like this one. Totally the opposite of the massive, multistory parking garages at Denver International Airport.

A figure emerged from the passenger seat, closed the door, and stood next to the car. Anna held up a hand as she approached and watched as Kaipo's smile went from bright and sunny to nonexistent as he took in Tūtū's grouchy face and whatever hers looked like. She mentally noted she now had to look up to meet his eyes when she reached him, blinking as drizzle droplets fell on her face.

His inky-dark hair stuck up in tufts like ruffled feathers, and the same old owl pendant hung on the black cord around his neck, resting on his aloha shirt.

"Hey," Anna said, extending her fist. They bumped twice, knocked ankles, then slapped palms, wiggling their fingers. Still had it! Anna grinned. "Thanks for the gummi bears."

"Looks like they weren't enough to stop the hangry," he replied quietly, darting his eyes back to Tūtū, who had stowed her purse in the back seat and was popping the trunk.

"I'll fill you in later," Anna muttered as she walked past him to put her bag in the trunk. They all climbed in, Tūtū and Anna in the front, Kaipo in the back seat. Tūtū started the car. "You buckled?"

"Yes," Anna and Kaipo dutifully chorused.

"Okay, we go," Tūtū said, and they left the airport in stuffy silence.

The sky cracked open again as they headed south, sheets of rain beating a familiar pattern against the windshield, welcoming Anna back to the rainforest. They drove out of the small town of Hilo and continued on past numerous villages that broke through the jungle on either side of the highway on their way to Tūtū's house.

Anna pulled a carefully folded postcard from the plane's magazine out of her pocket and jammed it into her backpack. The postcard boasted a turquoise sea and glittering white sand with *Aloha from Hawai'i* splashed across the front in large, swirling font. Maybe she could give it to Ridley. She could pretend she had a true Hawai'i experience this summer. Well, true in the way that would matter to her classmates. Too bad that image wasn't her reality. No matter how many times she made this trip, Anna was still disappointed when she got off the plane in a gray-skied jungle with no sunny, sandy beaches of the airline's postcards in sight. In her tūtū's sleepy hometown of Volcano, the weather was ten degrees cooler than the sunny beaches of Waikiki, and it was just as likely to be overcast and rainy as it was to be sunny.

Kaipo shifted in his seat.

"Your tūtū got a great parking spot, didn't she?" he said with fake cheer. "Any farther away, and you'd have been soaked."

"She sure did," Anna said, glancing nervously at Tūtū. Was she going to ignore her the whole drive?

"She made sure we got there early. Didn't want you waiting," he said.

"Thanks, Tūtū," Anna said. "I loved spotting you from the escalator." *Please take this peace offering*, Anna quietly begged in her head.

"Pah, didn't want you to wait in the rain is all," Tūtū grumbled.

"Hey, this was your first year in Intermediate, yeah? How'd it go? Did you and Ridley make it to finals in your snowboarding club over winter break again?" Kaipo swiveled in his seat to face her and asked rapid-fire questions.

Anna winced at Ridley's name. "Yeah, she placed. I made it to finals but didn't place, though."

"What was that face for?"

Anna brought her left hand up to her forehead, pretending to scratch it while she got her emotions in check. "Um, Ridley's kind of trying new things this year."

Kaipo was silent, reading into the pauses and nuances of that statement. Anna could practically hear his brain churning, attempting to decipher her tone. He knew all about Ridley, and Ridley knew all about Kaipo. In Anna's head there would be a summer someday in the future where Ridley would come to Hawai'i and Anna could introduce her best friends to each other, her worlds melding. That vision washed away as they continued through the storm.

"That sucks," he finally concluded. Anna blinked back tears at the sadness evident in his voice. He always seemed to know just how much she didn't say. "I found a neat gecko's nest we can check out . . . ," he continued, changing the subject.

"Fun!" Anna said with a sniffle. Gecko eggs *were* pretty neat. Anna loved watching them every day till they hatched. Probably wouldn't be interesting to Ridley, though, like swimming with dolphins or manta rays would be. Anna sighed, straining to see out the window.

When they finally pulled into the long gravel driveway, the pounding rain was beating so loudly on the car, even Kaipo had given up on conversation. Tūtū parked in the covered carport. Then she got out of the car and went inside, letting the screen door slam behind her.

"Yikes," Kaipo said as he closed the door and moved deeper into the carport to escape the rain.

"Yeah," Anna said. "I definitely should have given the gummi bears time to hit my bloodstream before opening my mouth." She swung her backpack onto her back and grabbed her suitcase out of the trunk. "I need to go talk to Tūtū. Wanna hang out here until—" A loud crash followed by continued banging from the kitchen interrupted Anna.

Both ducked their heads and looked toward the screen. "Nope," Kaipo said, wincing. "Last time your tūtū banged pots it was because *you* brought that feral cat into the house, and it tore up her curtains before I got it back outside. You go talk to her. I'll be back when the rain stops."

Anna looked up at the metal roof. He was right. She needed to try to fix this or it'd loom over her whole vacation. Zero chance of exploring Kona if that happened.

"Ugh, fine," she grumbled. "Chicken."

"Good luck."

Anna hauled her bags up the stairs and into the kitchen to apologize.

"Tūtū, I'm sorry about what I said. I'm just tired from the flight," she began, toeing off her sneakers on the mat outside the door. She needed to remember to just ignore Tūtū when she went on about legends and lore.

"You're twelve now," Tūtū said, chopping green onions. "Gotta start taking our moʻolelo seriously. I'm not gonna be around forever, and you're old enough to learn everything. Our stories and history been passed down for generations. This is your summer. You gotta step up and become the next keeper of the moʻolelo. Pretty soon you'll be too busy with life. Might stop coming to visit. Hafta learn it now."

Might stop coming to visit? Yeah, right. Mom and Dad would be sending her here forever.

"Okay, sorry," Anna said again, determined to make Tūtū understand. Her entire seventh-grade success hinged on the events of these next few weeks. "But, Tūtū, I don't need to memorize all these stories. There are so many others already written down that if I ever want to tell a story I can just Google it."

"Maybe you need to stop thinking like Anna and start feeling like Leilani," Tūtū snapped. "You feel the pull here, no?" She pointed to her naʻau. "Try, Lei. Try breathe."

Tūtū closed her eyes, took a deep breath in, and let it out slowly.

Breathe? How could she breathe slowly when there was a very real chance that she could become a middle-school pariah? "Tūtū," she said sharply, "it doesn't even matter. Online—"

"That's not our 'ohana's stories!" Tūtū slammed the knife down and wiped her hands on the cloth hanging from the stove before turning to face Anna. "You going to just read other stories instead of your family's? How you going know where you came from? What you made of? Who you are? You think Hawai'i was always this way?"

"No, but—"

"No. Our kūpuna were crying in front of the palace when the haole's men took down our flag."

Anna flinched. She was very aware that word could also be used to describe her and hated that it always made her feel lumped together with people responsible for a painful time in Hawai'i's history.

Tūtū continued, not noticing Anna's discomfort. "Our kūpuna were separated from their 'ōlelo. Talk Hawaiian in school? You get scoldings. The chants passing down our mo'olelo were almost forgotten. If that happened, we woulda lost everything. *That* is why it is important. *That* is why you need to know *our* story. The story of us: the Kama'ehus. Pah!" Tūtū threw her hands in the air. "I gonna lie down. I need one nap."

That was ancient history! Anna struggled to keep her anger inside. Years of training on respecting Tūtū were about to get flushed down the toilet if she didn't get hold of herself. *Take a deep breath and count to ten.* She made it to two.

"You didn't even listen!" she called out to Tūtū's retreating back.

Zero reaction.

Anna spun and caught herself right before punching the wall.

Whoa. Definitely time to get out of this too-small house. She grabbed her suitcase and stomped down the short hallway, past the long line of family photos and the singular one of her and Kaipo, her arm slung loosely around her best friend's waist. He was pointing to the pathetically small fish she had caught and was holding on a line during their day in Hilo last summer. Ridley and Hennley would *definitely* not consider that a cool Hawai'i photo.

Throwing a glare at Tūtū's now-closed bedroom door, Anna turned left across the hall to the tight back room that was hers every summer. She dumped her backpack on the rocker that had been here since her dad was a baby. Her suitcase thudded next to the futon. Then Anna grabbed her rain jacket and slammed her way back outside to the front lānai. Trying to calm down, she paced in front of the old wicker loveseat, caged in by the storm. Pulling at the twisted hair band on her wrist, Anna barely noticed the slight stings of the elastic snapping back again and again. The drumming of rain on the metal roof eventually slowed, then stopped.

Anna fumed as the rain puddles shrank, draining into the porous lava hidden beneath the gravel drive. She had *tried* to be respectful and quiet during Tūtū's stories. But she couldn't anymore. She wasn't a little girl. She used to beg Tūtū for just one more. She found it fascinating how history here blurred the line between reality and myth. Anna's mom's parents lived in Buffalo. They were Polish and had a family tree with no mentions of gods or goddesses anywhere in their history. They didn't talk about being born from the earth mother and sky father. Totally boring. Which is why Anna used to love coming to this little home in the jungle for three weeks every summer for the last seven years.

Key words there: *used to.*

Every time she asked Tūtū why she thought Anna'd be able to remember them if her dad didn't, her grandma would snap, "Pa'a ka waha; nānā ka maka; hana ka lima," and give Anna a chore to do to distract her and keep her busy. Anna eventually stopped asking. She still didn't know what the big deal was. Why they couldn't just write it down and be done with it?

When the puddles were mostly gone, Anna jumped over the three steps to the gravel drive, eager to burn off the squeezing in her heart and muscles. She crossed the grass and made her way to the boundary of the trees.

The smell of damp earth, too-sweet rotting guavas, and the hint of ginger all blended together in a perfume that spoke to some of her oldest memories. She used to love playing in this jungle, bouncing on the spindly guava-tree branches and pretending the hāpu'u ferns were magical boats that could take her wherever she wanted to be. Tūtū didn't have cable or internet, and Anna's cell phone service was horrible out in the middle of nowhere, so she couldn't even stalk Ridley's vacation on social while she was here. Couldn't check in and see if she was having the most epic of all summers without Anna. Maybe if Tūtū took her on a drive, she'd get service somewhere. Otherwise it was the jungle and Kaipo as her sources of entertainment. She squinted into the trees looking for movement. No sign of him yet.

With one heaving sigh, Anna turned back to the carport. There was no way she'd shake off this anger on her own. She needed the machete.

Listen to Tūtū

Anna tightened her grip on the machete handle, her sweaty palm warming the old wood. She swung back the semi-rusted blade and then brought it in front of her with a scream.

"Aaiiiieeeee ya! Ya! Ya! Ya!" Quick chopping motions followed her mighty swing, and green leafy bits flew. The jungle outside Tūtū's house had thickened over the last year. Tangled branches and ribbons of vines twisted into one another and pushed in on the small, manicured space Anna's grandma called her yard. She brought the machete down again on a particularly stubborn uluhe fern with a grunt, taking her frustration out on the jungle like older black belts going at the punching dummy in her kung fu class.

"I just don't get why the Pele thing was such a big deal," Kaipo said.

Anna glanced at him. He'd finally returned and was keeping her company while she worked, twirling a small piece of vine between his fingers as if he didn't have a care in the world. But the crease between his brows gave him away. He was worried for her. Again.

Anna shook her head and went back to whacking the plant in front of her. It was hard work keeping her tūtū's yard clear, but Anna was happy to help out so her grandma wouldn't have to deal with it. And it let her blow off steam. Win-win. Another strand of hair had fallen out of her ponytail, and she used her arm to get it off her face. Her whole body was sticky in the humidity.

"Sure, your classmates may not have heard about her before, but Ridley had. Why didn't she say something about Pele *and* plate tectonics?" Kaipo asked.

Anna looked at him. Apparently if everyone else in your class is brought up with the same stories, it's hard to fathom how unbelievable they sound to others. "Ridley didn't want to look like an—" Anna checked herself just in time. "We had a plan. We both were trying to expand our friendship horizons this year. Ridley's just better at it than I am."

"Expanding generally means to get bigger. Pretty sure she can keep you *and* make other friends."

Anna rolled her eyes at his literalness. "Thank you for that clarification." She hacked at another plant, remembering back to exactly when it had all gone wrong.

After a killer first half of winter break with their snowboarding team, Anna went to Buffalo to visit her mom's family and Ridley stayed in Boulder. No big deal. Well, except apparently in middle school it is a Very Big Deal because vacations are when friendships are altered: when they weaken and when they are made.

When Anna got back to school, Ridley was in with Hennley.

Anna tried. And Ridley tried, too! Anna saw it and couldn't blame her friend at all. Ridley would save Anna a seat, laughed at Anna's jokes (even the ones Anna knew weren't great), and tried to talk about their snowboarding stories.

But Hennley wasn't interested. Which meant that *her* friends weren't interested. Which meant that by the time March rolled around, Anna's volcano outburst really pushed Ridley to make a choice . . . and she chose cool.

By May, Ridley was so busy with her new group of friends, Anna didn't even see her anymore.

"She tried. Hennley—she's the ringleader—is kinda particular about who she welcomes in. I just thought if we could do some cooler things this summer with Tūtū, maybe that'd help." She struggled to sort through her tangled-up thoughts. "If we could go to Kona, maybe check out a resort with an amazing pool or snorkel with sea turtles. Something that'll impress them."

"Why would you want to? They don't seem very nice."

She punctuated her thoughts with swings of the machete. "Ridley's"—*chop*—"nice"—*thwack*—"and she's"—*slice*—"with them."

Anna's breath caught, and stepping back next to Kaipo, she bit down on the inside of her cheek to counteract the sudden sting in her eyes. She bent to drop the machete and grab a bunch of clippings. Kaipo picked up another armload. "I don't think Ridley would stop being your friend though, right?" he asked as he led the way into the jungle to toss the scraps onto the compost pile. "Don't you think you'll just get back together when you get home? Maybe she needed a little break."

"You weren't there," Anna said, pulling up next to him at the mound of clippings surrounded by ferns and guava trees. She caught him wince out of the corner of her eye. *Dang! Tread carefully.*

"I mean, come on. You know how much I wish you were there, too. Then at least I'd have someone to sit by the trash cans with." She grinned and elbowed him, trying to get him to smile. His brow stayed furrowed. He got quiet whenever she accidentally made careless comments about him missing out. She knew how crappy that felt. "Ridley said she's hanging out with one of her new friends this summer. She'll probably forget all about me and my not-cool summer and my not-cool shoes."

"Your shoes?" Kaipo, with confusion, looked at her shoes.

Anna dumped her compost and turned to Kaipo. "Never mind, it's a Colorado thing. I have to do something awesome here to rival whatever they're doing, to even stand a chance at getting back in next year." She went back to pick up her machete.

"Ah," said Kaipo. "So, you feel like you're stuck here while everything is happening over there?"

"Yeah, kind of," Anna said. She saw hurt flash again in Kaipo's brown eyes and hurried to correct herself. "I want to be here, too!" Anna told him, scrambling. "Come on, you know that. It's just . . . it's complicated." She frowned. How could she explain to Kaipo that she really did love spending time with him and Tūtū in the heart of Volcano, the little town so perfectly named for its location on the side of an active volcano? She couldn't wait to take a trip out to the black-sand beaches in Hilo, and she loved the good Pacific Rim food she couldn't get on the continent, like legit shave ice and Tūtū's homemade kalbi ribs.

And then there was Kaipo, always waiting to hang out with her when she came back every summer. He never laughed at her.

"I love it here, too," Anna said. "But come on." He just stood there, watching her. "Look at me!" She fidgeted as his eyes scanned her body, from frizzy hair to green-stained shirt to jeans and sneakers. He didn't say anything. "Kaipo, I'm not lōlō enough to think I fit in here. Even if I do know a couple of Hawaiian words."

"But that's why—"

"I swear, don't even come at me with reasoning Tūtū's stories. Seriously. You remember when we went to Hilo last year?"

"Yeah . . ."

"You and I went grocery shopping. Tūtū wanted us to grab stuff for musubi."

"Okaaaay . . ."

It sounded like he didn't remember, but that day scarred her brain as vividly as that volcanically craptacular day in class. It was a sunny day, and they'd finished up swimming at Waiuli and swung by KTA before heading back home. She and Kaipo were in the rice aisle, trying to find the kind Tūtū wanted. The air-conditioning was freezing, with her wet hair and damp suit under her sundress, and she was bouncing on her feet in her slides trying to stay warm. Another girl a little older than her was there, too, waiting her turn. Anna had tried to hurry, grabbing an orange box that looked vaguely familiar. The girl behind her snorted.

"Figures," she had mumbled.

"Huh?" Anna didn't know what she meant.

"Hmm? Oh, nothing."

"What 'figures'?"

The girl looked at Kaipo. "You gonna show her what kine rice she should get? Gotta help a haole out."

Anna was speechless. She just looked at Kaipo, then down at the box in her hand. It was white, wasn't that good enough? Kaipo took it from her and put it back. He grabbed the bag off the bottom shelf. Anna remembered how hot her skin felt as the girl squeezed in front of her, grabbing the same brand Kaipo had picked up, and headed to the front of the store.

"Either kind would have worked," Kaipo whispered. "This kind is just stickier. Which makes it better." He grinned, trying to cheer her up. She left the store with her head down.

Anna jogged his memory of the incident and raised her eyebrows.

"Oh, come on, Lei. That was minor," Kaipo said. "Hardly a reason to feel like you don't belong."

"Mm-hmm," Anna said, looking at her friend.

"Well, I'm sorry you feel like you don't. I *know* you do," Kaipo said. He nudged her arm with his elbow, and she half-smiled back before turning to fully face the tangle of ferns in front of her.

"I don't know." Anna sighed. "What if I don't want any of it anymore? When I try to get into it, I end up taking it home with me. And it's messing things up there. I don't want the stories. I don't want the history. I don't want the rice. Well, scratch that, the rice is really good. I'll keep the li hing mui gummi bears, too. But I just want to come and visit like a tourist. Go walk around the national parks. Go lie on a white-sand beach all day and sip a fruity drink with a paper umbrella in it. Do you know in all my years here I have never had a drink with an umbrella in it?" Anna was breathing heavily, her frustration pouring out again. "Tūtū is trying to make me into something I'm just not. She had her chance with Dad. Just because he doesn't remember what he should about our history, doesn't mean that it is all on me now. I quit!"

She raised her arm to chop again.

"Wait!" Kaipo shouted. He darted in front of her just as she was bringing the blade down.

"What the—!" Anna cried. She pivoted quickly, trying to change the direction of the machete's momentum away from her friend's body. The blade sliced through the air, missing Kaipo's head by an inch.

Anna, hands shaking, dropped the machete and staggered back. She braced herself on a tree and took belly breaths in through her nose.

"*Kaipo!* Do you have a death wish? I could have cut your arm off!" Anna said, still panting.

Kaipo seemed completely oblivious to how close he'd come to a maiming and was focused on something in front of him. Anna craned her neck to see what it was. Kaipo slowly turned toward her and held up a leaf to expose its underside.

"Check it out—nananana makaki'i, the happy face spider," Kaipo said.

A little, yellowish-green spider with long legs and clown-mask-like markings on its back smiled up at Anna.

"A spider!? You jumped in front of a machete for a *spider?*" Anna shouted.

"They are native to Hawai'i. Only found here. Gotta take care of them," Kaipo said. He carried the leaf into the jungle, out of harm's way, and Anna followed along. "The mamas care for their young for weeks," Kaipo explained. "They are just like a real 'ohana, too. A real family. Different than a lot of other spiders whose young are on their own as soon as they hatch. This mama has to pass down all her moʻolelo to her keiki, her young, so they know where they came from."

"I think I'm being taught a lesson," Anna grumbled, feeling ganged up on.

Kaipo placed the leaf gently onto a shiny shrub, another part of his world safe. He tugged at the owl pendant around his neck and looked directly at Anna. "I get that you don't care about your tūtū's stories. That you don't think the moʻolelo is important. But it is. It is who you are. It's how we carry on our history, our legacy. We can't lose that. It will help you feel more connected to this place."

"Kaipo, Tūtū's stories are just that. Stories," Anna told him, suddenly needing him to understand. To have him solidly on her side. If she could convince Kaipo, maybe he'd help her convince Tūtū, and instead of spending the next three weeks learning the moʻolelo, maybe they could explore the island and do touristy things. "There's *actual science* behind all these myths. Like"—Anna looked around, spying a red flower on a nearby tree—"Okay. Look at this flower."

"ʻŌhiʻa lehua," Kaipo said.

Anna rolled her eyes at him. "Yeah, I know what it is, sheesh." She wasn't a *complete* foreigner. Everyone knew about the ʻōhiʻa lehua and the myths attached to them. Their spindly, scraggly branches with their small, oval, green-gray leaves were bursting with red blossoms. Each of these lehua flowers were made of hairs instead of petals, looking sort of like one of Mom's old makeup brushes where the bristles were all spread out.

"According to Tūtū's legend," Anna said, "if I pick this flower,

Pele will make it rain. But it just isn't true. It's a story. This flower has zero to do with rain cycles."

Anna reached out to grab the blossom, but Kaipo swatted her hand away. Anna looked up at him, eyes wide.

"Sorry. Just, don't. Okay?" Kaipo said. He looked at the ground and rubbed the back of his neck, trying to downplay his reaction.

"Kaipo, come on, let me—"

He knocked her hand away again.

"You're being ridiculous. It is just a flower." She reached her hand out again.

"Come on, let's go check on the gecko eggs." Kaipo grabbed her hand and tried leading her away. His hand was warm, and a rough callus brushed her palm. Ordinarily Anna would have let him pull her wherever he wanted. But not today. Anna shook free and planted her feet.

"No! We're settling this now. Everybody here is obsessed with these stories!" Anna threw up her arms, voice rising. "I'm sick of it! I want a summer for me!"

"Okay, calm down—"

"Don't tell me to calm down!" Anna yelled, feeling the sea of anger she'd tamped down since her discussion with Tūtū swell and roil. How could Kaipo not be on her side? "I can't spend another year by the trash cans!" Kaipo's eyebrows shot up.

"I'm not even asking for a lot! I just want seventh grade to be better. I just need a break from all the stories and all the"—Anna waved her hands around the 'ōhi'a lehua—"precious flowers!"

Kaipo took a step toward her, hands outstretched in an attempt to placate, which only infuriated her more. He wasn't even looking at her. He was still looking at the dang flower!

"Kaipo, my eyes are up here." Anna picked the red blossom, ignoring his gasp, and brought it up to her face. He tracked it as if it were a live grenade.

His eyes frantically darted back and forth between hers and the fragile flower she cradled in her palm. His normally dark complexion had noticeably paled, and his mouth hung open. Anna shifted on her feet, suddenly feeling guilty for picking the flower, if only because it bothered Kaipo so much.

"It's okay, Kaipo," Anna said softly. "I told you. The old stories and myths aren't real." She twirled the fine bristles against her palm, enjoying the feather-light tickle.

And then, suddenly, the earth started to tremble.

They were little tremors at first—barely perceptible—that easily could have been overlooked. Then the pebbles on the ground began to hop, and the leaves in the trees rattled against one another.

Anna threw out her arms and bent her knees, trying to keep her balance as she backed away from the 'ōhi'a lehua tree, the bloodred flower still clutched tightly in one hand. *No way*, Anna thought. The shaking magnified, and an inhuman groan rose up from the ground.

Plucking the flower hadn't made it rain—but could it possibly have caused an earthquake?!

Long Walk off a Short Trail

"**O**kay, okay, just** a random earthquake," Anna said. She grabbed the nearest tree, which happened to be the one she had picked the lehua from. The rough bark trembled in her hand. "Cool timing, huh?" She shot a nervous smile at Kaipo. Her friend's eyes were wide as saucers.

"What have you done?" Kaipo asked. The tremors rattled the rainforest. A guava tree next to them shook so violently, the riper fruit flew off, becoming gooey projectiles. One hit Anna in the stomach, and she grunted at the surprising force, watching as it split on impact. Pink, wet guava meat and seeds oozed against her white shirt.

"RUN!" Kaipo shouted. They both took off, racing back down the path in the direction of Tūtū's gravel driveway. Kaipo glanced up the mountain, but Anna couldn't tell what he was searching for. Through the trees, she heard cracking and a crashing roar. It sounded like a rockslide Anna had been close to on one of her hikes back in Colorado with her dad. It grew louder and louder.

Anna glanced behind her to see the jungle being swallowed up into a gaping sinkhole. The burn in her pumping legs was easy to ignore as she pushed herself faster. Tūtū's story about getting buried alive flew through her mind in a flash, and her stomach churned. She was going to puke up a rainbow of gummi bears. *What a waste!* Clenching her teeth, she focused on Kaipo. He was running ahead of her, bare feet flying over the mossy stumps and dirt.

The longer they ran, the more Anna realized something wasn't making sense. They hadn't walked that far along the trail. They should be out by now. Where was the clearing and Tūtū's driveway? The blurring trees they passed all started to look the same as the crashing got closer, and yet there was no sign of the vegetation opening up ahead of them as there should have been. Anna was positive they hadn't walked this far.

"Kaipo!" Anna shouted through her heaving breaths, chest burning from effort. "We should have made it to the house by now!"

The roaring of the earth consuming itself continued behind them. Anna's mind whirred through possible reasons they hadn't made it out yet, but each felt slippery and brittle.

All her snowboarding and kung fu at high elevations back home in Colorado made running at sea level easier for Anna, but she couldn't keep it up forever. Kaipo was slowing, too, and he turned to look back at Anna, eyes bulging as something in the sky above her caught his attention.

Anna followed his gaze and froze, her heart jumping out of her chest.

Above them was a giant flying beast. It looked like a hawk but was the size of a small plane. Its wings, white and brown against the gray sky, stretched out wide over the trees around them.

Anna's mind went blank, all logic gone.

"'Io," she heard Kaipo whisper.

"What?" Anna said, still stunned.

"Shhhh. Get down." He tugged her hand till they were both crouching on the damp jungle floor. Anna watched the large hawk pass by overhead. This wasn't possible! There just weren't birds that big in the world. Not anymore, anyway.

Anna rubbed her eyes and lowered from her crouch to a kneel, and her shifting leg snapped a branch.

Crack!

The creature screeched, eyes zeroing in on the sound as it wheeled back in their direction.

"Oops," Anna said, attempting to swallow the choking fear. She was seconds away from screaming her head off and making a break for it, but her tired, quivering leg muscles held her in check. Kaipo's hand was shaking in hers, and she gave it a squeeze that was meant as reassuring but may have come off more like a death grip.

Kaipo looked at Anna, eyes wild. "Listen," he said. His voice cracked, and he started again in a low voice. "I know this is going to seem—well, I know you don't believe the legends, but you need to go talk to your tūtū. Tell her what happened. Show her the lehua . . ."

Anna looked down at her other hand, surprised to find her fingers still tightly clutching the fiery red blossom. "Okay, wait," she said, still trying to make sense of everything. "I know the timing with the earthquake and all was a coincidence, and that bird thing is freaky, but you don't honestly think . . ."

Kaipo shook his hand free from hers and took Anna's shoulders in his hands. "Don't give up till you find me. Till you find Pele."

Anna frowned. "Don't give up till I find you? Pele? Kaipo, what—?"

Before she could finish, Kaipo shoved her down into a shallow hole under the log and stood. He lifted his arms out to either side of his body and cried, "'Io! I am here!"

The huge hawk circled him and let out a piercing cry as it dove, enormous wings locked in tight as it plummeted toward him.

"*Kaipo!*" Anna screamed.

The bird spread its wings at the last minute, extending its talons and pouncing on her friend. Anna dropped to her stomach in her hiding place as dirt and debris flew in the strong draft, stinging and scratching her face and arms. She forced herself to look up and saw the hawk wrap its long talons around Kaipo's slender arms, pinning him to the ground.

"*No!*" Anna shrieked, crawling out from under the log.

Kaipo's teeth were clenched tightly, his hands balled in fists. *What do I do? What do I do?* Anna's mind raced. She searched the ground and found a small guava tree that had been uprooted in the wind. The hand holding the lehua shielded her face, and the other grabbed and waved the big stick in the air as she fought her way through the gusts over to the bird. It screeched at her as she connected with one of its wings.

"Get off!" Anna yelled, whacking it again. The hawk lowered its beak and snapped at her, missing Anna's arm by inches. She jumped out of the way and landed a massive swipe against the back of the bird's head. Its beak darted at her again, snapping her sapling in two. "No!" Anna cried. She tossed the stick aside and looked frantically for another weapon.

With another deafening cry, the bird pumped its wings and lifted Kaipo off the ground. Anna darted forward to grab one of Kaipo's legs.

"Gahhhh!" Kaipo shouted.

Anna immediately let go. She'd hurt him worse by yanking him through those razor-sharp talons. Blood was starting to stain his shirt where the talons had shredded the fabric and sliced the skin.

"Go tell Tūtū!" he shouted down at her, his eyes squeezed shut.

"Kaipo!" Anna cried, running after him. She was looking at the bird and not the ground, and she tripped over a branch that had fallen in the wind.

From the ground, Anna watched as the hawk gave one final screech and soared above the trees and over the sinkhole, Kaipo dangling from its steel grasp. Then it flapped its mighty wings and headed over the jungle, up the mountain. Anna was all alone.

How Bad Could It Be?

hen she and Kaipo had tried to escape the sinking earth, they had run for a long time without ever breaking through the trees to Tūtū's driveway. This time, on her own, Anna easily entered the clearing, and the gravel path came into view. She shivered. It felt as if she had been released from a hold she couldn't see, as if the jungle knew the deed had been done and freed her.

Anna ran to the house.

"Tūtū! Come quick!"

She leaped up the steps to the lānai, kicking off her sneakers mid-stride, swinging the screen door open so hard it slammed against the back wall. Her still-damp socks made footprints on the dark wood of the living room before Anna stepped onto the woven lauhala mat that covered the majority of the floor space.

"Tūtū!" Anna called again, running through the bedrooms, then back to the kitchen. The house was empty. Had something taken Tūtū, too?

A piece of paper on the counter caught her eye. Tūtū's familiar handwriting was scribbled across.

Aunty Charlotte called. I gotta go help with her screens.

Musubi in container. Back by dinner. Be good.

Honis, Tūtū

Anna exhaled. Tūtū was safe at her sister's. Anna paced the kitchen. Dinner was hours away. No way she could wait that long to do something. She could call Aunty Charlotte! She grabbed the ancient corded phone on the wall. Wait, no. The dial tone hummed in her ear as she thought it through. Aunty Charlotte lived in Waiākea Uka. It'd take forever for her to get home, even if she left now, and who knew how far away the hawk would be by then. Oh, the police! They'd know what to do, and they showed up fast in emergencies. She hesitated so long that the steady dial tone changed to a *beep-beep-beep* signal. She hung up, counted to two, and picked it back up again. Ugh, old tech. Okay, dial tone was back. Was 911 the right number?

Anna slapped the lehua blossom she still held onto the kitchen counter and opened Tūtū's cupboard to see the taped list of emergency numbers. She dialed the nonemergency local police.

"Hawai'i Police Department, how can I direct your call?" a calm voice said.

"Hi, um, my friend, Kaipo, um . . ." She really should have thought through what to say before dialing. Dang. Too late now, time to wing it. "Kaipo was kidnapped. He is about thirteen, five six or so, brown hair, brown skin, brown eyes, blue-and-white aloha shirt, owl necklace, bare feet—" The words poured from her.

"Slow down, you say your friend was kidnapped? When?"

"Just now."

"Where?"

"In the jungle by my tūtū's house." Anna gave them the address.

"Were you with him?"

"Yeah."

"Okay, can you describe the kidnapper? Any helpful details?"

Anna chewed her lower lip, then plowed ahead, "Well, I know this is going to sound ridiculous, but it was a giant hawk, wingspan of, I don't know, maybe seven feet? Twelve feet? It was huge! The talons were big enough to crush my head! It was brown on the top and lighter underneath."

Silence. Then a sigh from the other side of the line. "A giant hawk took your friend?"

Anna grimaced at the skepticism dripping through the phone. "Yeah, I know it sounds—"

"Listen, do you have an adult with you that you could put on the line?"

Not good. Would Tūtū get in trouble for leaving her home alone? Mom and Dad were cool with her being alone back in Colorado, but what were the laws like here? Anna panicked. "Oh! Look! Kaipo just walked in the door. Kaipo, what was all that about?" Anna pretended, her voice squeaky and strained. "Guess everything is all good here. Never mind and sorry for calling!"

"Listen, this is an official police line." The voice on the other end got stern. "It needs to be kept open for people who actually need our services. If you crank call again, action will be taken."

Anna gulped. She wanted to blurt out that this wasn't a joke but didn't see a way that this conversation could end well. She squeezed her hand into a fist, fingernails biting her palms as a swirl of angry frustration filled her veins.

"Understood." Anna hung up the phone and rocked back on her heels. Okay, time to think this through.

Some of her last words to Kaipo were that the old stories and myths weren't real. She had been so sure.

It just didn't make sense. Anna paced back to the living room, then down the hall and back up again. So she and Kaipo fought. It was their first fight, but that didn't mean anything, right? She picked a flower and there was an earthquake. It had to be a coincidence. She was sure she'd picked lehua before. She racked her brain, trying to remember a time she would have done it but found it utterly impossible to focus.

Fact: Her friend was gone.

Fact: She yelled at him right before it happened.

Fact: She picked the flower.

Fact: . . .

Well, she didn't know what other facts to consider. What else was important. What else there could possibly be other than that she yelled, she picked the flower, and Kaipo was taken. It didn't make any kind of sense at all. She paced back to her room, feeling like she needed to explode trying to make sense of giant birds and earthquakes and potential connections to . . .

Her brain hit the brakes and swerved hard left.

Don't think about goddesses yet or you'll curl up into a freaked-out little ball and never leave the room.

Right. Okay, avoiding any of *those* thoughts.

Anna grabbed her backpack from the rocker, her heart beating so loudly in her ears that it was hard to hear the jumbled thoughts her brain was yelling at her. There was no moment that she made a conscious decision. No *"I'm going to venture into an unknown jungle and find my friend"* light bulb in her brain. Her body just knew what it needed to do, even if her brain hadn't caught up yet. As she dumped everything out onto the floor then quickly rifled through it, her mind settled into the familiar rhythm of packing for a hike.

Because that's what she was going to do.

Hike into the woods and get her friend back.

How bad could it be? Kaipo had led her through this jungle a gazillion times; she'd just get back to the sinkhole and follow the route the hawk had taken up the mountain. Maybe there'd be a lava tube that would lead her straight there so she wouldn't need to deal with bushwhacking.

Anna stuffed a rain jacket into her backpack. She could protect herself from the elements. Next went her headlamp, first aid and safety kit her dad always made her pack, and metallic-looking emergency blanket she got from space camp.

Anna traded out her damp socks for dry wool ones and stashed another pair into her pack before zipping it closed and swinging it onto her back.

She hurried to the kitchen. Having the plan, even as loose as it was, ignited something inside her. She grabbed her water bottle, filled it from the tap, and stuck it in the mesh side pocket with her phone before putting her arm through the second strap. Anna took the Saran Wrapped musubi from the plastic container on the counter and a few Saloon Pilot Crackers from the cupboard. Her hands were shaking so badly, she nearly dropped them before stuffing them into her bag. She could hear Tūtū saying she was going too fast and needed to slow down. Ground herself.

Anna closed her eyes and took a big inhale through her nose . . .

Nope. No na'au. This was just too much.

Everything seemed to be happening all at once, not computing in her brain at all because she kept shying away from the *big thing.* Ignoring it wasn't going to make it go away, though. She took another deep breath and focused on the most absurd possibility ever in the whole world.

"There is just no way a mythological fire goddess sent a giant hawk to kidnap my friend," Anna muttered, instantly feeling better but also ridiculous for even giving voice to that theory. She flexed her hands, reaching for the pad of paper under the phone.

And then the second earthquake hit.

Before Anna could react, the shaking stopped. *What in the world?*

Anna took a few shallow puffs of breath, trying to get her heart back down into her chest from its current position somewhere in the stratosphere. Two earthquakes in one day were two too many. She cautiously moved to the window, scared of what she might find. The sky was clear, pale blue with thin white clouds.

No signs of giant hawks.

But what in the . . .

A fountain of glowing lava spurted taller than all the trees on the mountainside. Anna was stunned. It had been years since Kīlauea erupted, and she had never seen it erupt from that location before. Why, that was directly uphill of . . .

"We are in its path," Anna whispered to herself.

No FREAKING way. The coincidences were piling up too fast.

Luckily, lava, unlike coincidences, moved slowly. Years ago, her dad made her stand with him next to an active pāhoehoe flow while her mom took a picture. She was scared out of her mind, feeling the heat wafting off the ropy ooze next to the asphalt road. Anna shuddered out of the memory, focusing on her priorities now. She had some time before it reached Tūtū's. Anna needed to find Kaipo and bring him back as quickly as possible. They'd figure out how to move Tūtū and all of her stuff out of her house together. If this whole mess was her fault, and Kaipo ended up hurt and something bad happened to Tūtū's place, she'd never forgive herself. Tūtū was so proud that their family had been able to hang on to the land since Hawai'i was a kingdom.

Anna rushed back to the kitchen, grabbed the notepad and pen, then scribbled a quick note to Tūtū.

Tūtū,
~~So, funny story~~
~~Something bad happened~~
~~Kaipo told me to tell you~~
Kaipo found a pueo nest he wants to show me. The owl isn't there now, so it's a good time to check it out. Be back in a few hours.
Love you,
Anna
PS Thank you for the musubi!

There. That sounded plausible and would buy her some time. Anna couldn't bring herself to say this had anything to do with Pele.

She'd have to be fast. Maybe the thank-you note would put Tūtū in a better mood when Anna got back. *If* she got back. "Shut up, brain," she muttered, looking around the house to see if she'd forgot anything.

Anna went out onto the lānai to put on her shoes. If she went back down the same footpath, would she be able to find where the sinkhole was? It seemed as good a plan as any. Standing, Anna took one last look back into Tūtū's house, then squared her shoulders and took her first steps off the porch.

Stuck

Anna hurried down the drive. The muggy, heavy air settled on her arms like an unwelcome coat. It was practically mocking her with its lack of rain at this point. No precipitation from picking the flower, just a huge hawk and fountain of lava. At least there weren't any plane-size birds in sight now. The gravel crunched under her feet as she tried again to reason out the events of the day in a way that made sense and didn't involve vengeful goddesses and curses.

This time, she came up blank.

It was exhausting trying to constantly deny what Tūtū would say was standing on her toes all along.

Fact: She said Pele was a myth, and an earthquake created a sinkhole and a giant hawk took Kaipo.

Fact: She said Pele was a myth (again, because she was apparently as outspoken as her mom criticizing the flaws in the Marvelverse when it came to these things), then another earthquake hit, and the volcano—Pele's home, according to Tūtū—erupted.

Anna remembered back when Ridley would excitedly listen to all the stories she'd learned from Tūtū over summer. Did they believe the stories then? Or did they just think they were fun, like sharing creepy thrills around a campfire? Anna wasn't sure, but it was definitely hard to ignore them now. The jittery sensation under her skin magnified to a pressure-filled hum as she considered the possibility. The chance. The theory. That *maybe*—just *maybe*—there was a ticked-off goddess waiting for her at the top of that volcano.

Not. Good.

She slowed as she approached the footpath that disappeared into the jungle. Anna's hands were clammy as she peered into the vibrant green tunnel. Ferns and leaves swayed gently in the breeze, beckoning her forward. The machete lay in the grass where she'd dropped it earlier. For a brief moment, she considered bringing the blade. It'd be comforting to have a legit weapon with her. But she'd never actually used it on more than overgrown jungle before and didn't think it'd be much good against a . . . goddess. Her mind stumbled over the word, still trying to come to grips with the shift in reality.

If Pele were up there, approaching with a machete in hand would be a bad power move. Definitely not the vibe Anna wanted to give off.

With a sigh, she stepped over it, into the trees.

Everything looked the same as it had pre-earthquake. The path was still the mix of brown decomposing foliage and mossy green growth. The birds were still singing to one another, and she could still smell the rotten fruit. Not having Kaipo with her was the only difference. A huge hole where her happy was supposed to be.

The shade of the trees did nothing to alleviate the hot, sticky humidity. Nothing ever truly dried out here, which was part of what made this rainforest so lush. Anna's eyes adjusted to the darker jungle as she started forward, pulling a guava from a tree. She stuck it in the mesh pocket of her backpack, opposite her water bottle, and collected a couple more that overhung the path as she moved forward, unsure of how long it'd take to find her friend.

Uluhe ferns covered the jungle floor, forming a tightly woven web of waist-high plant life on either side of the cleared footpath. Anna walked quickly, thinking about the best way to placate a goddess.

She pictured a tiny version of herself inside her head turning on a light in a dim, forgotten section of her brain, walking through an echoey neural pathway to a dusty file cabinet labeled *mo'olelo*. She mentally pulled open the metal drawer, squeaky from nonuse, and started sifting through the stories accumulated over years of sitting at the foot of Tūtū's rocking chair. It was hard to actually see what was written on those files—it had been years, after all. But words and images drifted back to her. Songs, chants, different gods and goddesses, and pieces of her own genealogy. They flitted through her mind and flew away before she could grab onto them and make them stick.

Frustrated, Anna shook her head and turned to check her progress. The clearing to Tūtū's house was no longer visible. On and on she went, but she never found the sinkhole. Chicken skin broke out on her arms as she remembered the sensation of running and not getting anywhere with Kaipo. Time for some research. Anna grabbed a branch from a nearby guava tree and bent it back on itself at a joint. It was stubborn, not wanting to break off the tree, so she then twisted it around and around.

Tūtū's voice rang in her ears: *"You gotta ask permission! Be humble."*

Anna rolled her eyes at the memory. "Oh, lovely guava plant," she joked, tugging on the branch, "would you please allow me use of this littlest of sticks?" The stick broke so fast she fell backward onto her butt. She glared at the tree, frowning, as she stood. *Hmmph, no way.*

Anna used the broken-off stick to carve a big arrow in the footpath pointing in the direction of the sinkhole, going over it many times to make it deep and wide, ensuring it wouldn't be missed if she did need to backtrack. Carrying the stick, Anna started forward again, turning around every few steps to look back at her arrow.

This went on for what felt like hours, and while it seemed like she was getting farther away, she could still see her arrow. She started to run, facing ahead longer before looking back. She watched the trees as she passed them, trying to distinguish a pattern. Guava, purple flower vine thingy, hāpu'u with the heart shape, guava, guava, hāpu'u, vine, hāpu'u, ferns, guava . . . Every time she looked back, she could still see her arrow, and there was no sign of the sinkhole. Snapping the hair band on her wrist, Anna huffed. This was ridiculous. Time to get mega-intense. She flat-out sprinted as fast as she could away from her arrow. Throat tight, chest heaving, her feet pounded down the path until her muscles burned and she had to stop. She put her hands on her legs, bending over, gasping for breath. She turned around and crumpled to the ground in frustration when she saw her arrow still behind her, no farther back than it had been when she started her sprint.

It made no sense!

"Aaaaarrrrrggghhhhh!" Anna shouted out, punching a fist into the ground next to her.

She was tired, and she wasn't making any progress. She should have made it to the collapsed tube by now. She felt moisture seeping through her jeans where they touched the wet ground, so she pulled her rain jacket out of her backpack, spread it on the path, and sat cross-legged with her backpack in her lap. *Okay, Anna, pull yourself together. There has to be a reason why you don't seem to be getting anywhere. Maybe you just need to clear your mind. Focus on something else to get unstuck.* She pulled and snapped at the extra hair band on her wrist and tried to clear her mind.

"Oh sure, Anna. Just focus on something other than your missing friend." The fern in front of her bobbed in the wind, looking like it was either agreeing or laughing at her. She stuck her tongue out at it and instantly felt ridiculous. If Ridley and Hennley could see her now . . .

Actually, that wasn't a bad idea. They couldn't see her *now* now— she still didn't have reception—but it'd be good to start capturing this journey. She pulled her bag around and grabbed her phone. Confirming it was on airplane mode and battery saver, she snapped a quick selfie in front of a wild orchid and ferns. The lush greenery was definitely way different than the aspen, pines, and columbines she'd see on hikes in the Colorado mountains.

Animals in both places were pretty different, too. In Colorado, they had to use bear bags to protect their food from brown bears on backpacking trips. Mountain lion and coyote warnings were posted at trailheads. Here, the scariest thing to run into would be a wild boar, a pua'a. Anna put her phone back and thought back to her encounter with one in this very jungle.

It also happened to have been the first time she'd met Kaipo.

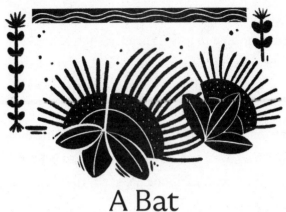

A Bat

It was Anna's first summer after moving to Colorado—right after kindergarten and her first snowy winter that seemed to stretch on and on. She'd been so excited to go back to what she still considered her home to stay with Tūtū for three weeks. Tūtū had all her favorite meals planned, and they hit the shave ice place on the way to Tūtū's from the airport. It was basically heaven.

A couple of days into her visit, Tūtū was hanging laundry, making the most of the sunny day while Anna wandered around the corner of the house to explore the edge of the jungle. Anna could hear Tūtū humming in the distance, and she hummed along, collecting wild orchids into a bouquet. Sudden movement in the ferns snared her attention.

A pua'a.

The wild boar was partially hidden—only its two tusks and wiry black mane poking off the top of its black head was visible. Anna froze. She'd only ever seen them from the kitchen windows as they trotted across Tūtū's lawn from time to time. This close, it was huge, especially since she was so small. She slowly backed away, but her shoe got caught on something and she'd fallen. Her sudden movement caused the boar to toss its head. It snorted and took a step toward her, coming out of the brush.

Anna remembered sucking in a huge lungful of air, sure she'd be able to scream loud enough for Tūtū to hear her, but it all went whooshing out when a boy stepped out of the jungle between her and the wild boar. He was just a little taller than her but didn't seem worried about the mean-looking pig at all. He offered her his hand and helped pull her to standing.

"You see that guava tree over there?" he asked in a quiet voice, pointing behind her. Anna could still recall the eerie calm that emanated from him. It felt like a weighted blanket, holding her together. A warm hug.

Super weird to feel after being terrified a second earlier. She'd wondered about it later, but in the moment, she was grateful to have help.

Anna had looked quickly over her shoulder to the tree and nodded. "Good. Go slowly and climb it." Anna focused on his face for a minute, then decided it seemed like a good-enough plan and backed up a few steps. As she moved away from the boy, the sense of calm dissipated, and her fear broke back through. She turned and wanted to run. All her muscles twitched and jumped; her brain screamed, *Get away!!!*

"Slowly," the boy reminded her, staying where he was by the pig.

How could he be that chill? Anna clenched her fists and took huge, slow steps. As soon as she reached the tree, she took hold of the lowest branches and pulled herself up, up, and up.

Suddenly, his voice came from right under her. "That's enough."

She almost let go of the branch in surprise. How'd he get to her so fast?

She looked down into the calm eyes of this strange boy.

"The pua'a is gone."

Anna looked back, and sure enough, the wild boar had disappeared. Relief was so strong that she promptly forgot about any weirdness. She lowered herself out of the tree and ran to the laundry line, pausing only once she reached Tūtū's skirt to look back. The boy lifted a hand and turned back into the jungle. When she questioned her grandma, Tūtū said the boy was Kaipo. She said he was safe and lived nearby. Anna remembered watching the edge of the jungle, sure she'd see either the boy or the pig pop back out.

Kaipo kept her waiting till the next day. He showed up at Tūtū's door, inviting her to go pick blackberries. Since then, Kaipo had been a near constant fixture at Tūtū's house. And Anna hadn't run into a wild boar since.

Movement from above caught her eye, dragging her back to the present. A wild boar had found her! Anna zipped straight into flight mode as she backpedaled frantically before realizing pigs didn't fly. And they certainly weren't smaller than her face.

As her heart restarted, she studied the small flapping creature. It darted about, circling above her head before descending lower and lower until it landed on a skinny branch in front of her and hung upside down. It was as small as her hand and kind of furry. It was mostly brown, with a patch of white behind its left ear. She'd seen bats before, typically at campsites zigzagging back and forth above their heads at twilight when they camped in Colorado. The tiny creatures never stayed in one place long enough to get a good look at them, but this one was pretty still now. Anna froze, afraid to scare it off. Hawai'i had bats? Huh, she never knew.

Its tiny eyes seemed to be watching her intently, so Anna slowly packed up her bag. Maybe she was close to its house or something. Were bats territorial? Dusting off the bottom of her jacket, still damp from the ground, she tied it around her waist and slowly scooted around the bat, giving it as much space as possible on the narrow footpath. The bat took flight again, swooping up the trail, and stopping once more to hang from a branch at Anna's eye level, just ahead of her. Anna paused and looked at the bat.

"Okay, I see you. I'm not trying to bother you or your family, little guy," she said as she moved carefully around it yet again. *Don't bats have rabies or some other bad disease? Could this one be sick? Maybe it is stalking me and wants to bite me. Where IS that sinkhole?*

The bat flew ahead again, this time brushing Anna's shoulder. Anna did a full-body shudder and rubbed the spot of contact. No traces of drool or foam. There'd be drool or foam if there was rabies, right? Or was that a mad dog?

The bat landed on a guava branch in front of her and started to open and close one of its wings, as if trying to get her attention.

"Just stay back! I'm trying to give you your space. You can fly off and go find some bugs to eat somewhere." Anna ducked under the bat and kept walking only to feel a bump on her shoulder. "Okay, now I KNOW you did that on purpose," she said, checking the spot again. "What the heck?" She stopped and the bat flew in front of her again and hung upside down on a branch, frantically opening and closing both wings.

Anna huffed. "So you're just going to come with me, then? Are you trying to tell me something? Should I know flagging code like those guys at the airport who direct the planes that I always try to decode on my flights over here? Okay, two wings—left wing—right wing—left wing—two wings—right wing— Hey!" The bat flew right at Anna's head. She ducked, almost losing her footing as it flapped around in her hair, then returned to a tree in front of her. Anna pulled out her hair band and quickly gathered the loose flyaways before drawing it back into a tight ponytail. *I swear it looks like its little hands are on its hips and it's glaring at me.*

"I don't know what you want!" Anna shouted at the tiny bat, putting her own hands on her hips. "Why are you getting mad at me? I'm stuck in the jungle on a path that doesn't seem to be taking me anywhere, trying to find my friend who was kidnapped by a giant hawk, who I guess could be tied to Pele. And I haven't found the sinkhole, let alone started to make any progress on hiking up the volcano, and now I'm talking to a bat and half expecting an answer! What do you want from me?!"

"Ho, it's about time!" the bat said.

The Fissure

Anna stumbled backward, tripping over a root in the trail, and landed on her butt, which was thankfully still covered by her rain jacket that she had tied around her waist.

"Wha . . . wha . . . what?! Did you . . . did you just . . . No, I must have imag—" The talking bat was likely a stress-induced hallucination, like the stress-induced headaches her mom sometimes got when she was working on some big physics problem. Yeah. That made sense.

"Oh, for flap's sake!" the bat said in a girl-boss-vibey voice, waving one of her wings in Anna's face like she was shaking a finger. "Don't even *think* about going back down that road. I mean, I know Kaipo said you were a struggle, but I didn't think you'd be this obstinately oblivious."

Obstinately oblivious? Wait. "You know Kaipo?"

"Keep up. I said I did. Oh, are you, like, one of those kids who likes to play jokes on people? And I thought I had it rough with Kahi."

Kahi? Who? What? Anna's brain scrambled to keep up.

"Come on, kuewa, we go. You do want to find Kaipo, right? I

would think you'd want to help him out before Pele gets bored. She's ended many 'aumākua that way."

Anna, thinking she'd lost her mind, looked up from her spot on the jungle floor. The bat used "we go" like Tūtū did.

"Right. Sure. Ended 'aumākua," she repeated. The word tickled something from her memories, but she ignored it, closed her eyes, and counted to ten the way she'd seen her mom calm herself.

"Kuewa, you coming or not?" the bat said. This time, Anna picked up on the word but not the meaning. *Kuewa?* Anna opened one eye. The bat was still there. Very persistent hallucination.

"Okay," Anna said. She nodded really fast and frowned, trying to think it through. Right. If at first it doesn't disappear, maybe go with it? "So we're going to go together. Because you're a bat. So yeah, nothing weird at all about me following you to search for Kaipo." *This is the most bizarre day ever.*

"Finally," the bat said, and she unlatched from the tree and flapped her way down the trail.

"I wasn't serious! That was sarcasm!" Anna called out after her. "I'm defending my sarcasm to a bat," she muttered as she got up, dusted off her butt, and jogged down the trail after the winged mammal.

"Hey, if you're really a bat, and I'm really talking to you, go grab that purple orchid and pick it," Anna said, testing the creature.

"Are you like this all the time? No wonder Kaipo is the master. You'd drive me batty in a day." The bat dove close to Anna's face and fluttered there a beat.

Anna blinked. Kaipo was a master what?

"For real? Not even a smile at the 'batty' thing, huh? Figures you don't even have a sense of humor. I'm *so* not picking a flower for you," the bat said.

"Ha! I knew it," Anna said, relieved. "You're imaginary. A weird stress creation. Don't know why I felt it when you bumped into me, though . . ." Anna pondered this, and her jog slowed to a walk. The bat grumbled some Hawaiian under her breath that Anna couldn't pick up and flew to the purple orchid. She started patting at it with one wing while the other wing flapped furiously, keeping her up.

"Here! Happy now? Is this good enough for you?" Then the bat flew up and continued down the path muttering to herself about having to cooperate with a human that wasn't even her human.

What in the name of sandy beaches was going on? With all the things she'd seen and, well, heard, Anna felt like her brain was swelling so much, it'd pop out of her ears. Apparently the bat was . . . real? If that were true, then . . . crud. Anna's armpits started sweating, and she knew it wasn't just the humidity. Definitely in over her head here. But maybe the bat—and she couldn't believe she was thinking this—could help her. She snapped the extra hair band on her wrist, the sting grounding her in her new reality, and started jogging again.

"Hey, how do you know about Kaipo?" Anna asked when she caught up. "Have you seen him? What's going on? And what's a kuewa? My tūtū didn't teach me that one."

"You acted all akamai when you picked Pele's lehua, why don't you tell me?"

Well, she had her there. Picking the flower was proving to be the least-smart thing Anna'd done in a while.

"I didn't mean for Kaipo to get taken," Anna said. Mega understatement.

"Oh greaaaat. You didn't even *mean it*, and you managed to call the goddess of the freaking volcano. Next time, keep your Doubty McDoubterness to yourself," the bat said.

Fair point. "You said you know Kaipo? Kaipo's talked to you? Do you know where he is? Can you help me find him?" Anna asked, following the bat.

"I don't know, can I? Do you think you need help? Or are you too all knowing, all powerful, all human?"

"Ummm, I mean, I am human . . . ," Anna said, not sure how to respond.

The bat flipped over so she was flying backward, like a backstroke in midair, and watched Anna. "Are you always like this?" She shook her little head. "Look, I'll try to explain it nice and slow so even *you* can understand: I need. To get. Kaipo. Back."

"Watch out for the—" Anna interrupted, but the bat zipped over the frond that extended over the trail right before crashing.

"We fliers stick together," she continued, fully into her rant. "He was helping me with something. Something important. Something I need him to complete. But I can't complete it, can I? Because somebody ticked off Pele and had him kidnapped." Was the bat glaring at her? Her furry face was so little, it was hard to tell. What had she called herself?

"Wait, what do you mean, *fliers*?"

"Fliers? Did I say fliers? I meant . . . Breyers. Yeah, we have an ice cream of the month club." She turned to face away from Anna again.

"Whatever, stop interrupting. If Kaipo didn't tell you, it was prob-ably because he knew you wouldn't listen. You don't deserve him."

Whoa. Anna stopped short, feeling the quick burn of tears prick her eyes. The bat flew on for a bit before she stopped and hung on a branch, facing away. Mean talking bat. She didn't know what Anna was like. Anna wouldn't have ever hurt Kaipo on purpose.

Sure, there was the time she squished his fingers when he tried to boost her up into the guava tree and she accidentally stepped on his hand. Or the time they had pails of rainwater they were randomly swinging around to see who'd get dizzy and fall down first (the lack of things to do led them to try some truly interesting things), and she accidentally let go of the handle, and he tried to catch it before it went through Tūtū's window, and it hit him in the head. Okay, and yeah, there was that time that a wasp in the blackberry bush freaked her out, and she essentially shoved Kaipo out of the bush ahead of her, and he got scratches on his arms. But those were never intentional.

Anna's stomach turned like she'd eaten some bad mango, the sweet memories overpowered by her bruised pride. She knew what she had to do. Kaipo was this creature's friend, too. With her crummy attitude, maybe the bat didn't have too many. It'd explain why she was so mad at her. Anna knew what being friendless was like.

"I'm sorry." Anna looked at her toes as she apologized. "I hate that he's gone. I didn't know."

"Don't get all mushy on me. Let's go. I don't want you out here in the dark. Guessing you can't see as well as I can," the bat said.

"Wait, I thought you were blind and used echolocation?" Anna couldn't help herself.

"Musubi, musu-bye," the bat said. "Same difference. It's how I don't bang into things. You coming?" The bat flew down the trail.

"Do you know where we're going?" Anna asked.

"I'm a talking bat, what do you think?"

Anna hesitated. The bat didn't answer her question. Really, she hadn't given her any information at all. But she was a talking bat who was a friend of Kaipo's. The odds of that happening had to be, like, a gazillion to one. So, the tiny mammal had to be special, right? And special creatures knew things, right? Why else would the bat have come to find her? Obviously they were going to form some amazing team and go rescue Kaipo. Like Batman and Robin, but more just Girlbat and Human.

Anna made to move forward, but her pack snagged on a branch behind her. She turned to free it and gasped.

"My arrow!" Anna said.

"What now?" the bat groaned from up ahead.

"It's gone!" She couldn't believe it. "My arrow is finally gone! We're moving forward!" Anna grinned from ear to ear and jumped up and down, the branch releasing her bag in the frenzy. The bat remained silent. Trying to calm her giddiness, Anna stilled.

"Ya good?"

Anna nodded, feeling heat creep up her neck. Her body didn't know how to handle all these emotional swings. From utter devastation of losing Kaipo to chatting it up with a moody bat to being thrilled beyond belief not to see something as simple as an arrow. The past few hours had been wilder than a roller-coaster ride at Elitch Gardens.

"Of course, we're moving forward. You're beginning to see," the bat said.

"There was a sinkhole up ahead. I'm going to go in and see if there is a tube that leads ma uka, up to the volcano. ʻIo took Kaipo to Pele's ʻōhiʻa forest," Anna proclaimed, trying to raise the bat's opinion of her by sharing her current working theory.

"Sure, kuewa. How are you gonna find Pele's forest if it's hidden in a traveling mist?" the bat asked, and Anna was sure she felt her roll her little beady eyes.

Pele's forest was in a traveling mist? What in the salty sea was a traveling mist? Clearly the bat did know something she didn't. Anna's shoulders sagged.

"Name's Anna."

"Oh, is it?" the bat asked.

Anna hesitated, unsure if she should have used her middle name. Of course the flying know-it-all pounced on her indecision.

"What, you don't even know your own name?"

"I'm Anna," she firmly called back. Kaipo and Tūtū called her Lei, but sticking to what she was most comfortable with, not pretending to be someone she wasn't, sounded good here.

"Mmmkay. Sure it is. No matter. All I have to do is make sure you get Kaipo back before Pele destroys him. I need him to finish what he helped me start. Instead, he's gone and I'm stuck out here with a biped struggling to see straight."

"I see fine," Anna said. "What are you needing to finish with him, anyway?"

"You see fine?" The bat ignored her second question. "Betcha didn't see me coming, did you?"

Anna frowned and opened her mouth to repeat herself, but the bat cut in. "I'll fly just a bit higher up to see if I can get a feel for where we are. We can be like Messi and Biles. We're on the same team but don't have to like each other." She flew up above the tree canopy, zipping around eating bugs while surveying the land below. Anna decided to drop the question of what Kaipo and the bat were doing for now. Instead she tried to puzzle out that random analogy as she walked along in the speckled daylight.

"Do you mean the soccer player and the gymnast? They aren't even from the same country or sport, let alone team." Anna questioned her own earlier thought of Girlbat and Human. Whatever. Anna would put up with the attitude until she figured out how to rescue Kaipo and deal with the masquerading mist or whatever it was.

"Ugh." The bat didn't even try to fix the analogy; she just flew up a little higher to catch a moth. Definitely questionable knowledge there.

"Hey, what's your name?" Anna asked, watching the bat flit around above her as they continued down the path.

"Ilikea," she answered, mouth full of moth wings. Anna grimaced, watching the pale delicateness crumple in the sharp tiny teeth. "And watch out that you don't fall into the—"

"Aaaaaaahhh!!"

"—fissure." Ilikea drifted down to Anna. She hadn't made it to the main part of the sinkhole yet but had fallen into a smaller crack that had radiated out from the large crater. *Smaller* being a relative term; the crack was still large enough to swallow a human.

"Ow," Anna said, stunned, sitting on her butt for what she hoped would be the final time today. Thankfully, she hadn't fallen far; if she stood, she'd be able to reach the dirt rim and pull herself out. She took off her backpack and rooted around for her headlamp. Growing up backpacking in Colorado had her always prepared to spend the night in the wilderness whenever she went on hikes. Clicking it on the lowest brightness to conserve the battery, she took a look around.

The floor she'd fallen on sloped downward away from her, and she could see that the walls opened up and were concave, forming a sort of tunnel. It smelled like old rain, and she could hear dripping. The hairs of hundreds of roots protruded from the walls and the rim, where the ceiling of the tunnel hadn't caved in completely. The walls were slick and ropy, made of an old lava flow. She had about a football field of broken rock to scramble over before she'd reach the smooth, intact tube. It was slow going, clambering over the remnants of the tube's ceiling. She was looking forward to not having her feet twisted and turned over the jagged broken pieces. They were almost past the section that had collapsed, and the darkness of the intact tunnel loomed ahead.

She saw an 'ōhi'a tree in the rubble. Her palms tingled in recognition. It was the same tree that she'd picked the lehua blossom from, now uprooted and mangled in the debris. She was back at the scene of the crime. Kaipo'd tried to warn her. Ignoring him had been the worst idea in the history of ideas. Anna squeezed her hands into tight fists, nails biting palms.

Folks who lived in the area knew that it came with risks that weren't common many other places. There were rare years when everyone worried about their homes being consumed by a new lava flow. When that happened, Anna's dad would fly out to help Tūtū pack up all her stuff in the back of her old pickup truck and drive her out to stay with Aunty Charlotte or one of her friends. They'd stay there for a few weeks, sometimes longer, and wait for Pele to decide whose land she'd spare and who'd be starting over. So far their family had been fortunate. Tūtū's house had stood for decades, but just below the superficial layer of soil was solid lava rock from an old pāhoehoe flow that came through the area sometime before her ancestors were given the land. It was evidence that this side of the island only existed because of the awesome power of Pele. At least, that's what many of the locals believed.

The earth trembled a little, and she marshaled her thoughts. *Don't upset the goddess while in the belly of her home!* Anna stayed completely still, waiting to see what unbelievable thing would happen after this earthquake. One second passed. Then another.

Nothing.

Ilikea darted around her head, into the tube, then back out again. "Kuewa, you're not stopping now, are you?"

"It's Anna," she replied. She looked ahead of her into the tube. All flows should lead to Pele, right? This tube could get her there, like following an ant's tunnel uphill back to the queen.

Anna released her breath, straightened her spine. "Let's go."

Scrambling over the final bits of collapsed rock, her footsteps echoed as she headed into the lava tube.

A Goddess

The sound of Anna's shuffling steps moved in a steady rhythm, at odds with the chaotic plips and plops of water in the tunnel. Anna pulled her phone out of the side pocket to check if it had been damaged in the fall. The screen was okay, and she snapped a picture of Ilikea fluttering in the tube in the waning light. Anna wondered if she'd be able to record Ilikea talking to her, or would it come out as whatever bat noises sound like? Either way, Ridley would think being this close to a bat was cool, right? Did it even matter what Ridley liked? It was probably Hennley she needed to impress.

"Clench your teeth any harder, and they'll fall out," Ilikea said, fluttering down to Anna's shoulder.

"That's not a thing," Anna said. But she subtly opened her mouth and wiggled her jaw around. That felt better. *Lighten up, Anna. Don't let Hennley get to you from the other side of the world.*

"Happened to a friend of mine. He was the most stressed-out bat ever. Constantly worried that he was eating too many moths and depleting the food chain. And whether or not Harry and Stylez would get back together. And if the moon was going to crash into the sun."

"Harry and Stylez?"

"Our best DJs. Ugh, never mind. I don't know why I even bother with you and your smooth brain." Anna thought about asking more questions but decided against engaging. Ilikea flew back up toward the ceiling, and the sound of drips filled the cave again.

What she wouldn't give to have Ridley or Kaipo with her right now. At least she knew she'd be getting Kaipo back. If she didn't . . . Anna shuddered and focused on her other missing friend. Losing Ridley was like losing a piece of herself. She didn't even know what she actually liked or didn't like, thought or didn't think anymore. She was so used to sharing her mind with Ridley, deciding on everything together. They'd go see the big movie over fall break, then analyze the heck out of the outfits, acting, and songs afterward, determining if they liked it or not. Books? Same thing. Discussed at length and came to the same conclusions. Teachers? Classes? Yup, every "slaps" or "stinks" outcome was mutually agreed upon. It felt empty considering everything on her own, and more than a little shaky, but she was pretty sure that they'd agree that walking this kinda creepy tube with a cranky bat stinks. Anna tried to push those thoughts out of her mind.

The last time Anna went on a tour of a lava tube, she was on a rare vacation with Mom and Dad. It was maybe second or third grade. Tūtū took them to the national park in Volcano and they all walked through Nāhuku lava tube. That tube had orange lights that dimly lit the entire length of the tunnel so visitors didn't get their feet soaked in the patchwork of puddles on the floor, but it cast strange shadows on the walls. Her dad had explained how the faster-moving hot lava flowed through the cooling outer crust like water through a straw, eventually leaving only the exterior shell behind.

In the orange glow, it had been all too easy to imagine another flow would come while they were down there, and they'd be trapped and burned to death. She started to panic, tugging her dad's hand to turn around and go back the other way. Dad had picked her up and walked quicker through the tube to help her feel better. Her mom said funny things like "donkey butt" and "snail toots" that echoed over and over down the tunnel, causing other visitors to turn and look at them. Tūtū's cackle and Mom's words kept Anna laughing until they all emerged unscathed.

Dodging a puddle, Anna shouted, "Goat snot!" She smiled as "ot . . . ot . . . ot" echoed around the tight space.

"Is this the part where I try find a rock to hit you over the head with to put you out of your misery as you begin your descent into madness?"

"Never mind," Anna muttered. "Just something my mom did." Ilikea was a pretty crummy stand-in for her real family.

"Mm-hmm."

"So, tell me what you know about Pele," Anna said, changing the subject. Over the course of the day, she'd seen the ground open, her friend get scooped, and a volcano erupt. Oh, and a talking bat. And the day wasn't over yet. Clearly it was time to open up to the possibility that there might be more going on here than she thought. "I've heard legends from my tūtū. What do you know about the fire goddess?"

"Look at you, asking helpful questions. 'Bout time!" Ilikea said as she slowed her darting and settled into a weaving pattern just in front of Anna, following all the bugs drawn to the light from her headlamp. The white spot of fur on her head seemed extra bright in the beam. Anna rolled her eyes.

"No one knows for sure where Pele came from, but we know that when she came to the Hawaiian Islands, she stopped at Kauai first . . ."

"Wait," Anna interrupted. "This part always confused me when Tūtū told me the stories. She *came* to the islands? She didn't *create* the islands? I thought the goddess of the volcano would have made them all." She glanced up briefly at Ilikea as she asked, then quickly returned her eyes to the floor to try to keep her shoes dry.

"Yes," Ilikea said. "Pele came to the islands. Maui had already pulled the islands out of the sea—"

"Maui, the demigod?"

"Yes, kuewa—"

"*Anna.*"

"—do you know another Maui?" She continued, ignoring Anna's interruptions, "You need me to break into song and dance for you?" Ilikea lowered her voice and started singing while bopping her head to a nonexistent beat. "Mischievous, marvelous, magical Maui. Hero of this land." Then she stopped.

Anna grinned, automatically getting the ancient Israel Kamakawiwoʻole song stuck in her head. Her dad kept it on his playlist and sang along every time.

Ilikea continued. "Or no, you look like you might be more of the"—the bat spun around and spread her wings wide, doing little batty shoulder shrugs, and sang—"'So what can I say except you're welcome' type."

The song from the old Polynesian Disney movie started weaving in and out of Anna's brain, too. She hadn't seen that one in forever!

Ilikea interrupted her thoughts with a shaking head. "So distractible. At least pretend like you're staying on task."

"Hey—" Anna frowned. The music was catchy! Sheesh, she *was* focused. And she knew who Maui was.

"*Any*way." Ilikea cut off her protest. "When Pele was looking for a new home, she started at Kauai and continued her way down the chain, settling briefly into Maunaloa's Mokuʻāweoweo caldera before moving on to Kīlauea's Halemaʻumaʻu crater, her current home."

"But why did she come here? Why didn't she just stay wherever she came from?" Anna asked, stepping over another massive puddle, feeling something wet plink onto her head and run down to her headlamp band.

"For flap's sake, do you want me to get to Kaipo or not?" Ilikea replied, swooping down in front of her face and flying back and forth to glare into each of Anna's eyes individually. The bat's tiny body danced in the beam and threw chaotic shadows on the walls of the tube.

"Gah, yes," Anna said, her steps faltering a bit at the sudden flapping in front of her. "Don't get your wings in a tizzy."

Ilikea seemed as eager to find Kaipo as she was. It probably had to do with whatever Kaipo had been helping her do. Anna reminded herself to circle back to that next, but figured it'd help to know a bit more about Pele's backstory. But if the bat steered her wrong, forget it. She'd go on her own.

"Pele got banished from her family home in Kahiki, a far-off island somewhere in the Pacific Ocean. She had a notoriously bad temper and messed with someone she shouldn't have messed with. She was no longer welcome there. So she got in a canoe and took off, looking for a new place to call home. She brought her little sister Hiʻiakaikapoliopele with her, carrying her like an egg in her armpit—"

Anna looked at Ilikea with raised brows. Ilikea's echolocation must have been working overtime to sense it. "Yes, an egg. Not all families look like yours, you know. The two sisters don't always get along, what with Pele's temper and irrational jealousy issues and all. We don't see or hear from Hi'iaka much these days. Word is that they are fighting again, and Hi'iaka is lying low somewhere. Pele tends to get upset if people don't pay her the respect she feels she is due and lashes out when slighted. Combine that with the fact that she pays close attention to her pua, her flowers—" She flew down to her face again and gave her the batty glare.

"I know what 'pua' means," Anna mumbled.

"Oh really? You could have fooled me. You were foolish enough to pick a goddess's flower. You, in all your 'I'm from Colorado and don't believe these stories anymore,' as you pick one of Pele's lehua blossoms. You were just asking for it. The attitude pushed her over the edge and got Pele extra fired up. A little rain wasn't gonna be enough, oh no. For such in-her-face-ness, she took your—"

"I know, I know, you've already ranted about all this. Wait. How'd you . . . Were you there when I picked the flower? And how do you know I'm from Colorado?" Anna sputtered. "Were you watching us when it all happened? Why didn't you stop 'Io or help me then? And sidenote, since when does Pele kidnap friends just for picking a flower? I thought the whole legend was just that she'd make it rain?"

"Maybe if you weren't all showy-offy when you picked the flower, you might have just gotten rain, but you can't go mocking Pele openly in front of your . . . your friend, and not expect a goddess-size smackdown," Ilikea said. "Plus, come on, me helping you then? Please. Think about it, what would you have done if you saw me, a tiny bat, right when a giant hawk took your friend? Would you have thought I was there to help you? Were you ready to hear me?"

"Well, maybe not, but . . ." Anna ducked to avoid a lower bit of rock before straightening again.

"*Didn't think so*," Ilikea said in a smug, singsongy voice. "You weren't ready. Besides, I wasn't there when it happened. Makani came to find me to tell me what happened. I came as soon as I heard and waited for you to arrive back in the jungle."

"Makani?" Anna asked.

"Yes, Makani. The breeze. They were here after the rain and saw the whole thing."

Anna froze. Huh? She stuck a finger in her ear and wiggled it around, sure she heard Ilikea wrong. "The breeze saw the whole thing, found you, and told you about it?"

"Is there an echo in here or is it just my locator?" Ilikea laughed at her own joke. Getting nothing from Anna, she sighed. "Oh come on, open up. You're talking to a bat. Why would a breeze be any different? Haven't you felt them brush your skin? Heard them whisper in your ear? When you were young, some of your best ideas came from Makani. They're who invited you up into the guava trees to play, who led you around the corner of your drive to find the best blackberries, who helped you catch your first wave. Just because you don't remember hearing them doesn't mean they've stopped talking. It means you've stopped listening."

A Bad Plan and a Worse Plan

Ilikea perched upside down, clinging to a root in the ceiling. "Uh-oh. Did I break your brain? Kuewa? Can you hear me?"

Anna remained locked in place. Her pulse pounded in her temples as she tried to absorb this latest bit of information. The wind was alive? Like, a person, but not? What was that word . . . *sentient*. Mom explained it to her one night when Dad went off on how the ring in *The Lord of the Rings* was all feeling.

"For real? You're supposed to be going in to save Kaipo from Pele, and *this* has you freaked out? The *wind*? Okay, this trip is apparently over. I'm out."

The mention of Pele pierced Anna's daze. "I'm here. I'm good." She snapped her hair band and started putting one foot in front of the other again.

"Oh, you're *good*. What a relief." Ilikea's tiny voice shook with sarcasm. "Here I thought you'd decided to have a massive freak-out session just because of a little breeze. I mean, *hello*, you're battling *lava* soon. Toughen up, buttercup."

Anna didn't bother to respond. Light from her headlamp bobbed ahead, illuminating the walls of the lava tube. Her footsteps echoed off the chamber, and the burn in her thighs let her know they were hiking an uphill slope.

She could vaguely remember climbing the guava trees, a gentle breeze urging her higher, lifting her spirits and adding to the sense of excitement as Kaipo climbed nearby. Their favorite game of pretend was imagining they were pirates on the high seas, the wind whipping through her hair as she stood high up on the mast, searching for an island to bury their treasure. Once they were so busy playing, they missed lunch.

Tūtū had come by looking for them, carrying sandwiches. When she spotted Anna so high that she couldn't even reach her feet, Tūtū almost dropped the food. As soon as Anna's toes touched the ground, her grandma scolded her, telling her how dangerous it could be if she was to fall from such a height.

Anna didn't know how to explain to Tūtū that she felt completely secure in the trees, no matter how high she went. She made sure Kaipo took them deeper into the rainforest before climbing after that, so Tūtū wouldn't see her and worry. Now she wondered if Makani shared in those adventures and if she'd recognize them again. *At this point I wouldn't be surprised if the old guava tree itself popped by to say hello.*

But it didn't matter how many people or things she met. Ilikea was right. At the end of this she still needed to face Pele, and Anna had no clue what she'd do then.

"Could you—" Anna's voice cracked, and she swallowed again, trying to clear her suddenly dry throat. "Could you tell me something about Pele that could help me? What does she enjoy? What are things that I can do to make her happy?"

"What can you do to make Pele happy? Pretty simple. Praise her; she loves sincere flattery. Make her feel like you respect her. Honor her. People have honored her for years with hula. That'd be a good place to start. Can you dance hula?"

Hula? Crud crackers. Maybe it'd be better for lava to just come finish her off now. Anna rubbed the back of her neck. "I took lessons when I visited years ago but haven't practiced since I was eight. The hālau I went to closed, and Tūtū never found another that she liked close enough to want to take me. She said she'd teach me herself, but I never had the patience. It's just so slow!"

Anna didn't mention that she always felt so out of place at the hālau. When she was really young, she fit in fine. As she got older, though, she noticed how much more advanced the other kids were. Three weeks of lessons a year never got her very far. One day the kumu asked her to come to the front of the class so she could watch her more carefully and give her instructions. The red-hot burn of embarrassment at being singled out wasn't something she ever forgot.

By the time she was eight, it was clear that she was just a visitor and not a local who could take classes year-round. Entering the large dance studio, she felt about the size of one of Kaipo's precious happy face spiders. Girls bunched in tight groups would look toward the door at the sound of her footsteps, then instantly look away, leaving Anna alone and awkward. She tried to ignore the giggles and snatches of "haole" in whispered conversations. Anna knew her pale skin and Colorado way of talking were clear signals she wasn't from around here anymore, and she just wished Ridley were with her so at least they could be awkward together. She was secretly thrilled when the hālau closed and she didn't have to endure the silent water breaks where she'd stand alone watching the other kids practice pieces of the dance together. She wanted to shout that she was one of the top snowboarders in her age bracket. That she was good at something. But that sport held zero value in this tropical place. And Ridley hadn't been there to talk it up with her.

"Is there anything else she likes?" Moving on past that awful memory.

"Hmmmm . . . oh!" Ilikea made a fluttery flourish as she remembered. "She loves he'e hōlua. Can't resist a good competition."

"Hōlua?" Anna asked. "Oh, like the sled races, but on lava rock instead of snow? I remember Tūtū talking about it, the story of Pele and her sister Poli'ahu racing."

"Wait, whaaaat?" The bat got all sarcastic sounding. "You actually have some helpful information in that brain after all."

"How is that helpful? Wait, you think that would be an option for me? Racing the Hawaiian goddess of fire down a hill of lava. You really are batty."

"Hold up, did you just make a bat joke? Did she just make a bat joke?!" Ilikea swooped around the tube asking the shadows.

Anna cracked a smile, but it fell quickly from her face. "Pele's gonna take one look at me and laugh. I'm not a worthy adversary."

"I mean, truth. Check what you're wearing. Your shoes are questionable. I don't even know what you were thinking there, kuewa."

Anna bristled. She mentally made a note to ask Tūtū what *kuewa* meant as soon as she got home. And why the dig on her shoes? First Hennley and her crew and now a bat who probably hadn't seen the inside of a school before, so how did she even know what to wear?

"Um," Anna said, stomping through the tunnel, "basically that they're comfortable, and I shouldn't have to conform to anyone's propaganda of what is trending on social to earn friendships."

"Huh?"

"My shoes. I picked them for comfort, not to be on trend."

"On trend? Whatever. I just meant I don't know how you can go around with those big, enclosed shoes on. I'd feel so cut off from the 'āina."

"Oh," Anna said, a prickle of heat climbing her neck. *Whoops.* "Sorry. Sore subject. Pele's gonna think I'm just a haole from the continent who doesn't belong here."

"And what do you think?" Ilikea asked.

Anna looked down, not wanting to admit that she'd just voiced exactly what she thought. *Focus on the facts.* She spoke up again. "It doesn't matter what I think, why do *you* think she'd race me?"

"She's raced mortals in the past," Ilikea said. "Most have died fiery deaths, encased in lava for eternity." She gave a shrug, like, *Eh, what can you do.* "One was able to escape out to sea in a canoe never to return. He kind of won, but Pele took her anger out on his entire village, covering it in lava. Let's just hope it doesn't come to that! Go the honor route, for sure. We'll find Pele, you'll show her super-serious, intense respect. And, if she's still ticked, you have the racing option to fall back on."

Anna turned the idea of a sled race over in her mind. How different than snowboarding would it be? Falling on lava basically sounded like the worst option ever. *Ouch.*

A loud rumbling echoed against the tube. Anna's cheeks got warm, and she peeked up at Ilikea. *Maybe she didn't notice . . .*

"Really, kuewa? I talk about fiery death, and your stomach growls loud enough to wake the spirits." Ilikea flapped up toward the ceiling.

"Sorry, been a while since I ate that last guava. And it's Anna." Anna pushed on her belly to try to muffle its complaints. She swung her bag around and rifled through it, searching for a musubi.

"Pah. I am NOT your . . ." Ilikea appeared to struggle with what to say for a bit. "Never mind, just don't get used to this." With those strange words, Ilikea left Anna, flying back the way they had come in.

"Wait! Where are you going?" Anna called after her, but Ilikea either didn't hear or decided not to answer. In another second, she was gone. Swallowed up by the inky blackness of the cave. *Okay, then . . .* Anna breathed deeply through her nose. *No big deal.* But it was. Being stuck in a cave with Ilikea was one thing. Now? Alone? Terrifying.

"Pig Puss!" she shouted, trying to scare away her mounting anxiety. Anna swung her headlamp back around, in the direction they had been walking, all thoughts of eating gone. Beyond the edges of her beam, the darkness filled the vacancy left by her light whenever she slightly moved her head. Anna trained herself to not look outside the beam, knowing her overactive imagination would have her seeing all sorts of fanged, horned beasties. Nope. No good. Focus on the light. Stay within the lines. Why was the darkness getting closer, though? Anna slowed her pace.

Closer.

Closer.

What in the . . . *thunk*.

She walked into the wall.

"Hey!" Anna took off her headlamp, rubbing the sore spot on her forehead that it had bumped, then reached out a hand. Solid rock.

A dead end? No way. Anna shined the light right, then left. Not a dead end.

A junction.

Both directions looked the same. Black. Roots glistening in her light. Damp. Anna chewed her lip, not sure which way was uphill. She could wait here. Ilikea would probably come back. But maybe she could get through this without the bat. Was there anything from Tūtū's stories that could help her out of this? Anna thought hard.

Nothing from the legends came to her.

But something from science class did.

She put her headlamp back on. Reaching around, she grabbed her water bottle, careful not to let her phone drop. After taking a big swig of water, she carefully unscrewed the cap and crouched down.

Tipping the bottle over slowly, she watched water pool on the floor of the lava tube. The small puddle grew and grew, and finally a skinny tendril broke free from the surface tension and pulled to Anna's left. The tiny finger of water moved slowly at first, creeping around bumps and getting stuck in divots. Anna didn't want to waste too much water but needed to know the slope of the floor. She added more water to the puddle. The tendril flowed faster, growing in size as it searched for a crack to seep into, revealing the slight slant of the cave that was imperceptible to the naked eye. Satisfied, Anna put the lid back on the bottle, stood, and turned right. Uphill. Ma uka. Where the lava came from, and where Pele lived.

Looking back where she'd come, there was no sign of Ilikea. "Ili?" Anna yelled. *ILI . . . Ili . . . ili . . .* echoed around her. Then, nothing but the drips and plops. Goose bumps broke out along her arms as she imagined a million invisible eyes opening at her call, staring at her.

Time to move.

Her headlamp crawled over the ground around her until she spotted a small section of finely crushed stone in a low point of the junction. She bent over and, using her index finger, inscribed an arrow pointing right. *Can a bat see . . . or echo feel . . . a shallowly pressed arrow?* Anna looked around one more time, simultaneously hoping for movement and fearing it. Nothing. "I'm heading right," she called to the darkness, just in case Ilikea was within hearing distance.

At first, the tube continued as it had, roots and puddles dotting the space that was roughly the size of the train tunnels at the Denver International Airport. But after about a hundred yards, the sound of her footsteps changed. They got higher pitched. She slowed, not wanting to run into a wall again, and shined her light on the ceiling. A cool, wet drop fell into her eye, causing her to flinch. She blinked quickly, rubbing the moisture away. Looking up again, the roots were definitely getting closer. The tube was shrinking!

Anna picked up the pace, hunching over now to avoid having roots grab and tug her hair, but soon it was unavoidable. The walls pressed in on either side, funneling her forward in tighter and tighter spaces as the moisture from the ceiling and slimy roots rubbed onto hair and shoulders, feeling like skinny fingers crawling out from above to hold her down here forever.

She'd been in caves before in Colorado. She even went on a trip where they had to slither on their bellies through mud into tiny openings. The tight spaces always opened up.

Her heart pounded in time to the echoing drips. She dropped to her hands and knees and crawled, inching forward. Her jeans got soaked in cold puddles, and her backpack scraped along the low ceiling as she pushed ahead, needing to find a way through this labyrinth.

And then it stopped. Dead end.

No, no, no, no, no!

"Argh!"

Anna put her forehead down on her hands, conking it a few times in frustration. She had been so close, she could feel it! No point in wallowing, she had to go back the way she came and try the other direction. Anna swung her head around to look over her shoulder. But when she started scooting in reverse, her shoes hit something solid. She kicked out her feet, searching for the exit tunnel she'd just crawled through. Everywhere they reached, they bumped rock.

The opening was gone. Sealed.

She was in a lava casket.

Fear skittered up her spine, digging its claws deep into the muscles in her back. This didn't make sense. Anna's breath came in quick pants. She tried to grasp logic, with her heart pounding so loudly in her ears she was worried the tunnel might collapse from the noise.

Find facts. But she couldn't. Science deserted her. She was totally out of her element. Scrunching her eyes shut, Anna worked to calm herself.

But her thoughts kept gnawing at her: Why was this happening? Why couldn't this trip have gone her way from the beginning? Anna tried to imagine it. She could have come down the escalator at the airport, and Tūtū could have said she had a surprise in store and whisked her away to Kona with Kaipo. Anna could currently be lounging on the beach, fruity drink with fun umbrella in hand, sun on her skin, laughing with her friend, taking pictures to show Ridley and Hennley. She could practically feel the cool breeze in her hair . . .

The breeze! Her head jerked up, bumping the roots on the ceiling, causing a cascade of water droplets to fall on her hair and back. Anna maneuvered her hand in front of her face. Sure enough, a slight breeze was coming from the wall. There must be something on the other side!

Hope sparked a low burn that raced through her veins. Anna knocked, then pounded on the wall. A dull sound echoed through the space, but no matter how firmly she hit it, the wall stayed in place.

Anna racked her brain. She needed something harder.

Her *water bottle.* She reached back and awkwardly pulled the metal canister from her side pocket, scraping her elbow on the wall next to her. It was closer than it had been a minute ago. The tunnel was shrinking! She heard her phone fall to floor. No time for that now. She rolled to one side of the cramped space, lying on her hip, and propped up by her elbow, her headlamp illuminating the target in front of her. Closing her eyes and taking a deep breath, Anna braced herself for impact.

Sometimes You Need to Ask

Releasing her breath in a powerful *whooosh*, Anna thrust the water bottle forward as hard as she could, into the lava wall. A loud crash of crumbling rock reverberated through the tiny space as her bottle, hand, then arm went through the stone and cool air poured into the new opening.

"Cheehoo!" Anna busted out Tūtū's celebratory cheer, high-pitched and happy. She sucked in the fresh air as the *OOO . . . ooo . . . ooo* bounced away from her. Anna twisted to follow the echo. The tunnel behind her had reopened, and the walls next to her expanded.

"Eh, what the flap's going on over there?"

Ilikea! The small bat flew into her headlamp beam. "Just working through the tunnel system," Anna said. "Got it figured out. You wouldn't even believe—"

Ilikea's tiny raised brow cut her off mid-sentence.

"Okay, maybe you would," Anna finished with a grin. She reached back to grab her phone off the ground, took a quick picture of the hole she'd created, then stowed it and the water bottle safely away. Anna faced forward again to look out the new hole.

There, on the other side of the rock, was a cavernous space. It was the size of her classroom at school. In the middle of the floor, there was a small pile of rubble. Something was off. Anna squinted, trying to figure out what was tickling the back of her mind . . .

She could see! There was no way her little headlamp would reach that far into the room, yet the crumbled stones in the center were clearly illuminated. Anna lowered her head to the ground, resting her ear on the cold rock floor to be able to see up to the room's ceiling. Yes! An opening! Her cheeks stretched even farther in a smile, and she looked at Ilikea, proud to have come to the end.

"What?" the bat asked, unable to see past Anna in the small space. "You gonna go or just lie here? Oh yeah, take this." Anna looked over. A small banana was clutched in the little batty feet.

"It's raining again, but I found a banana. Not that I care, I just wanted you to pipe down. Tell your 'ōpū to quit complaining," Ilikea said.

"Oh!" That was surprisingly nice of the bat. Now that the imminent threat of being crushed by the tube was gone, hunger came slamming back full force. Anna still couldn't reach for the fruit in this smallish space, though. "Can I get through first?"

"Fly all the way out there, and this is the thanks I get? Ungrateful little—"

"Thank you!" Anna said, cutting Ilikea off before she called her whatever she was going to call her. "I'm going to try to lower myself headfirst out of this hole." Anna crept forward, bracing herself on the crumbly ledge of the hole, then slowly walking her hands down the sloped side of the space till she was doing a weird handstand on her belly and her toes were hooked on the ledge, her backpack falling forward and bumping the back of her head. Her arms trembled under the weight of her body. How had her phone not fallen out yet? The water bottle must really have it in snugly. Swinging her legs down out of the hole, she got herself right side up and stumble-jogged down the sloped wall to the bottom of the cavern, waving her arms, narrowly preventing herself from completely eating it.

"Oh my GOODNESS," she said, sucking in deep breaths of fresh-ish air while standing on her tiptoes and stretching her arms over her head. "That *sucked*! Forget this plan. No way am I going to last underground all the way. I need to get back up aboveground, out of Pele's veins." She pushed her toes into the ground, flexing the shoe through the sole of her foot in an attempt to squeeze the water out that had soaked in while lying in the tunnel.

The jeans might dry, but these shoes? Never. Ridiculous five bazillion percent humidity. She shuddered, remembering her old purple bathing suit with the black polka dots. After swimming at the beach, she forgot it in her bag for a couple of days, and by the time she found it, it had grown some moldy plant life from the fungi kingdom and smelled like a swamp.

"Yeah, how you gonna do that, kuewa?" Ilikea drifted closer, offering the banana.

"It's Anna." Some of her hair had come out of her ponytail, and short tendrils stuck to her cheek and forehead. She tucked them behind her ears before taking and peeling the fruit while she looked around her new space. It was an apple banana, her favorite kind. They were smaller than the usual ones they'd get at the store in Colorado. The tart bite tasted almost like a regular banana that wasn't quite fully ripe yet, but oh so much better. Anna found herself drawn to slightly green bananas back home in a poor attempt to replicate the taste.

The ground in the room was relatively smooth, with sporadic puddles and cracks. The light was coming from a small hole in the ceiling about the size of an extra-large pizza. Anna stopped directly underneath and looked up. The good news was that the rain had stopped and the weak filtered light that passed for sunshine in Volcano was attempting to break through the clouds. The bad news was that the ceiling was out of reach. Anna finished the banana, put the peel in her pack, and tried to reach the rim. She stretched her arms up and jumped, but the lip of the hole remained stubbornly beyond her grasp. Anna turned off her headlamp and stuffed it in her bag, then backed up to get a running start. Grinding her foot down, she crouched, then sprang into a run.

Step . . . step . . . LEAP!

The feeling of flying was pathetically short-lived, and her fingertips only grazed some of the wet roots hanging from the ceiling before she crashed back to the ground. Her knees and palms hit the floor, absorbing the sharp impact, and she rolled quickly to her side with a grunt the way her kung fu instructor had taught her. She pressed her scraped palms against her thighs.

Anna rose to her feet and winced at the fresh pain in her knees. Practicing the moves on a padded floor in the studio was way more comfortable. Ilikea continued to flutter above her head. She wasn't sure how long she'd been down here, but surely time was ticking.

"Hey, Ilikea? So, *if* we assume that this whole Pele moʻolelo is legit and what we're working with, is there, like, a time limit or something on how long I have to find Kaipo? I mean, in all the other stories, there's some big mean person saying, '*When the sun sets in three days, a plague upon your houses*' or something like that. Three is typically kind of the magic number, right?" She backed up and got ready for another jump. "Genies gave three wishes, Rumpelstiltskin gave the queen three tries to guess his name." Anna leaped and missed again. This time she rolled a bit more gracefully. That lip was just too high. She put her hands on her hips and scanned the room. "Oh! And then there's the whole Three Little Pigs, Three Blind Mice, Goldilocks and the Three Bears, and the Three Billy Goats Gruff thing. So, is Pele giving me three days to find Kaipo?"

Ilikea stared at her. "What are you even going on about right now? Fairy tales? This isn't a fairy tale. We're trying to rescue Kaipo and have to do it ASAP. You want me to predict how much time Pele is giving you? You might as well try to predict the weather."

Anna cocked her head. "Um, meteorologists do that. It's a thing."

Ilikea blinked at her for a second, like she was shocked by the news before shrugging her bat wings. "Whatever. Point is, Pele's unpredictable and can change her mind whenever she feels like it, so maybe we have three days, maybe we have three minutes. Heck, maybe you'll meet three strange helpers before finally encountering the goddess herself in this part of the jungle. Fairy tales. *Pfft.* Come on, kuewa. We have to keep going and quickly."

"Wait. Do you think she already k-k— . . . hurt him?" Anna couldn't bring herself to say *killed*. A lump in her throat the size of Lānaʻi prevented it.

"Nah, not yet."

Anna rubbed the inside of her elbow. "Why not? Why would she even give me the chance to get him?"

"Have you never even *tried* to think like a goddess before? I mean, come on. You go around just killing subjects willy-nilly, and then what? Who you gonna hang out with next?"

Anna winced at the casual use of the *k* word.

"Fine, so assuming he's alive, that's good. We can just go, apologize somehow—"

"Apologize with hula—" Ilikea interrupted.

"*Somehow*—"

"Hula."

"Maybe with hula, and get him back," Anna finished.

Ilikea did a somersault. "Oh my goodness, you really have no idea, do you, kuewa."

"Well, at least I'm trying to think of something, *Ilikea*," Anna mumbled, emphasizing her name since she'd apparently never use hers. "Where would I even learn a hula, anyway?"

Ilikea shrugged. "You realize at some point you're gonna have to start figuring these things out yourself, right? I can't help you with everything. Wings would get lost in translation." She mimicked a couple of moves pathetically and almost fell to the ground before swooping back up and perching on some roots. "Don't go breaking your brain again trying to do too much at once. Focus on getting out for now."

As much as she'd hate to admit it, that was decent advice. Anna examined the ladder-and-staircase-free walls of the space. There were a couple of holes ranging in size at various intervals, suggesting other tunnels. Anna definitely wanted out of there. No more earthworming for her. But where would she go aboveground?

"Here's an easier question: Do you know where we're going once we're out of this cave?"

Sweat began to pool at the base of her spine. This was not looking good.

"Do I know where we're going? *Ha! Pssh! Fssnnn! Snuh!*" the bat continued before falling silent. Anna waited a beat.

"Well, do you?" Anna's voice squeaked at the end of the question.

"Hmmm? Oh yeah. For sure. Definitely. But if I revealed all my brilliance to you at once, you'd be stunned and just fall over weeping in gratitude, and we'd never get anywhere."

Anna raised an eyebrow in disbelief.

"Hey, look, a moth!" Ilikea zoomed over to the far side of the cave to catch some bug that was invisible to Anna's eye. *Right.*

She cleared her throat and tried to do what her mom always said: focus on what she could control, which right then was getting out of there and finding Kaipo. With or without this bat. Letting herself spiral into a pit of despair while actually stuck in a pit, though tempting, would be completely unproductive. Right? Right. Focus.

"Well," Anna said, snapping her hair band and deciding to keep it basic, "I'm going to get out of here and just keep heading ma uka till I get to the top of the mountain and look down into Pele's home. Maybe find a doorbell or something to ring to let her know I'm there. Seems realistic."

Ilikea stayed quiet.

Fine. Silence it is.

Anna moved to one wall and placed her hand on the cool stone, feeling its ropy surface for any sort of handhold. The flow of lava polished this cave generations ago. There was no way Anna could scale the wall and maneuver across the ceiling on her own. Overhead, some of the roots that were poking through the ceiling were wider than others. *If I could make it up to there, I'd be able to do it.* She put her hands on the surface again. *Come on, there has to be an old gas pocket or something I could grab onto . . . aha!*

Anna's fingers sunk into a small indent way above her head. She held on tightly and attempted to pull herself up. In all her years of hiking and backpacking, she'd only gone rock climbing a few times. She was okay at it, but the heights freaked her out. Two feet on the ground was definitely more her jam.

There is no way I can pull myself up with this tiny handhold.

"Gah! I could really use some HELP!" Anna shouted up to the void, frustrated at coming so far, being so close, and not being able to get there.

A strong wind blew through the tunnel and abruptly stopped. Ilikea looked at her expectantly.

"What?" Anna asked.

"Well, did you call Makani here or not?"

"Makani? Oh, the wind that told you what happened? Wait, they're here?"

"You must have sincerely asked for help and opened up a bit. Are you ready?"

"Ready for wha—oooohhhhhh!" Makani formed a strong burst of air, lifting Anna off the ground.

Slimy Monkey Bars

Anna **instinctively crouched** and bent at the waist, putting her hands back down on the ground. "Ilikea! I'm not doing a wheelbarrow race right now!"

"Makani is only trying to help. Do you want to get up that wall or have you decided Kaipo isn't worth it?" Ilikea snarked.

Anna twisted her neck so she could look up at her. "Okay, so my feet are up. Now what?"

"If you're going to face Pele, you've gotta start getting creative."

Okay, so the bat was a "tough love" kind of coach. Or maybe she didn't know, either. That was a scary thought. Remembering the burpees her snowboarding coach made the team do to "maintain overall fitness," Anna attempted to kick her legs back into a plank position with her feet in the air. Her nose stung as a memory of her and Ridley hit her. A couple of years ago at training, they both did burpees faster and faster till they were barely even straightening up at all on the jumps. Coach was not pleased. They both had to do a five-minute plank hold at the end of class for goofing around, and her abs were like jelly for days after that.

A drip of snot fell from Anna's nose onto the damp floor of the cave. She quickly sniffled in the next drop and put one hand in front of the other, over and over. Her triceps trembled and palms stung from her earlier fall. Makani provided a light pushing from behind, helping her move across the tunnel floor.

When she got to the wall, she scooted her hands back toward her feet that were still hovering above the ground in Makani's grasp. Wobbling slightly on the uneven wind, Anna slowly stood, using the wall to brace herself, holding her breath. Finally upright, she exhaled and looked up at the curve of the ceiling.

As soon as she redirected her attention, she felt the wind give her a little nudge toward the ceiling of the tube, and Anna grabbed onto the roots that were dangling. *It's just like when I was little and Dad supported my feet as I struggled across the monkey bars. I'll focus on that and maybe get out of this tube before I freak out that I'm currently being held up by nothing more than a helpful weather phenomenon!*

Anna hadn't factored in how slippery the roots would be. It made sense: all the water dripping off of them for days, months, years; of course they'd be slick. Anna clutched onto a particularly slimy root, and it slipped right out of her hand.

"Oop! Yeah, those are usually a little slick," Ilikea said, watching the slow progress while hanging on a root.

"Thanks for the warning," Anna said through gritted teeth. Her hand slipped off the next root, and she fell again, slowly, buffered by the wind. Her arms pinwheeled, finding no purchase until she was back on the ground. Ilikea spoke from her perch.

"You can't have Makani do all the work. They aren't that powerful.

You've got to pull your own weight. Or are those puny little arms not able to?"

Anna wiped the root slime onto her jeans, adding one more smudge to all the filth. Smug flying flier.

"My arms are just fine, thank you very much. Makani and I were just getting to know each other again. It's been a while." Time to remeet an old acquaintance for the first time. "Um, hi, Makani." The breeze blew her hair back off her face, cooling her. Anna closed her eyes and smiled. "All right, you and me. We got this. Let's show that bat."

A deep inhale through her nose—not *quite* down to her naʻau—prepared her for the next climbing attempt. There was a slight tremble to her step, which she hoped Ilikea wouldn't notice, as she approached the wall. She talked to the wind. *Mm-hmm, no big deal. Just an old friend about to help her out of a lava tube. Cool, cool.*

When she felt Makani swirl around her legs, she braced herself on the wall and looked up. Anticipating the rise this time, Anna focused on finding the largest, most gnarled roots that would provide the best handholds. She grabbed one root, holding strongly while testing the slipperiness of the next, transferring her weight only when she was sure she had a solid grip. She took shallow breaths and flinched when water dripped onto her face from the ceiling. Trying to keep her flailing legs under control resulted in twinges and tweaks as Anna tried to make Makani's job of supporting her easier.

"If I didn't know better, I'd think you were grabbing onto live wires and getting shocked with every root," Ilikea said. Anna bit her lip and reached for the next hold.

Three more roots to go.

Two. *Bah, that was a big drip, gah don't let it be a spider. Nope, just a waterdrop.*

One. *And . . . I'm . . . THERE!*

Anna gripped the edges of the opening, her legs and body dangling in the tube below. She felt Makani swirling around her as she ran her fingers along the ground searching for purchase. The ledge was paper thin in areas and crumbled under her touch. A cascade of dirt and rock fell onto Anna's face, into her eyes and open mouth. Anna looked down, blinking and sputtering furiously, trying not to lose her grip. Her hair swirled around her head, a side effect of Makani's efforts.

"Come on, kuewa, don't lose it now," Ilikea said from somewhere nearby. Blindly, Anna worked her hands around the hole, the wind helping her rotate, and finally found some holds that remained firm under her weight. Using all her strength, she pulled herself up, first getting one elbow up onto the ledge, then the other, and pushing herself upward while Makani heaved her legs up from below.

As soon as Anna was high enough to get her knees on the wet, mossy ground, she scrambled quickly away from the opening on all fours, not able to see where she was going. Ilikea flew up out of the hole behind her, and Makani brushed the wisps of hair that escaped her ponytail back from her face, letting her know they were still there. Anna wiped her filthy hands on her equally filthy jeans, then carefully tended to her eyes, pulling their corners out to the sides to form tears that washed away the dirt and grime.

There was no way her brain, clamoring for a logical explanation, could dispute the fact that she was almost buried alive by Pele's lava tube. Or that Makani had definitely helped her get out of the cave.

What would Tūtū say if she could see her now? Blinking the cleansing tears away, she surveyed the jungle in front of her. Whoa.

Well, click her heels and call her Dorothy, she certainly wasn't in Volcano anymore.

Or at least not the Volcano she knew.

This jungle was somehow wilder looking than it was around Tūtū's. An ancient-looking hāpuʻu fern grew five feet sideways before taking off toward the sky. The coils of the young ferns emerging from the trunk looked part octopus—strange tentacles about to unfurl and grab you with their suction-cupped appendages. Anna felt Makani whisper to her the way they used to when she was little. She remembered standing on the lower soggy trunk just a little off the ground while holding on to the tall, lacy ferns erupting from the top of the L-shaped tree and pretending she rode an alien beast while Kaipo would gallop around, over, and through the trees nearby.

It was so dense there she couldn't tell which way was ma uka.

"I'll head up and take a look to figure out which way to go," Ilikea said, as if sensing her indecision.

Anna waited while Ilikea ascended. Looking back toward the hole in the ground, she pulled out her phone, wiped the dirt off the lens, and took a quick selfie with the opening in the background and her mouth in a grimace. Makani caught the vibe she was going for and blew the hair in her ponytail up, so it looked like she was falling and freaked. Laughter bubbled out of her at how ridiculous the picture looked. It'd be perfect to show Ridley. "Nice. Thanks, Makani!" They swirled around her.

"Oh yeah, by all means, let's stop and do a photo shoot," Ilikea cut in. "Ma uka is that way, FYI." Her batty wing thrust indignantly to the right.

Anna's cheeks heated, and she bristled at the implication she was wasting time. "Hey, you were checking on direction. I had time. I'm already done." Anna stuffed her phone away with more force than necessary.

Makani swirled away from her. As Ilikea grumbled to Makani about loyalty and missions, Anna looked where Ilikea had pointed. Some of the weblike tendrils of the uluhe fern undergrowth had been cleared away between giant trees, leaving space to walk without being caught in their tangle. Someone or something must walk this path frequently to keep the area so clear.

"Hey, you two." Anna tried to interrupt Ilikea's lecture. Makani was getting their two cents in by spinning the bat around in a mini hurricane. Anna knew laughing at Ilikea's frustrated exclamations of not getting proper respect would be treasonous, so she struggled to keep a straight face as she asked, "What do you think made this path?"

Which Way Do We Go?

The swirling stopped, and Ilikea almost hit the ground before she got her wings out. She made big, haughty flaps that carried her to a frond over the trail, giving Makani the cold shoulder. Makani tickled the inside of Anna's elbows with a gentle touch, and Anna smiled, letting them know she was cool with the shenanigans, especially since they got her out of the cave.

"You don't think you're the only one in this jungle, do you?" Ilikea said as a nonanswer to Anna's question.

"I know, I was just wondering. It looks like whatever it is comes here a lot, and I want to be prepared to come face-to-face with it."

"Well, it could be anything, right? What were you saying earlier? Oh, billy goats, Wrinkledstickskin, bears, pigs . . ."

"So basically you have no clue. Super." Why couldn't Kaipo have been working with a more helpful bat? "The trail is going uphill, so at least that feels like the right direction. Let's go and see if we can find an overlook or clearing," Anna suggested.

"Fine. You ready? We go." Ilikea huffed.

Makani took off ahead, bounding up the path, pushing fronds and branches out of the way for Anna. Ilikea stayed higher up, almost hidden, sulking. Birds sang in the canopy completely unaware of her stress. Normally, Kaipo would have been walking ahead of her, telling her what birds those were, helping her connect more with nature. Sometimes she'd hide behind a tree and wait to see how long it'd take him to notice she was no longer "mm-hmming" to his comments. Once he went out of sight before noticing she was missing. Anna had jumped out as he passed, and he tackled her. She'd peed her pants a little from laughing so hard with him. The birds he'd been identifying took to the sky, annoyed at their ruckus.

Now she'd give anything to see him running around the curve ahead. His absence ached like a three-day-old kick in the chest—a dull throb with every breath. Heading up the trail, Anna caught herself more than once turning to point out a huge hāpuʻu fern to him, knowing he'd share her wonder at the size of the feathery leaves, and the fact that he was gone would come slamming back into her, taking her breath away. He'd love this place.

Anna snapped the hair band on her wrist, refocusing on the path and the crew she was with. Ilikea was being too silent. Did her feelings seriously get *that* hurt by Makani? What would Kaipo do? He'd figure out a way to make everyone feel important and valued. Maybe the bat needed to feel needed.

"Ilikea, can you fly above the trees and see where the volcano is? Is it still erupting? My lack of wings is a bummer right now," Anna said, making a show of standing on her tiptoes and straining to see through the canopy. She wasn't exactly sure where Tūtū's house was, but there was no massive fountain of lava visible anymore, so maybe Pele had slowed the newest flow? Or maybe they were just at a bad viewpoint. Anna kept her eyes on Ilikea and held her breath.

"Ugh. I'll do it for Kaipo," Ilikea said. She ascended above the treetops, flew in a circle, and called back down to Anna, "Okay, looks like that new fissure is still bubbling and spewing, flow is moving toward . . ." Anna held her breath. The bat was quiet.

"What? Toward what?" Anna asked, voice high with anxiety. Ilikea dropped lower and actually looked nervous, making quick, jerking movements. "Where is the lava going, Ili?"

"Toward your tūtū's house."

"Okay." Anna's brain started churning. This was nothing new. The lava was heading that way when she had left the house. "Can you go up and see if there is a lime-green car parked in the carport at all?"

With zero snark, Ilikea went up for a look. "A car is there. Can't tell color, though."

It had to be Tūtū. She was home. In the line of fire. A fresh wave of panic crested over her. Anna scrunched her toes, trying to ground herself and focus on what to do next other than curling into a ball, plugging her ears, and singing "John Jacob Jingleheimer Schmidt" at the top of her lungs till this entire horrific day was over.

"Change of plans, team." She talked fast, twisting and tugging at the hair band so hard she was surprised it didn't snap under tension. "I need to get home ASAP. Ili, can you point me in the best route?" The bat stuck her furry nose out to the right. Right into the uluhe fern thicket.

Goat snot.

"Do you see a plan B at all?"

"Nope. You want to get down to the house, that's the fastest."

No way was that going to be the fastest. Anna ran full speed at the thicket, got caught by the tight mesh of waist-high vines, and bounced back out. She lifted her leg and tried to step onto the tangle, but her foot sank through the top layers and became ensnared in the chaos. Anna fell to the side and worked to free her foot, then stood hopping while she pulled her sneaker out of the plant.

"Through and over aren't looking so good," Anna said as she sat on the ground to put her shoe back on. A crawling sensation prickled across the back of her hand, and she shook it off.

"Yeesh!" She shuddered, and she watched a gecko fly off and land on the ground next to her. Instantly contrite, she dropped on all fours to apologize. "Sorry! I thought you were a spider!" The gecko chirped once, looked at her, then looked to the thicket. With a final chirp, it ran and disappeared right under the plants.

Hmmm. "Makani, could you lift up the uluhe so I can go under?" Makani swirled around her and took off. Anna watched in awe as the vines bent and stretched in the wind, forming a low, narrow tunnel. "You rock!"

"No, they wind." Ilikea hovered in the trees. "Come on, we need to move. I'll stay up high to make sure you stay on track so we can get back to rescuing Kaipo faster."

Anna scrambled into the greenery. She went as fast as possible in a low hunch, her thighs burning and back aching from the tight position. The uluhe scratched her arms and pulled her hair, forcing her lower. A chirp from the ground caught her attention. The little gecko was ahead of her, running down the clearing! With chirps and flicks of the tiny brown tail, the gecko would dart off in different directions, and Makani would quickly shift, dropping the vines they were holding up and lifting the vines where the gecko went. Anna hoped the gecko knew where it was going, but Makani seemed content to follow it.

"And now we're taking the lead of a reptile," Ilikea said, flying low behind Anna.

"Be nice," Anna warned, not wanting to offend the creature that was hopefully taking her home.

"You do realize that Makani could basically be playing a fun game of chase right now, right?"

Anna tripped on a root. "What?"

"They can get distracted."

Anna weighed this new information. A chirp sounded from farther ahead. "I need to try this," she insisted. "Kaipo loved geckos. It stands to reason, given everything I've seen, that maybe they love him, too? I don't know." She felt like a balloon was expanding in her chest as she tried to absorb exactly what she was saying. Her mouth was going, but her brain couldn't keep up. "He'd help the geckos. Heck, he almost died trying to protect a spider from me. I vote to keep going." She nodded to herself when she heard that decision. *Yes. Solid reasoning. High five, self.*

Ilikea stayed silent through twists and turns after that. Whether she agreed or thought they were all fools, Anna wasn't sure. With a chirp, their gecko guide jumped onto a tree up ahead. Anna watched it disappear around the trunk. "Wait!" Slipping on a patch of soggy moss, she stumbled, then pushed herself faster to find where the gecko had gone. She circled to the far side of the tree, looking for any trace of its bubble toes.

"Um, Anna?" Ilikea said.

"Wait, I know the gecko was helping." Anna searched frantically, not wanting to get an *I told you so* from the bat.

"Anna . . ."

"He's got to be here somewhere."

"Anna! Turn. Around."

Makani spun her around. There, in the clearing, was Tūtū's house.

Anna's heart leaped into her throat. She gave a cry and took off running, past the car, up the steps, and into the kitchen.

"Tūtū!"

Her grandma was there in the kitchen, the very picture of normalcy. Shoes kicked off, Anna rushed over and wrapped her arms around Tūtū, pushing her face into Tūtū's silvery hair, inhaling the familiar smells of rice, ginger, and pikake that were distinctly her grandmother. And then she remembered the lava.

"Ohmigosh. Tūtū. I'm so glad you're okay. I pissed off Pele, and lava is coming. Don't you see it? We gotta get you out."

"Eh, slow down." Tūtū turned around, wiping her hands on the dish towel hanging from the stove. "Where's Kaipo? I thought you were out with him. Been waiting for you guys to get back. I got some stuff in the car already. Grab your bag." Then she *really* looked at Anna and gasped. "Aiya! Whachu been up to?"

Anna swallowed hard. Truth-bomb time. "Kay, so you know that I was mad that you weren't listening to me, and I wanted to go to Kona to show my friends that I can have an epic summer vacay, too?" Tūtū's lips pressed into a thin line, and she gave a curt nod, staying silent.

"Yeah, so I tried to explain that to Kaipo, but he totally took your side of things, saying I needed to listen more." Tūtū's lip quirked up in the corner. "I know, of course, right? So very Kaipo. Well, I didn't take it well. I kind of got mad and pickedalehuaandyelledatPele." Anna sucked in a lungful of air. "You'd think that an all-mighty goddess wouldn't pay attention to little ol' me, but hooee does she hate being insulted." Tūtū's brows pulled together. Anna kept going, plowing through to the finish. "So Pele sent 'Io to grab Kaipo. I'm trying to get to him, thinking he is up at the top of the crater with her. I was on my way but needed to come tell you that, um, some, um, *lava*"—Anna kind of whispered—"*is coming. Here. This way. Now.*" She was so quiet by the end, unsure if Tūtū heard.

"Ho-kay." Tūtū nodded and dusted her hands together, taking no time at all to process all the weirdness. "That explains things. Here's what to do, Lei."

Anna sighed with relief, extremely grateful to let her grandma take charge.

"You go get Kaipo back and fix this with Pele. I going stay here. We got an evacuation plan, and I gotta help Mrs. Lottie and her keiki. With the new baby, she needs me to corral the others. Then gotta help Uncle Higa round up his goats. The new flow has been all over da news. Das why I came home early. Folks packing up and heading out."

No way. Anna rubbed her ear, sure she heard that wrong. "Hold on. You want me to go back up there? What if you come, too? I mean, I know you have people here to help—" Anna felt guilty even asking, but come on! Shouldn't Tūtū care more about helping her own granddaughter than other neighbors? Wasn't there some sort of family code or something? "I don't want to do it by myself." A bit of a whine crept into her voice that she hated, but it was better than breaking down and crying.

"Eh, look at me." Anna raised her eyes to Tūtū's warm face. "Were you by yourself?" Tūtū asked, one eyebrow raised.

"Well . . . no." A glance at the window confirmed Ilikea wasn't visible.

"I figured." Tūtū's eyes twinkled. "Come here."

Tūtū held out her arms. Anna walked into them and let out a huge sigh, relishing the comfort in the chaos. Tūtū's cheek was on her hair, and Anna could feel her jaw move when she spoke again.

"Sometimes our actions have consequences bigger than we can imagine, yeah? Butterfly flaps its wings and makes a hurricane . . . tiny ripples can make big waves . . . you one smart girl, you get it. Main thing is that you don't run from making it right again, yeah? Otherwise, those waves? They going drown you. Go get Kaipo. Apologize to Pele. Hurry. Still get chance to stop the flow before it hits houses."

Anna felt Tūtū's warm lips brush a kiss on her forehead, and then she was released. Anna frowned and looked outside.

"The lava tube took forever to get through."

"Eh, you ready to listen to my suggestion now?"

Anna's eyes snapped back to Tūtū, ready for anything to avoid that death trap. "Absolutely!"

"There's an old trail off the back of the lot. Between the two biggest hāpu'u ferns. I let that part get overgrown so you wouldn't go wander up there on your own when you were little, but it should get you ma uka faster."

Perfect. "Thank you, Tūtū!"

"Here's one musubi. Remember, Lei, you have our moʻolelo in you, yeah?"

Anna tried to smile, but it felt tight and phony. With one last hug, she grabbed the seaweed-wrapped rice with salty red ume spread—she was not a Spam-fan—biting into it the instant she was back out the door. She laced up her shoes and ran across the clearing, scooping up the machete on the way. The massive hāpuʻu ferns that stood like ancient sentinels created shade over whatever path there may have once been. Grateful for the machete, Anna finished the musubi and started swinging.

"Yeah, yeah, you told me, guess you had more faith." Ilikea's voice was carried over on a breeze. "You don't need to push, I'll get there when I want to get there."

"Huh?" Anna said. She turned around to see Ilikea getting bounced around by Makani as they worked their way over to her.

"Nothing. You decided to come back, eh? What, your tūtū kicked you out? She didn't want to be in cahoots with a fugitive?"

Anna went back to hacking through the vines, breathing hard through the ridiculousness but glad to see the snarly bat. "There's a trail back here that'll get us up the mountain. Tūtū has to stay and help folks in town." As she moved under the ferns, the last of the tangle gave way, and a path was visible. The ferns and jungle hugged the space from above, but a ground trail was clear, moss and dirt free from trees and roots winding under the foliage. Anna pushed forward, hacking at the tendrils that reached out and coiled around her ankles, trying to slow her down.

"The mighty warrior swings her sword." Ilikea spoke in a bored, monotone voice. "She thrusts and parries. How impressive. How strong. No evil can stand in her way, not even the jungle."

Anna stopped swinging for a second, her chest heaving. She swatted away a coil that reached for her ponytail. "Kay," she gulped out between breaths. "I hear the judginess. Spit it out."

"Is this really a battle?"

"Um . . . yes? I need to get to Kaipo fast, so yeah."

"And how's that going for you?"

Anna looked back. She was barely past the two massive hāpu'u ferns. "Not great."

"So lose the machete, Mulan."

Anna considered it briefly. She sure wasn't sprinting up the mountain the way her feet were itching to. With a sigh, she tossed the machete back onto the grass in the clearing. Makani swirled around her, lifting her ponytail back up as she turned around. Her jaw dropped as she watched in disbelief as vines that were reaching for her a second ago curled up on themselves. Ilikea flew over her shoulder and used a bat wing to close Anna's mouth.

"For flap's sake, don't just stand there. Let's go!"

Was this really still her tūtū's Volcano? A low hum under her skin started as she approached the vines, considering them closely. The uluhe felt the same, silky-smooth spine and slightly pokey fern edges. Was it her imagination, or did the ends of the plant start to curl toward her finger, like it was returning the greeting?

"Thank you," Anna whispered under her breath, not wanting Ilikea to hear if this was all just her imagination. A breeze rustled the plant, and Anna looked up the path. She had so much to ask Kaipo.

The path continued to clear as Anna, Ilikea, and Makani headed ma uka. Anna took a swig from her water bottle. The higher-pitched sloshing signaled she'd be out soon. She should have filled it when she was back at Tūtū's. Definitely time to find more. Maybe there was a river nearby. As Anna stuffed the bottle back into her pack, she paused to grab another guava off a tree to replenish her side-pocket stash, picking a second one to eat.

The ferns a few feet away rustled. Anna froze.

An enormous snout framed by four curved ivory tusks poked through the growth. Anna's insides turned to blooping jellyfish as it snuffled loudly, turning in Anna's direction. Zero chance of screaming. A huge block of fear lodged in her throat, preventing even the tiniest of squeaks. Preventing breath. The pressure in her head built as the animal came closer. This boar must have been as big as a black bear to have a nose that size. Right when she thought she was going to pass out from lack of oxygen, the snout retreated into the ferns. Anna listened as the beast moved away quickly through the brush.

Anna bent over, sucking in huge lungfuls of air.

"Are you coming or not?" Ilikea called.

Anna struggled to marshal her innards into some semblance of solid bone and organs. When her spine and legs decided to co-operate again, she straightened and marched toward the bat.

"Did you see that boar?" she croaked.

Choking on the sudden dryness of her mouth, Anna grabbed her water bottle again and drained it. The trail stayed free and clear of large mammals, but Anna kept pausing, listening for any signs of intruders.

"Hmm?" Ilikea hummed. Makani blew Anna's hair back off one shoulder then over onto her other.

Anna coughed, trying to clear her throat, and tried again. "The ridiculously large, about to eat my face, giant boar? Did you see it?"

"No, but boars don't eat people. You're fine."

Um, false. Well. Partly false. They might not eat people, but they could definitely mess them up. As she continued up the trail again, Anna remembered what Uncle Tiny had told her.

Her uncle, Aunty Charlotte's son, was a pua'a hunter. Last summer, Anna and Tūtū made the drive to Waiākea Uka for dinner. They sat in Aunty Charlotte's fancy, two-story house with an interior built-in koi pond, a lava-rock pathway, and an atrium with actual trees planted in the floor stretching up to the light streaming in from second-story windows and skylights. Anna loved visiting because they had hunting dogs. No, they weren't the friendliest animals, kept for tracking pigs and for keeping folks off the property. They weren't any discernible breed, just random poi mutts, but she loved them, and they tolerated her.

She sat on the cool concrete of the back patio surrounded by hot doggy breath. Tūtū and Aunty Charlotte played cribbage and talked story while Anna listened to Uncle Tiny's latest horror stories of other hunters or their dogs getting gored by tusks or trampled by the boars.

At the time, Anna had brushed him off as being dramatic,

figuring he was talking like a fisherman overexaggerating the size of the fish that got away. After all, he never had any scars or injuries. Remembering the size of the tusks on the boar she just saw, Anna could definitely imagine the pain and damage they could inflict, and she didn't want anything to do with it.

"Fine. Maybe not dead, just maimed. Pretty sure that's what was making the paths we saw earlier." Her mouth was completely dry. "Hey, is there a river around here?" She cleared her throat again. It'd be good to fill her water bottle.

"Yeahhhhhhh . . . ," Ilikea said, long and drawn out the way Anna did when she tried to pretend she knew what she was talking about but had no clue and needed to buy time to think. "Oh! Water! Kuewa—"

"Anna," Anna said automatically.

"—Whatever. I almost forgot, there's a cave over here that I've heard about. There are scales inside that would help you against Pele." Ilikea sounded livelier and more animated than she'd been yet on this trip.

But Anna had no clue what she was talking about.

"Scales?"

"Yeah, scales!" Ilikea said. Makani swirled the tiny creature up into the air, getting into the excitement. "Hoohoo, are you gonna be thanking me or what? Who's the best bat? This bat. Who's the best bat? This bat."

Ilikea flapped and fluttered in a wonky motion that Anna assumed was a batty dance as she chanted her little song. Every time she said, "This bat," her batty fingers at the tips of her wings would point at herself, and she'd momentarily drop toward the ground and

Makani would swoop in to lift her back up so she could continue her cheer.

"Water's this way."

"Okay, but what kind of scale? How is it going to help me?"

"Oh . . . well . . . so." Ilikea circled for a bit. Then she put on a super attitude-y tone and said, "The scales are long known to provide protection for travelers on journeys throughout our islands. It's rumored that a scale was what protected Kamehameha and helped him to unite the islands."

"Tūtū said it was because he had guns from the haole and a sweet heiau in honor of his war god."

"Okay, but how did he *get* the guns and the heiau? The scale!" Ilikea said. "Just go in the cave, pick up a scale, bring it out, and it'll protect you. You're the one that is saving Kaipo. What, you don't know what you're doing?" Ilikea broke into mocking cheer as she flew ahead. "C-L-U . . . E-L-E-double S. She's clueless, what, what? She's clueless!"

"Fine, okay, a scale," Anna said with a frown. A cave full of scales? Like, the ones in the doctor's office to check weight? What would that do against Pele? Or was it more like a fish scale? This sounded majorly sketchy. Where was Kaipo, with his all-knowing everything, when she needed him?

Oh.

Right.

He was trapped somewhere because of her being, well, a donkey (or another word for one). Anna felt the hot prick of embarrassment as she pushed on behind the bat. At least they had a plan.

Ish.

Anna tried to picture what Pele might look like. Years ago, when the Jaggar Museum at Hawai'i Volcanoes National Park was still open, Anna had come face-to-face with a depiction of the goddess going through a transformation from beautiful maiden to old woman. Anna had stopped, transfixed, and Tūtū came up behind her, placing a hand on her shoulder.

"Ah, I see you went find Herb Kane's vision of Pele," Tūtū said of the mural. The haunting image was so vivid and powerful that Anna couldn't help but believe that he had seen the goddess with his own mortal eyes. She looked at the rest of the painting.

"The snow on that mountain is a lady in white!" Anna said, peering way up at a corner of the mural.

"'Ae, that's Poli'ahu, the snow goddess of Maunakea. Remember the story we used to read about the hōlua?"

"Oh yeah," Anna had remembered, "that epic sled race down the mountain between the goddesses. Pele threw that major tantrum when her sister Poli'ahu won. I loved the picture of Pele trying to burn down the whole mountain with her lava. Who's that below her? Next to the boar?" Anna asked, pointing at a man whose shoulder brushed against a breadfruit plant.

"Ah," Tūtū answered with a smile. "Those are some forms of Kamapua'a. He can be a man, a pig, or even a kukui nut tree. He and Pele have one interesting relationship. Sometimes he's Pele's boyfriend; sometimes he's her enemy."

Anna had puzzled over how someone would like their enemy.

"Kuewa! Watch where you're going!" Ilikea's resonating voice shook Anna from her cozy memories, and she came to a quick stop.

Heart pounding in her ears, she surveyed the glittering crystals suspended inches from her nose. A giant, raindrop-covered spiderweb of an overly ambitious arachnid spanned the trees ahead of her. A shiver worked its way up her spine. Way too close for comfort. She definitely needed Kaipo back to lead the way and break the webs ASAP. Anna hugged herself as she went off trail to avoid being coated in spidey thread, picking her way over decaying logs and around the trees.

"Thanks for the heads-up," said Anna, her heart slowing to its regular pace as she grabbed her phone and snapped a quick shot with her hand held in front of it for scale, Ilikea hovering blurry in the background. Hmm. Ridley wouldn't consider a massive web proof of an epic vacation.

She deleted the shot and tucked her phone safely back into her side pocket. The high pitch of birds in the trees was a constant this deep in the rainforest, but a new low tone filtered through the trees, adding an undercurrent to the melody.

"Water!" Anna moved more quickly, tripping and stomping toward the welcome sound of a rushing creek.

Anna moved a couple of hāpu'u fern fronds out of the way and gasped. A dark turquoise pool of water enclosed by lava rock lay just beyond the jungle border. A frothy, white waterfall tumbled into the pool and a creek flowed out over the far lip, cascading over boulders and smoothly rounded pebbles in a creek bed. The pool itself was about the size of Tūtū's living room, and a cave winked in and out of sight behind the mist at the base of the waterfall. Kaipo would absolutely love this place. He must not know about it, or he'd have brought her here. Or maybe he wouldn't? Maybe he would have worried that she wouldn't have appreciated it the right way. That she would have teased him if he treated it with his calm, quiet manner that she could now see was a sort of reverence for the natural world around him. Like she had with that spider he'd found.

Or maybe he worried about her just using the place for a picture to show her friends on social, not caring about the risk of it getting crowded with others wanting to come take the perfect shot of themselves next to these pristine waters.

But now? Now Anna could sense it, too. This place felt too special to share with just *anyone*. Too . . . sacred? Yeah, that was the right word. "Don't worry, Kaipo, I'll keep this a secret."

The hum started under her skin again, and Anna pulled out her water bottle. She approached the falls cautiously while keeping her eye on the mouth of the cave. Did it really house a scale that could protect her from Pele?

My, What Big Eyes You Have

"**I'll be back,**" Anna shouted over the rush of the falls.

"You're really going in?!" Ilikea squeaked. Then she coughed and lowered her voice, "I mean, yeah, do it."

Anna paused and tilted her head. "You told me there was a scale in there that would help protect me."

"Well, yeah, there is. They are probably all piled in a corner. No biggie. Just hurry up, all right? We need to keep moving." Ilikea flew up to a branch and perched, crossing her bat wings stubbornly. Anna narrowed her eyes at the creature. What was up with her? The bat definitely seemed anxious about something, but a scale of protection would be pretty epic. And facing Pele on her own didn't sound like a great plan.

With a deep breath in through her nose and out through her mouth, Anna turned to the falls again. Her sneakers slipped and slid on the wet ferns surrounding the pool. The mist chilled her to her bones, and goose bumps broke out along her bare arms.

She crept closer, extending her empty hand till it touched the cool, smooth lava rock wall that the waterfall cascaded down.

"Hi, beautiful falls," she murmured. "Thank you so much for your cool water. I really appreciate it." Her other hand brought the water bottle in to fill on a side trickle. Her shoes slid off the slippery grass and onto the slipperier boulders. Old fruit covered many of the rocks, adding to the sliminess. The dose of rotting reality marring the pristine beauty shook Anna out of her peaceful calm as she struggled to regain her balance. The stench of earthy decay coated her tongue. She gagged, then clenched her teeth and took shallow breaths through her mouth.

Anna stepped gingerly onto a flat-ish-looking boulder, testing her weight. Invisible slime plus gravity worked in cahoots, and her foot went flying. She shrieked and attempted to dig her fingers into the rock wall but couldn't find any purchase. Her left leg shot out to another rock, but it was covered with pebbles that all went skittering and splunking down to the pool below. Anna sat, hoping to stop her downward momentum. Her butt slid for a minute on the disgusting grime, and she spread her feet out between two different stones, wedging herself in the middle of them. Finally, about an inch before her foot ended up in the pool, she stopped sliding and silenced herself, breathing hard. Small rocks that she'd dislodged continued to fall into the water around her, and her butt was getting wetter by the second as the rotting juices seeped through her jeans. Anna removed her hand from the wall and tried to swallow her heart down from her throat back to her chest.

She wouldn't have noticed the first tremors if it weren't for the ripples that emanated out from the rocks around her. Her breath caught, and she watched, transfixed. Ripples . . . ripples . . . ripples . . . in a steady rhythm, almost like a heartbeat . . . or like footsteps.

Uh-oh. Anna stood and instantly slipped back down to her butt. She stayed there, frozen, as the ripples grew deeper. Then she could feel the rock itself shaking. One hand on the rock wall to keep from sliding into the water, Anna waited, eyes glued to the falls.

The churning curtain parted as a lizard's head emerged. First the tip of its snout, plated in shimmering blue scales, each roughly the size of tea saucers. Then, beautiful golden eyes stared, unblinking, as the arrow-shaped head—bigger than the end table next to her couch back home—came through the water and turned toward her. The nostrils flared and its long, forked tongue flickered, tasting the air around Anna.

Anna's mouth went dry. A moʻo! Tūtū had told her stories about these legendary creatures guarding waterfalls, harassing people, and battling gods. The pools in lava were the results of many of their fights, according to her grandma. Anna's heart jumped again, beating so wildly she was sure its tongue would sense its vibrations and know just how much fear she tried desperately to conceal. *Okay, not really a dragon, but not quite a giant gecko, either,* she thought to herself, all the while absentmindedly admiring the color of the scales the way someone might find a tiger's stripes beautiful as they were being stalked.

Scales!

Ilikea never said anything about them being *attached* to a moʻo.

Goat snot.

The moʻo's neck extended out of the cave, and then a front foot the size of a big dinner plate reached out and over to the side of the pool near where Anna stood. She quickly backed away from the claws at the end of each of its five scaly toes. They easily pierced the lava next to her, sending broken chunks tumbling into the tranquil pool. The tongue flickered again in her direction, stopping just short of her nose. Anna shrank back, wincing. And then the creature spoke.

It had a floating, singsongy voice.

"'O wai kou inoa?"

The water bottle bobbled from her grip, and she nearly lost it in the pool. Her hand slipped, and she felt a rock cut into the soft flesh of her palm. "Ow!" Anna yelped, then quickly clamped her teeth together, sucking a hard breath through them as she clenched her muscles and fought to remain upright on the slippery surface. *'O wai kou inoa . . . where've I heard that before?* She stuck her water bottle back in her pack.

Anna's mind flashed back to when she was younger, sitting on the lauhala mat at the foot of Tūtū's rocking chair. Tūtū always tried to teach her as much of her native language as possible in the short three weeks they had together every summer. Tūtū wanted to have Anna become as familiar with her moʻolelo and Hawaiian roots as she had become with her American culture. It didn't really eliminate Anna's feeling of being an outsider, but at least she knew the stories. One of the first songs Tūtū taught her was a name song:

"'O wai kou inoa? What is your name?" Tūtū'd sing.

"'O Leilani koʻu inoa. That is my name!" Anna'd answer.

They'd repeat the lyrics, asking each other's names and making up silly names like Nīele Nancy and Kolohe Kimo to extend the song. Easier to remember words in a song than if Tūtū said, "Repeat after me: *Nīele* means overly curious. *Kolohe* means rascal." *Could Tūtū have ever guessed that I'd one day be asked that very same question by a giant lizard at the foot of a waterfall?*

"'O Anna ko'u inoa, of Volcano, oh wonderful and wise mo'o of the falls." Anna tried to sound obliging and humble. Last thing she wanted to do was somehow upset a dragon-lizard thing and get eaten before she even made it to the fire goddess.

"Ah, you are one of the old kama'āina families," the mo'o said, fluidly switching from Hawaiian to English. "I can taste your tūtū's influence on your words. Tell me, *Anna*"—it almost sounded like it tested her name. Low and drawn out, not at all singsongy like the rest of the mo'o's words—"why did you scream and disturb my slumber? Have you come to join me? I've been bored and lonely since I ate my last pet."

Abort! Abort! Abort! Sirens blared in Anna's head.

What would Kaipo do? What would Tūtū say?

It took everything she had to hold herself in place instead of attempting to scramble as far away from this mythical monster as possible. Anna gritted her teeth. *Think, Anna. Think like Lei. The way Tūtū wants you to.*

"I'm so glad to see you, too," Anna choked out. She swung her backpack around to the front of her body, quickly rifling through it. She pulled out her last musubi, unwrapped it, and offered it up as omiyage. "Thank you for allowing me to visit your home." She bit the inside of her lip hard to keep from screaming as the mo'o craned its head, stretching till Anna felt the warm puffs of breath against her palm. Then, quick as a blink, the musubi was gone. Anna wiped her tingly palm against the rock, scraping away the sensation of smooth scales against the rough surface.

Okay, offering made, time to get creative. She came here looking for a scale. Maybe she could still get one. Remembering a story Tūtū had told her, Anna spoke. "I heard that Pele helped Maui destroy a mo'o over by Boiling Pots." The mo'o's pupil narrowed to a slit as it focused on her words. "That's not cool at all for her to get involved and play favorites like that, is it?"

"What are you getting at?" the lizard hissed.

"My friend has been kidnapped by Pele. I'm going to get him back," Anna announced.

The mo'o laughed once, sharp and bitter. "You? What makes you think you'd be able to rescue your friend from the almighty Pele?"

"I'll have your scale to help me," Anna said, trying to sound strong and sure of herself, hoping there was no tremor in her voice even as her knees shook. Even though she wasn't exactly sure how the scale would help.

The mo'o went silent. Its eyes shifted, sliding over Anna as if weighing her differently than they had a second ago. "I find myself intrigued, Anna of Volcano, and that has not happened in some time. I've been bored with no one to keep me company. Come into my cave, and we will talk."

No! Going into caves with creatures that ate humans definitely did not sound like a good plan for saving Kaipo.

"Oh, I think talking out here is good," Anna quickly replied, "Really. I can hear you better, and I think the cave will be a little too—"

"I said COME!"

The claws on the foot nearest Anna released the lava and wrapped around her torso. Anna's ribs squished painfully and she tried to pry herself out of them. The cool, iridescent scales overlapped delicately, forming smooth seams that slid silently as the joints flexed tighter. Anna gasped as the claws pricked holes in her shirt. Every breath she took caused the needlelike tips to dig into her skin, her backpack crushed to her back. No way could she pull away without getting pierced through. The giant lizard's body fully extended outside the cave. It was about the size of an elephant but low to the ground and with a longer tail. The giant lizard started retreating into the cave, carrying Anna with it.

Clean Cave, Happy Home

Anna held her breath as the mo'o pulled her through the falls, only to discover the water parted and didn't touch her. The mo'o put her down on the damp rock floor and paced to the rear of the cave. Anna turned to the bright falls and lifted her shirt to look at her stomach. The punctures from the claws were tiny. Her guts weren't spilling out. With a sigh of relief that she wouldn't bleed to death before getting to Kaipo, she lowered the shirt and turned to look back at the lizard. Now to work on not getting eaten.

The mist from the falls coated the interior of the cave with a slick sheen of moisture. Anna wanted to move toward the back of the cave to avoid the cold spray, but she didn't want to go too far into its lair or get too close to the mo'o. Having the waterfall and cave opening to her back and the lizard to her front helped her feel like she wasn't completely boxed in.

It was a fairly tidy cave, as far as caves went. Anna stood without hitting her head at the entrance, and if she stretched out her arms, she still wouldn't touch both sides of the opening. Dim light reached the back of the cave, showing that it widened even farther toward the rear. The lizard had settled in, lying across the rear wall on a large mound of decaying leaves. Anna couldn't help noticing that the cave's smell reminded her of autumn back in Colorado: pungent and organic. Its long tail, instead of curling around it like a cat's, stretched out along the side wall of the cave and reached about half the distance back toward Anna and the opening. There were a few puddles of water, some roots hanging down from the ceiling, and a pile of bone-looking things back in the far-left corner that Anna didn't want to examine too closely.

The mo'o's golden eyes seemed to glow at Anna from the rear of the cave, reflecting the little light that made it back there. Its tongue flicked out every so often, which she assumed made sure she hadn't escaped. But who knows? Maybe he was testing her emotions and gauging just how freaked out she was over all this.

"I like your cave," Anna said, figuring flattery made everyone happy. "It's very . . . clean. And cozy. Very cozy."

"Don't bore me with inane chatter now. You held such promise. It has been some time since I've had a human. They are so delectable that I find myself wondering if my interest in you was imagined . . ."

"No! No." Anna mentally scrambled, sweating through the freezing mist. "I told you I need to go to Pele, and I plan on using one of your scales to get my friend back, right? Um, so, do you have a scale I could have? And could you show me how to use it?"

She clasped her hands together. *Shoot!* Tūtū always told her to be more respectful of elders. Hopefully the mo'o remembered she'd offered it a musubi and didn't just go straight to asking for a scale.

"Please! I meant to say please. Don't know where my manners went—" Anna clamped her lips together, determined not to chatter and give the lizard any reason to get hungry.

"What's in it for me?" the moʻo asked from the back of the cave, its voice deceptively sweet. "I could be helpful, just eat you right now and end your agonizing over your lost friend. You won't even care once you're dead. And you do smell delicious." The lizard's tongue flicked out in her direction.

"Um, I'm good. Thank you for the offer of ending my misery, though. I'd like to be miserable a bit longer." Wait, that didn't sound right. "You're bored? You want entertainment, and I want a scale. I will tell you a story. A great story. One you haven't heard before. It will entertain you, and you could give me a scale. Does that sound good? Deal?"

"I've heard all the stories," said the moʻo.

"But what if I could tell you one you've never heard before? Would you give me a scale?"

The moʻo thought for a little bit. "Fine," it said, finally. "If you tell me a story I haven't heard before, I'll give you a scale and let you walk out of here."

"Great!" Anna said, breathing a sigh of relief.

"If I *have* heard it, I eat you."

Anna gulped. Well, that option sucked. *Kaipo. Focus on Kaipo.* Anna squeezed her eyes shut and clenched her fists, forcing the words out.

"You have a deal."

Fate sealed, Anna thought about the moʻolelo she learned with Tūtū. Which story wouldn't the moʻo have heard of? This creature had probably been around since the dawn of time. Most of its previous storytellers would have likely told tales of Maui or the other popular Hawaiian legends. Anna paced back and forth at the opening of the cave, racking her brain. Wait! She should make up a story from back in Colorado. He wouldn't have heard one of those before.

"Okay," Anna said, coming to a stop in the middle of the cave. "I'll tell you the story of a girl from the land of rock and ice."

"That will do, girl," it said, crossing its front legs under its head and resting its chin on them, its wide eyes gazing in her direction.

Here goes nothing, Anna thought as she launched into the story.

"Once upon a time, in a land of rock and ice, there lived a girl," she started, her voice shaking as she twisted and plucked at the hair band on her wrist.

The lizard yawned, showing off a mouth full of daggerlike teeth. Anna gulped. "Boring . . . ," it said as it lay its head back down.

"She wasn't just any girl. She had a heart of ice. This girl never smiled. She never played with the other children. She didn't understand their games and laughter. All she did was stand on the edge of the playground and watch, silent and unmoving, frozen in place." Anna paused, watching the lizard. Its face gave nothing away. *Well, it's not moving toward me to eat me, so that's a plus. If I really am the keeper of the moʻolelo, now would be an excellent time to have that skill to invent a story unique enough to captivate a moʻo.* Anna continued the story, her voice smoothing out as she gained confidence. Kaipo needed her to do this. Tūtū said it was in her blood. "One day a—"

"Let me guess. One day a boy shows up and thaws her frozen heart. Boring. Heard it."

"Do you want to hear the story? No. A boy doesn't show up." Anna glared at the lizard. She had been getting in a groove! Where was she? Oh yeah, remembering the day she had met Hennley. *The beginning of the end.* Her lips automatically turned down, and she crossed her arms as she continued. "One day, a butterfly showed up." She quirked an eyebrow at the moʻo. The lizard stayed silent. *Phew!* "It fluttered over to her on a nearby tree branch. It studied the girl, her serious face, eyes trained on the other children.

"'I can help you,' the butterfly said in a whisper-soft voice. Now, you'd think that would startle the girl, having a butterfly speak to her out of nowhere. But since she had a heart of ice, she never felt fear or surprise. Instead, she turned to the small voice and inspected the creature. This was different.

"'Help me with what?' she asked.

"'Help you be more like them. Running and laughing and playing. Help you feel.'

"The girl considered it. She looked out to the field. Imagined what that would look like. What it would feel like to be just like them."

Anna lowered her arms and tried to shake off the shadow of the memories of her former friend. She needed to be smart here. She shouldn't give the whole story away without learning more about the scale. Maybe she could learn more about what it did. She knew that whenever Tūtū finally got to an interesting part of her story, Anna begged her to continue if she got distracted. She'd be willing to do anything, just to hear how it'd end.

So Anna stopped.

Right in the middle of the story.

"But wait, marvelous moʻo, I'd like to know, why are your scales blue?" Anna asked, breaking the cadence of the tale.

The mo'o lifted its chin off its lizardy hands and shook its head as if waking itself up. "Why did you stop the story?" it asked incredulously. "My scales are blue because I'm a water spirit. Blue scales allow me to become one with water, and they deflect fire. Now, get back to the story. How does the butterfly melt her heart?"

"One last question, well, more of a clarification really. Smaller geckos have a skin that they shed, not scales. Do you, um, shed?" Anna asked, rushing through the word commonly used for household pets, glancing around the tidy cave, not seeing any old scales or skins. Ilikea clearly didn't know what she was talking about—pile of scales.

At this, the irritated mo'o glided off its pile of debris and stalked toward Anna. She involuntarily took a step back before stopping and holding her ground, not wanting to appear to be scared or about to flee. She didn't want to provoke it into using its claws again, but she needed information.

"I have scales because in my large form it is easier for me to replace my scales individually as needed rather than shed my entire skin at once. Other mo'o may choose to inhabit space differently," the mo'o said, its raised, lyrical voice bouncing around the walls of the cave as it moved behind Anna. She forced herself to stay still and continued to face the back of the cave. Unable to see the mo'o, she focused on slowing her breathing. It had involuntarily sped up and become choppy as soon as those piercing talons had come close again.

The mo'o continued, "But I'm never sloppy. I put them into the pool and dissolve them so no one is able to use their powers. If humans knew what they were capable of, I'd be hunted for them." It finished its slow circle of Anna and headed back to its debris pile, where it lowered itself onto a bed of leaves once more.

Anna's body relaxed now that the claws were on the opposite side of the room again. *Okay, the scales DO have powers!*

"How do they work?"

"Anything is possible if you believe. But first you have to get back to the story. Does the butterfly beat its wings quickly over her chest to melt the ice?"

This had to work. Anything was possible if she believed? Heck, in this cave with an oversize talking gecko she felt closer to Tūtū's stories than ever before. She focused on that feeling—the warm, solid seed of truth that took root and started to grow in her gut as she returned to the story. "So the girl with the heart of ice said, 'Show me where this would happen.' The butterfly flitted off toward the back corner of the field, into a small grove of trees. The temperature cooled, not that the girl felt, noticed, or cared. She focused solely on the butterfly that promised change. 'What would it be like, being like them?' she asked.

"'Oh wonderful!' the butterfly exclaimed. 'You'll be able to share in their jokes, their stories, their triumphs and sorrows. You will be just like them!' The girl watched as the butterfly flitted about, weighing its words. She held out her hand. The butterfly landed delicately in the center of her palm, its wings lightly fluttering up and down, as if waiting for her agreement." Anna paused again, looking at the mo'o. It lay in the back of the cave, but with a definite lean in her direction, waiting to hear what would happen next. A spark of inspiration hit, and she held back a grin. Time to give this story the ending it deserved.

"The girl looked at the butterfly. Considered what it said. Its beautiful wings pulsed slowly. Orange with black outlines, like miniature flames flickering in her palm, promising to melt her icy heart. Then, faster than a blink, she brought her other hand over the butterfly and clapped. The winged insect was crushed. Killed in an instant." Anna watched mo'o's head snap up when she *clapped*, the sound echoing in the cave. The giant lizard tilted its head one way, then the other. Then it broke into shocked laughter.

Picture It

"**The strange ice** girl killed the beautiful butterfly?!" the mo'o asked in wonder.

"Yes." Anna's smile broke through.

"But that can't be it. What happens next?"

"I think this is a good-enough ending for now. It was a surprise and a new story. I have satisfied my end of the deal."

No need to rehash reality. Anna didn't know what would happen with Ridley. She shifted from foot to foot. Her whole life felt like one gigantic question mark right now. Taking a deep breath, she tried to ground herself, scrunching her toes in her shoes. One thing at a time. One friend at a time. Get the scale. Save Kaipo. Then figure out the rest.

The mo'o flicked its tongue. "Tell me more, first."

"A deal is a deal. I will tell you more if you give me the scale and your absolute word that I may leave no matter the ending."

"I want the ending."

Anna pretended to think, frowning a bit. "I don't think you want to know what's next."

"I do!" the lizard proclaimed.

"Mmm, I don't know. It's pretty gross." Anna scrunched up her face in a grimace.

The mo'o cocked its head. "Tell me."

"Are you sure? You can handle gross? And do I have your word I may leave with a scale no matter what?"

"Yes! I give you my word. Tell me now!" The mo'o was making little bouncing movements on its forelegs.

"Well, all right. But don't say I didn't warn you." Anna lowered her voice. "The girl with the ice heart opened her hands, looking at the crushed creature. The delicate beauty, dead. Flame of life, extinguished. And then . . ." Anna watched as the lizard leaned closer, hanging on every word. "She raised her hand, up, up to her mouth . . . and ATE it! Well, not the wings because those were nothing but powdery crumpled dust, but she ate the slender black body—legs, antennae, and all."

The lizard collapsed on the floor, laughing. "She ate the butterfly?!"

Anna continued, "Yup, ate it. Then the girl wiped her hands off on her pants and walked back to the edge of the field to watch the other kids playing. There was another girl standing there. That girl had a soul of fire and was full of rage and angst and love and every emotion imaginable. It was always too much and always simmering right below the surface.

"The girl with the ice heart stopped next to her, and they both faced the field. Their hands hung at their sides almost touching. The girl with the ice heart felt it thaw, just the slightest amount, and the girl with the fiery soul let out a long exhale. Together they stood in silence, watching the other children play." Anna finished, exhaling through all her energy. Her fingertips felt tingly, a rush of adrenaline shooting through her at finishing the story. Was this how it was for Tūtū?

"Hmm, I see what you are saying there," the moʻo said.

"You do?" Anna's brain scrambled trying to guess at what the ancient creature pulled from her impromptu story time.

"Yes. I like it. Don't trust pretty things that promise to change you, to turn you into something you're not. Trust those that stand by you and appreciate you for who you are."

Dang, that was good. As the words seeped under her skin, she considered what she'd been trying to do on this trip with the whole "winning Ridley back with pictures" thing. Surely that didn't really count, right? I mean, Ridley was her friend first. If anything, Anna was just trying to save her from Hennley's clutches, the way she was trying to save Kaipo. Chewing her lip, she decided to focus on another part of her story.

"Well, yeah. But also, friends bring out the best in each other and can be comfortable with each other's quirks. And that sometimes a little bit of change is okay."

It wasn't like she was making excuses. She and Ridley totally brought out the best in each other. Hennley didn't. Anna was just changing ever so slightly, not for Hennley but for Ridley. But even her own gut clenched at that fallacy. Clearly, she needed to improve her lying skills to pull off lying to herself more convincingly. She was definitely changing for Hennley. To get into that group. She scrunched her nose.

"Is there an odor I'm unaware of?" asked the moʻo.

"Hmm? Oh no. Just thinking." Anna turned her story over in her head. Would she be able to mend the rift between her and Ridley? Would pictures of an amazing summer really be enough, or would she have to change herself even more? And was it worth it?

Right now she wasn't sure, but she didn't have a better plan. Anna pulled out her phone, weighed it in her palm, then slowly slid it back into the pocket. It just didn't feel right to try to capture this incredible, impossible creature in a photo. She'd have to figure out a different way. This moment was hers alone.

"So." She clapped her hands nervously. "I'll get going now. May I please have a scale? It is time that I rescue my other friend."

"You seem to have difficulty holding on to your friends." The mo'o chuckled at its not-at-all funny joke. Anna forced herself to laugh along weakly. "Yes, yes. You may have your scale. Hurry, come closer."

Anna swallowed, wiping her clammy hands on her jeans. Okay. No big deal, just walk up to a giant monster that thinks you smell delicious and take part of its hide. She breathed through her nose and took measured steps forward, certain to keep her chin up and not give away the fact that it felt like a million buzzing bees were all trying to push out of her skin.

The mo'o lazily stretched its neck forward, reaching and clawing at the ground far in front of it, much as a cat would when roused from a nap. Its shoulders shifted back and forth in a feline manner, before settling back down onto the pile of old leaves.

"Take the scale from my shoulder above my right foreleg, closest to you." It leaned its shoulder toward her. "Come now, do it quickly."

Anna reached the torso of the mo'o, putting as much distance between her and its mouth as possible. Her skin crawled with dread at being close to those piercing claws again. Eager to have the protection, she stuffed her fear down her throat, trying not to choke. She gingerly reached out, balancing carefully on the balls of her feet so as to not put any of her body weight on the beast's heaving side and grasped the shimmering scale on its shoulder with her right hand. Her left hand put pressure on the scales just above to dull the pinch she imagined it'd feel from the scale extraction. Was it like someone pulling out a strand or two of her hair? May as well be as considerate as possible to the powerful being. A quick tug—*like ripping off a Band-Aid*—and the scale came off. It glistened blue in her hand, not dulling at all having been separated from its creator. *I can see why people would want to hunt it for its scales; they're beautiful! I wonder what it does and how I make it work . . .* Anna stared, momentarily stunned by the power she held in her hand. From the corner of her eye Anna caught sight of the lizard's tail flick and shook.

"Thank you, mo'o," she said as she backed away to her spot by the opening and the waterfall. She swung her bag to her stomach, wincing as it hit her tender punctures, and put the smooth scale carefully inside before returning it to her back. "Well, um, goodbye." Anna lifted a hand in a little half wave, not really sure if bowing was more the thing to do when leaving a mo'o's cave. Out of all Tūtū's stories, she had never learned lizard protocol. She turned toward the water, half expecting to feel the claws sinking back into her stomach if it changed its mind.

"Take care, Anna of Volcano. And remember, you're always welcome to stay." It started laughing as if it knew an inside joke.

Anna definitely did *not* want to stay. She made it to the edge of the cave and put one hand on the wall, ready to peer into the mist.

A pebble next to her foot that tumbled out of the opening of the cave made her stop to adjust her eyes to the daylight and listen as it bounced off the side of the cliff a couple of times before disappearing into the mist of the falls far below. This was not the same cave she had been brought into! She remembered, when she first went to fill her water bottle, the mouth of the cave was near the pond and the moʻo emerged at her eye level. Now she was practically Rapunzel in a tower in the sky. *I see how the moʻo keeps its storytellers with it. Think, Anna, think!*

Don't Look Down

A thin ledge of lava ran from the edge of the cave along the wall of rock toward the jungle beyond the pool. No wider than her foot, it had crumbled away completely in other spots, likely a result of the mo'o's claws and weight as it leaned out to greet visitors to its pond.

Anna carefully pivoted to put her right foot on the ledge, smooshing the toe of her sneaker as hard as she could against the cliff. Her shirt clung to her chest, pressed against the wet lava cliff. The weight of her backpack acted like a cruel counterbalance, tugging her away from the safety of the wall. Her hands grasped at the sparse ferns and small plants that somehow grew in this improbable environment. The grooves and cracks were smaller than the handholds at the indoor rock climbing gym she'd been to a few times for Ridley's birthday parties in Boulder. Why oh why didn't she go climbing in Eldorado Canyon when she had the chance? She'd be a pro at this!

Anna glanced down into the churning mist, and her entire body broke out in a clammy sweat.

Oh yeah, because she was scared of heights.

Anna squeezed her eyes shut and willed her fingers to grow suction cups. She had to do this. Scooting out a little farther, she balanced the balls of both feet on the ledge and began slowly edging toward the jungle.

The ledge crackled and crumbled beneath her feet, the lava more brittle and thin than she originally thought. She moved forward unsteadily. Her knuckles scraped the rough cliff and bled through shallow cuts. The palms of her hands stung as they slipped trying to grip the damp plants. Her feet cramped. She carefully moved her right foot forward.

Then right hand.

Left hand.

Then left foot.

Over and over. Warm sweat mixed with the cool mist of the falls and dripped down her back. She kept her focus on the wall in front of her, searching for her next handhold, when suddenly the ledge beneath her feet completely gave way.

"Whooaaaa!" Anna yelled, her knees slamming into the wall of the cliff as her body dangled. Hands slipping on the small fern she'd grabbed, she frantically scrambled with her toes, searching for any purchase. Nothing. She looked at the face of the cliff. A few small orchid plants nearby wouldn't offer the strength to hold her body. She looked down, stretching her foot toward the nearest ledge. She felt her hands reach the very end of the plant, continuing to slide.

And then she fell.

She didn't flip or bounce off the wall the way she had heard the pebble tumble out of the cave. Anna just fell straight down, feet first. The cool wind of the waterfall blew past her as the pool rushed toward her.

"Makani!" Anna called out.

The air around her warmed, and she felt pressure below her trying to stop her fall.

It didn't slow her enough.

She continued plummeting toward the rocks and rotten fruit below. "Makani, can you push me against the wall?" The warm air gathered behind her, and Anna slammed upright into the rock face. Instantly she curled her fingers into claws, tearing her nails as she slid. Finally, her feet found purchase on a tiny ledge and held her steady. Her cheek scraped against the rocks, and tears sprang to her eyes, but at least she stopped falling.

Anna let out a huge sigh. "Thanks, if you can just sort of keep up a pressure at my back, I'll climb my way over."

Anna worked on finding slots for her toes and new handholds. She'd fallen to a much rougher area, riddled with pits and divots from the churning spray of the falls meeting the pool.

With Makani's help, Anna picked her way over to the edge of the water. At last, one foot and then the other touched down on the jungle floor, and Anna dropped to her hands and knees. A warm tornado that acted like a blow-dryer instantly sucked her up, drying her soaked clothes and hair and eliminating her ever-present goose bumps. "Makani, I wish I could hug you. Thank you. So much." Anna hung her head for a minute in exhaustion.

She examined her sore fingertips, wincing at the sight of blood seeping from cuts and ripped nails. She pulled out her first aid kit and quickly cleaned up the worst of it with an alcohol swab, hissing through the pain. Frizzed-out hair hung around her face, so she braided it back, securing a hair band to the base. Movement out of the corner of her eye caught her attention, and she turned in time to see a hulking black shape disappear into the brush. Was something following her? Was it the boar again? She twisted the other hair band on her wrist when she heard a familiar voice.

Ilikea appeared, flapping above her. "Oh good, you're back. You get the scale, Kuewa?"

Anna was torn between annoyance at being called "kuewa" again and anger at essentially being sent into a deathtrap. Sure, she survived. But *barely*.

Anger won.

"Are you even kidding me right now?" Anna swung her pack to her stomach. "You told me there would be scales in the cave."

"Yes? And?"

"You failed to mention the scales would be attached to a mo'o!" Anna shouted, pulling it out and holding it in front of her.

In the clear light of day, the scale shone a beautiful crystalline blue that changed hues as she tilted it. Sometimes it would be the clear aqua of a morning sky; tilted the other way, it looked like the deep, dark blue of the pools in the lava rocks.

"Well, paint me gray and call me nēnē. Anna, you actually got one." Ilikea stopped flying around her and perched upside down on a nearby branch to better examine the scale.

Anna rocked back at the sound of her actual name on the bat's lips (well, mouth—she wasn't sure the bat had lips). When Ilikea reached out a tiny bat hand, Anna yanked the scale out of reach.

"No, you don't get to touch it. I almost died back there!"

"But you didn't."

"But I could have."

"But you didn't."

Anna huffed. This argument wouldn't get them any closer to Kaipo. "Whatever. We need to go. You can explain how to use this thing on the way."

Before Ilikea could answer, a shadow fell over them, and they both glanced up. 'Io!

Screeeeeeeee!

The massive hawk that had taken Kaipo screeched as it caught sight of Anna and the scale.

"Run!" Anna yelled.

"Fly!" Ilikea shouted at the same time. Anna threw her pack on, gripped the scale, and took off through the trees. The bird's shadow stayed over them as Anna weaved and dodged.

"Anna, duck!" Ilikea called from somewhere over her left shoulder when she went under a branch.

"Anna, jump!" she said the second after Anna jumped over a mossy trunk.

"Anna, 'Io's getting closer." Ilikea's voice was over her head now. "Go faster!"

"Ilikea." Anna panted. "Not. Helpful."

"Anna, the scale," Ilikea said. Anna glanced down. The scale was vibrating ever so slightly and glowing with a dull pulsing light, as if aware a threat was near. The hawk screamed again, tearing Anna's gaze back up to the sky. It tucked its wings, diving toward her.

Anna fell to the ground on her back, scale in one hand. 'Io landed on the other side of some trees. It hopped and scraped the ground, advancing on Anna. She scrambled backward awkwardly, trying not to drop the scale as 'Io's feet framed her body. The giant hawk reached for Anna. She rolled to the side, and its claws tore through the earth behind her. The air filled with the smell of soil. Anna looked up to see the other foot coming straight for her. She rolled back and forth to avoid the massive, striking talons.

A cloud of debris grew to surround Anna as the hawk continued its deadly dance. Pulse pounding in her ears, Anna used the dirt as cover. She rolled onto her belly and crawled under some hāpu'u ferns, knowing it would only buy her seconds. The dirt cleared, and 'Io came after her. It tore through the branches like ripping through wrapping paper, green fronds flying. There was nowhere to go. Anna looked around, for once wishing that the ground would actually open up and swallow her. *Where's a lava tube when you really need one?* She rolled onto her back, the scale held like a shield on her chest.

'Io pounced.

It brought one foot down directly on the scale, crushing it into her.

"Ungh." Anna's breath squeezed out of her chest, her eyes watering in pain. The hawk's other foot dug into the dirt near Anna's head. She flinched away from the daggerlike claws that had hurt Kaipo. The weight on the scale was intense. Her lungs felt like they might crush to the point of collapse under the hawk's pressure. She took shallow breaths to not pass out. 'Io screamed again, and Anna let go of the scale for a second to cover her ears from the deafening noise.

The instant she took her hands from the scale, the hawk gripped it with its beak.

"Anna, the scale! It's going for the scale!" Ilikea shouted. She darted back and forth over the monster's back.

"I . . . know!" Anna ground out through clenched teeth.

Her hands flew back to the scale, yanking it out of the sharp beak and holding it to her chest. No way was 'Io gonna get this away from her. The pulsing glow intensified, cool to Anna's touch. The hawk pecked at her fingers. Anna shifted them, playing the most dangerous game of hot hands ever to avoid a severed digit.

"Do something!" said Ilikea.

"You got any ideas?" Anna yelled back.

"Try blowing in its face."

Blowing it its . . . what?

"Why would I blow in its face?!"

"I did it to a cat once, and it left me alone!" Ilikea shouted while flying somersaults over the hawk.

"I don't think that works with hawks. It'll just bite off my whole head!"

"Fine, genius. You're so smart, you think of something!"

"Trying!"

Anna's right hand swiveled the scale like it was a steering wheel she was turning. She moved it down her chest until it was over her lower stomach. Using her elbows, she propped herself up just enough to be able to crane her head over the top of the scale. 'Io was focused on trying to peck her fingers and didn't notice her shift positions.

Crunching her abs, she brought her face close to the yellow foot pushing down on the scale. She pulled her lips back from her teeth and opened wide, trying not to think about where that foot had been.

Pushing up with one final burst of strength, Anna bit down.

Hard.

It's like biting into kalbi ribs, she tried to convince herself. A thin layer of meat over hard bone. She clenched her jaw as hard as she could and grimaced as she felt a warm trickle run down her chin. *Don't gag, don't gag, don't gag*, Anna thought, eyes squeezed tight.

'Io screamed again, jerking its foot off the scale and out of Anna's mouth. Wings spread, it took off in a flurry of ferns and leaves. Anna rolled to her stomach, keeping the scale under her belly.

"Pleh!" Anna spat onto the ground, gagging when small chunks of yellow flesh covered in drool hit the dirt.

She grabbed her water bottle from the side of her backpack and rinsed out her mouth, spitting again and again. Cautiously she touched her chin. Her fingers came away tinged with blood. Her stomach churned. She leaned over and squirted water onto her face, scrubbing frantically with her other hand trying to get all traces off. Finally, she straightened. 'Io was a speck in the distance, but Anna shouted, "That's for making Kaipo bleed, you oversize dodo bird!"

"Let's not get hysterical," Ilikea said. Now that the danger was gone, she had perched in a nearby tree while Anna cleaned herself.

Anna gargled one more time, spit a stream of water onto the ground, then wiped her mouth with the back of her hand, feeling wild and more than a little hardcore. She'd just bit a legendary hawk's foot. She grinned.

"Uh-oh," Ilikea said. "Makani, she's lost it."

Anna looked up at her. "Oh, come on. Aren't you impressed? I totally kept the scale away from 'Io. That's pretty awesome, right?" Anna did a little shimmy, proud of her victory.

"Sure. And when Pele's hawk comes back with a busted toe and no scale, then what? How do you think she'll react?"

Anna winced, bubble burst. Kaipo was gonna pay for her actions. Again. But seriously, what other option was there? Hand the scale over to Pele? She might as well just go home and let their house be swallowed by lava. No. Anna would fight this. And if she upset a goddess by hurting her minion in the process, well, boohoo.

Why did Ilikea always have to make her feel bad for everything? Anna shoved the water bottle and scale back in her pack with more force than necessary. If the bat was so concerned about Kaipo, why didn't she help more? She didn't even have any good ideas. All she did was repeat what Anna did.

"What was that back there, anyway?" Anna finally asked, swinging toward Ilikea. She yanked her pack onto her back, swiped the clumps of dirt off her jeans and shirt, and stomped up the trail, anger fueling her steps.

"What do you mean?" Ilikea said, fluttering behind. Anna glared back at her. She looked stiff, more guarded than usual.

"You," Anna huffed. "You were, like, the worst help ever. You basically played narrator the way my dad does when he drives the car, 'Okay, kiddo, hang on. Turning left here. Gonna check the mirror now. Clear to go.'" Anna looked ahead and continued up the trail. "I thought you said you'd help me get to Kaipo."

"Well, I did."

"Right. How in the world have you helped?"

"I got you to the lava tube."

"I almost got crushed!"

"I got you to the cave."

"I almost got eaten! Do you even know what this scale does? How to use it?"

"For flap's sake, you are just negative! I don't know if I like your attitude." Ilikea perched on a branch and folded her wings, turning her face away from Anna.

"You . . . don't like . . . my . . . ?" Anna spluttered. "No. *You* are the one with the crappy attitude. And zero people skills."

"Maybe I want you to learn for yourself?"

"Or maybe you're just a bat who doesn't know anything and is trying to get me killed."

"I *know* stuff. I just know that I don't want you to know what I know. Yet."

Anna's jaw dropped. "Are you kidding me? You know what? Forget it. I can do this on my own. I was able to get out of the tunnel on my own, get a scale on my own. I can go get Kaipo without you. Come on, Makani."

Anna felt the breeze swirl around her once, then watched leaves whirl as they blew over to Ilikea's branch, making it bob hard enough that that bat fell and bounced on the gusts of wind before spreading her wings.

"Fine! Go! You'll be back. No way can you do this without me. You still don't even know where he is!" Ilikea screeched.

"Maybe not yet," Anna spat, "but I'll figure it out."

With Friends Like These

Anna stomped her way through the rainforest, trying to forget Ilikea with every step. Most of the path was fairly easy and clear, but every now and then there was an impassable section of tangled uluhe fern. Anna felt at odds with the jungle as she fought her way through the tangled brush. Her fuming anger had her battling the twisted ferns while listening to the peaceful singing of birds hidden overhead. The happy sound felt all wrong given her mood. She punched through another vine.

Kaipo wouldn't have felt like this. He always seemed so at ease in the jungle. Her chest felt a sharp tug as she wondered if he was being tortured in the fiery pit of a volcano. Pele wasn't exactly known for mercy. She was the goddess of fire! Prone to fits of temper and rage, spite and malice and all the big feelings. *If* the stories were true. Anna sighed. Who was she kidding? The giant hawk, a massive dragony lizard. A lump formed in her throat, making it hard to swallow. The stories were *real*. Deep down, she had always known they were. And Kaipo was in actual danger. How long could a fragile little human last in the face of a vengeful goddess? What if Pele started melting off his fingers one by one? The lava would cauterize them so he wouldn't bleed out and the torture could last longer. Or what if Pele had her hawk peck at his eyes? Wait, was that Greek mythology? Do goddesses borrow other gods' torture methods?

All to say, Kaipo was in serious trouble. And it was Anna's fault.

She made a loud hack-coughing noise, trying to clear her throat and her thoughts at the same time. No use moping. She had a friend to save.

"Ew, sounds like you have a fishbone stuck in your throat," came a voice behind her.

Anna whirled around in surprise. A girl about her age, barefoot the way Kaipo often was, hovered a short distance away. She was wearing a maroon sleeveless dress that either was super good at hiding dirt and moisture or was amazing at avoiding all the damp ferns and trees surrounding them. Her dark hair was twisted into a bun that was almost as big as her head and secured with one of those cool wooden dual-prong combs that Anna had seen in her mom's drawer but had no clue how to use.

"Wha— Who are you?" Anna asked, looking around, half expecting to see more people emerge from the jungle.

"Surprised you, did I? Yeah, you looked pretty lost in thought. You can call me 'Ula. What are you doing out here?"

Anna chewed the inside of her lip, unsure how to answer. For some reason, this seemed to delight the strange girl.

"Oh, come on now." 'Ula held out her arms and turned in a slow circle. "I've been taking this walk every day for *forever* and never see anybody other than my family. *Bo-ring.* Then finally there's a girl about my age, and she doesn't want to talk? Figures." Then she stopped and faced Anna again. "What, are you on the run?" Anna didn't know how to answer that. "Seriously, you're right outside my backyard and not saying a word. Super cool way to make friends."

Anna's skin flushed with embarrassment. She definitely knew firsthand how boring it could be out here, though it was becoming more and more clear that maybe there was a lot to like about an eventless summer hanging out with Tūtū and not worrying about lava burning houses or your best friend dying.

"Sorry, no, I just hadn't seen you around before and you caught me off guard."

"I could say the same about you," 'Ula said with a smile. "So really, what are you doing here?"

Anna didn't want to make this girl think she was more bizarre than she probably already seemed.

"Just out," she lied. "Told a friend I'd meet him by the volcano and got a bit turned around. Figured heading ma uka was a safe bet."

'Ula cocked her head like she was trying to put some puzzle pieces together. Her brows pinched. Then her face cleared, and she smiled brilliantly. "Kinda dangerous, yeah? Meeting by a volcano? Didn't you hear it's erupting again?"

"Yeah . . ." Quick, what could she say that wouldn't sound like she had a death wish? Anna tried to think fast, grateful when 'Ula piped up again.

"But hey, you do you. You only live once, amiright?"

"Um, something like that." Anna snapped the hair band on her wrist. "Do you know of a trail around here that gets to the crater?"

"I mean, duh. Did you miss the part about me hiking around here *forever*? My . . . um . . . dog ran off years ago, and I know it's silly, but I'm always hoping I'll spot him. Especially with the recent flow starting back up. There is a trail this way that runs along the edge of the cliff that will take you up the volcano."

Anna watched 'Ula turn and head off on a spur trail. The stranger-danger advice wouldn't really apply to a bubbly girl her age, would it? Anna was pretty sure she could take her if it came to that. She shook her head. *Take her?* What was she even thinking? This was a random girl in a jungle, not some scary person out to get her. Still, she couldn't help the shocks that were zipping up and down her spine like she'd stuck her finger in a socket.

"You coming?" 'Ula called.

"Yup, just taking a quick picture." Anna grabbed her phone, took a shot, and then jogged to catch up to the girl. *IF* the stranger-danger feelings were legit and something happened to her, at least someone might find her phone and see where she was last.

"Oh neat, you have a phone! It's the kind that takes pictures?"

"Um, yeah," Anna said, a bit confused. What phone didn't take pictures? "Here, we can take one of us." Anna held it out over her head and leaned closer to the girl, whose massive grin filled the screen. It was contagious, and Anna felt her own mouth stretch into an answering smile, the two of them looking like they'd been life-long friends in the single shot.

"That is so cool!" 'Ula said. "Let's do another."

"Oh okay." Anna snapped another one quickly. "I'll upload them when I get back to service. Let's get to that trail you mentioned."

"Yeah, sure, it's just this way," 'Ula said, and walked ahead.

Anna had no idea where the clear trail came from, but it was wide enough that for the first time since leaving Tūtū's (well, aside from all the time in the lava tube), Anna was able to swing her arms while walking. Nothing touched her! It was blissfully easy, and she fell into a rhythm behind 'Ula, watching her bare feet pick their way over the dirt.

"So, have you been in the area long?" 'Ula asked.

"Me? No, not too long. Just visiting. But my tūtū's been in Volcano forever."

"Mmm, neat place. I like the art."

"Totally." Anna scrambled for something else to say. She didn't usually check out art with Tūtū. "I like the guavas." She squeezed her eyes shut. *I like GUAVAS?* What kind of doofus answer was that?

"Oh my gosh, I know, right?" 'Ula said. "I swear the skin on the guavas here isn't nearly as gross as the ones on O'ahu."

Anna had no clue what guavas on the outer island were like but was thrilled that 'Ula was just going with it like this was a normal conversation to have.

"Maybe it's all the rain?" Anna suggested, not sure what else to talk about.

'Ula nodded as if that was a very wise deduction.

"That makes a lot of sense. The rain could absolutely make the fruit plumper, fleshier. I like the way you think . . . wait, what's your name?"

"Anna."

"I like the way you think, Anna." 'Ula grinned her big grin again, and this time Anna's smile in response was fully authentic, spreading to her bruised fingertips. Makani blew through the trees overhead, leaving the girls to the stretchy silence of discovery. Could it really be this simple? Trying to make conversation with Hennley was like trying to play hot potato with dynamite—she constantly expected her words to blow up in her face whenever it was her turn to talk.

"Okay, I feel like I need to ask," 'Ula began.

Anna braced herself. *Here it comes, the big "You're not from around here, huh?" conversation.* Why couldn't she just blend in?

"Lilikoi or lychee?" 'Ula asked.

"Huh?"

"Which do you like more? For shave ice?"

"Oh!" Seriously? That was it? This she could totally answer. "I guess I'd go lychee. But really I'm more half strawberry, half li hing mui," Anna said.

"Yes! I always forget about li hing mui and just go for the lilikoi. But you're right, that combo is awesome. Hey, have you been to that ice-cream place in Hilo that has li hing mui ice cream?" 'Ula tipped her head back and made like she was drooling. "So 'ono!"

Anna let her shoulders droop, relaxing into this easy talk for the first time since Kaipo had been taken. "Ooh, no, but that sounds amazing. Have you been to the restaurant over by the park in Hilo with the haupia pancakes?"

"Yeah, that place is the *best*. Oh my goodness, I can never finish my food. Those pancakes are as big as hubcaps! You have good taste."

Anna beamed absurdly at this praise. Finally! *Suck potatoes, Hennley, I can totally do this conversation thing.*

"Hey, are you nervous about the eruption?" Anna asked. "Your place isn't in danger, is it?"

"Aw, you're so good to look out for me. I'm ma uka of the eruption, so I'll be fine."

Anna thought about maps of the area, trying to remember what could possibly be habitable north of the flow. She didn't think homes went up that far. In fact, Kaipo had told her a story once about how Tūtū's home was the farthest up the mountain.

A rustling in the brush to her right startled Anna out of her thoughts. She couldn't see anything in the wild growth. Was the boar back?

"Did you hear that?"

"Hmm?"

"Sounded like something big was right there," Anna said, pulse racing.

"Oh, I'm sure we're okay. It was probably just the wind."

Anna glanced up and raised a brow. She watched as an ʻōhiʻa branch bent horizontally, then wagged left to right. Makani's equivalent of shaking their head. Not them, then. She tried to let it go but kept stealing glances out to the jungle, unable to shake the feeling of being watched, but not wanting to say anything that sounded out of the ordinary that could crush this tender, new alliance with ʻUla.

Which was why she was completely stunned by what ʻUla said next.

"So have you seen the moʻo by the falls?"

Anna stumbled over a root. "W-what?"

ʻUla glanced back over her shoulder with the same easy smile on her face. "I mean, I hope I'm not being too much"—she widened her eyes—"but just thought I'd ask."

Anna couldn't believe her ears. This girl knew about the moʻo? Believed in it? Would she know about the scale? "I did, actually. It was . . . neat." She repeated ʻUla's word from earlier.

"No way! That's so awesome." ʻUla did a little spin and clapped her hands. Anna smiled, not really believing that this girl was enthusiastic about something this, well, unbelievable. "She give you anything?"

"She?"

"Yeah, well, I guess I shouldn't assume. But most mo'o are female, so." 'Ula shrugged her shoulders. Huh. Anna filed that nugget of knowledge to digest later. She hesitated and weighed her options on telling this new girl about the scale.

On one hand, if Anna didn't say anything, she'd just keep walking and hope she could figure out how to use it on her own. She'd had fairly decent success so far. She'd probably get up to the top of the mountain soon. But the image of Kaipo's hand being shoved into a fire flickered in her brain. She'd grown too comfortable. Time was of the essence.

If Anna told this girl about the scale, maybe 'Ula could tell her what it did. She already seemed more knowledgeable than Ilikea. Anna winced as she thought about the bat. Maybe she'd been a bit hasty in ditching her. After all, she was a friend of Kaipo's. Now all she had was this girl in the jungle. Sure. She'd see what 'Ula knew.

"Actually, I did get something." Anna swung her backpack around and unzipped it as 'Ula turned her way and walked closer. Anna pulled out the scale, the cool, blue firmness biting into her fingers. It felt as though there were the slightest tremor to it, like a tuning fork that had been struck minutes ago and was practically done vibrating. 'Ula's eyes grew wide.

"Whoa," she whispered.

"I know, right?" Anna replied. "Do you know what it does?" She held its broad face up to the sky.

'Ula stepped closer and the tremor increased. Anna tightened her grip and brought it closer to her chest.

'Ula paused and looked contrite. "I'm not sure. But I'm dying to check it out." She took another step closer. "I've heard stories about them. One said that a mo'o scale can help you breathe underwater. Was thinking it might help me find something I lost in the ocean. He—I mean *it* dropped in a while back, but it was super important to me. Here, could I hold it?"

The earlier tingles from Anna's spine struck through to her core, her na'au. No way was she about to hand off this scale. The mo'o trusted her with it, and she was going to protect it.

"I'll hold it for now, but have you ever used one before? Or heard of someone who has?"

'Ula stopped about a foot in front of Anna, her face twisted in confusion. "Wait, why won't you let me hold it?"

"I just . . . I can't right now."

"You can't? Oh, are you going back to being all mysterious? Aren't we past that?"

"Yeah, but—"

"I mean, come on, Anna, someone who likes the same guavas and shave ice can't be all that bad." 'Ula gave a clear-eyed grin. "Or, like, do you think I'm evil or something?" She screwed up her face like that was the absolute most ridiculous thought in the world.

But Anna couldn't shake the feeling. And that sucked.

"No, it's cool, I was just wondering if you'd used one before." Anna held it in one hand as she worked to open her backpack with her other, readying it to put the scale back in. 'Ula darted forward, closing the gap between them, and grabbed the scale.

Anna instantly recoiled, stepping back and pulling the scale with her. "No! Let it . . ."

Her words died in her mouth as 'Ula's fingertips closed around the scale . . .

Then passed right through it.

The scale melted where she came into contact, liquid oozing down and resolidifying over Anna's hands, its slightly thicker ridges like paint that dripped and hardened. 'Ula's eyebrows pulled together, and she grabbed again. Anna watched in fascination as the scale again melted out of 'Ula's grasp.

"Give it to me!" 'Ula screeched, her face contorting, rippling under the skin.

Anna gasped and jumped back as one of 'Ula's outstretched hands touched her arm. It was intensely hot, like she had a super-high fever. Or had been warming it over a fire. The image of Kaipo burning flashed in her mind again.

"No," Anna whispered. "No way."

She twisted away, moving as quickly as she could but not wanting to turn her back on this stranger who had squirmed her way into Anna's confidence. Arms wide, 'Ula started slowly approaching. The trees above Anna's head began whipping around furiously, showering the girls in leaves and branches.

"Makani, I need help!"

"I got you, Anna!" A familiar cry came from behind, and a small shadow darted over her shoulder up into the rioting branches. "Throw!"

Ilikea? "How? Where—"

"No time! Throw!" the little bat shouted.

Anna gauged the distance and threw the scale into the air over her head. She watched Makani guide the scale higher to Ilikea, and the bat caught it in her feet. Anna braced herself for it to fall back down to earth, figuring it'd melt as soon as Ilikea touched it.

But it didn't.

Ilikea took hold and, buffeted by Makani, she flew up into the treetops and out of sight. Anna breathed a sigh of relief and turned to face 'Ula.

She expected anger. She expected rage.

She didn't expect pity.

The scornful kind delivered by the mean girls who look down their nose at the poor unfortunate souls who dared to breathe the same air as them but would never use the oxygen to its fullest potential.

"Aw." 'Ula pouted. "Looks like you have a broken scale. Whoops." She covered her mouth and made her eyes wide in fake surprise. "*Had* a broken scale." She clicked her tongue and then laughed. Not a big, low, *muahaha* laugh. But a pretty, delicate, fancy laugh that sounded like freaking wind chimes. Anna hated it instantly. "Poor Anna, all that work for nothing. Hope you have a plan B for Kaipo!"

Anna froze. "How do you know about Kaipo?"

"Oh please, child. I know everything that happens in my jungle. You should hurry, I grow tired of keeping him alive."

Fear tinged with disappointment snaked through Anna. 'Ula was not just a girl going for a walk in the woods. Anna should have suspected something. Tūtū always said Pele could take on many forms. Granted, she never explicitly said one of those forms could be a teen girl with seemingly genuine offers of friendship, but seriously, what were the odds that she'd find an actual friend all the way out here in the middle of nowhere when she couldn't even keep one on the crowded playgrounds back home?

Anna wrestled with wanting to run far away, yell at the goddess for tricking her, and beg for Kaipo back all at once, but 'Ula evaporated into steam before she could act. Like, poof.

And instead of floating up or dissipating in the atmosphere, the earth trembled, and a crack opened up at Anna's feet. Anna jumped back and watched as the wisp that was 'Ula filtered down into the ground.

He's Not Who You Thought

"**W**hat in the . . .**"** Anna stared at the crack in the ground, not believing her eyes.

"Anna! Girl, we get in one argument, and you go running off to the enemy? What were you thinking?" Ilikea came back down out of the trees, struggling mightily with the massive scale in her batty toes.

Anna couldn't even say anything. She just kept staring at the crack. Was she a mean-girl magnet? How could she have been so blind? No. She wouldn't let this bring her down. It wasn't her fault that she was nice and open. Her gullibility and willingness to make friends didn't make her a pathetic sucker. The other people taking advantage of that were the ones who were messed up. Being a goddess was not an excuse for being awful and tricky. The adrenaline that had flooded through Anna's system moments ago drained out of her, and anger took its place. She kicked a flimsy fern and roared in frustration.

Until another rustling in the brush caught her attention.

"Did you hear that?" Anna asked, crouching into a kung fu ready-for-anything stance.

"Hard to hear anything other than my furious flapping . . ."

Anna made big waving arm motions at the tangled vines off the trail. A black shape separated from the shadows and took off deeper into the jungle. The boar!

"Hello? Earth to Anna. Could you take this scale? It's kind of a downer. Get it? It's pulling me down?"

Anna shook her head and relaxed out of her position. She looked at the bat. "Did you see that?"

"Can't. See. Anything . . . trying. To stay. Up."

"Oh yeah, sorry." Anna took the plate-size scale. It was still cool to the touch but was no longer vibrating. "You came back."

"Well, yeah. I wasn't gonna just let you go tromping off on your own. We needed to chill, take a breather, then go get Kaipo. Wait, wasn't that your plan, too?"

"Yeah," she said with a smile. "Totally doing the same thing. You just beat me to it." She put the scale in her backpack and shouldered the load. "Okay, but for real, though. I really could use some truth right now."

"What do you mean?"

"Come on, what's your deal? Why do you go from being awful to helpful? How do you even know Kaipo?"

Ilikea stayed silent so long Anna wondered if she'd ever speak. "Well?" she asked.

Ilikea heaved an enormous sigh, and her whole body rose up, then sank closer to the ground. She mumbled something low.

"What'd you say?" Anna asked.

"I said if you hadn't gotten Kaipo kidnapped, maybe I'd be better at the whole protector thing," Ilikea blurted out, then darted up into the canopy.

"Wait!" Anna called after her. "What does that even mean?"

"He was my kumu," Ilikea said, her voice filtering down through the leaves like the weak sunlight. "He was teaching me to be an 'aumakua."

Anna rotated in a small circle looking for Ilikea but couldn't find her in the shadows. "Hold up. Whoa, whoa, whoa. 'Aumakua?"

The word rattled around in her brain and unearthed the stories her tūtū had told her over the years.

"My tūtū said that 'aumākua are like . . . family guardians?" Her eyebrows furrowed as she tried to pull up the details. Something wasn't adding up. "I thought she said they were usually plants or animals or something nature-y. What do you mean, Kaipo was teaching you to be one? How would he know?"

Silence.

"Ilikea," Anna called out in warning. "Get down here and talk to me. How did Kaipo know?"

The bat drifted down out of the canopy till she was face-to-face with Anna, perched on a branch.

"Kaipo's an 'aumakua, okay?" The bat sniffled. "You *so* don't deserve him. You don't even *believe* in him, for flap's sake."

Anna's knees buckled, and she sat gracelessly down onto a lichen-covered fallen log. After 'Ula, this was all a bit too much.

"No." She shook her head. "No way. Kaipo's just a boy, I've known him forever. He's my *best* friend. I mean, he doesn't seem epic enough to be a guardian. Maybe for, like, spiders and things yeah . . ."

Were they talking about the same boy? Kaipo couldn't have hidden something this major from her. He was so regular. They had all that time hanging out on their own; he totally would have shared something like this, right? He could have at least *tried* to tell her. She would have listened. Maybe.

Anna frowned.

Maybe not.

Ilikea's voice faded into the background as Anna thought back on all her years with Kaipo. Them at the farmer's market and him finding the best avocados and pickled mangos every time. Was that actually a sign of being her 'aumakua? That wasn't very impressive. Or maybe it was how he always knew when she needed to get out of the house and would be there to listen? But isn't that just what a friend does? Or maybe—

Ilikea cut in at a near shout, "Are you actually kidding me right now?" The bat clapped her wings by Anna's face, a puff of air blowing back her baby hairs. "You ran off with Pele-freaking-honuamea just now and almost lost the scale, and now you're doubting me on your so-called best friend? Um, hello? Did you ever stop to think maybe the reason why you can't think of any major amazing things he's saved you from is because his very presence keeps the badness away? Maybe you're not as smart as you think, huh?"

Anna's shoulders crumpled. She was too exhausted to defend herself, and part of her knew Ilikea was right.

"I'm sorry," she whispered.

Ilikea sighed. "Whatever. You survived. You have the scale. Main thing is you don't go pretend to be the expert on what 'aumākua can be. They can change. Shift. Don't you think your 'ohana's 'aumakua thought you might not believe in him if he was in another body or shape? Maybe you'd be more likely to talk to a boy than a pueo?"

Anna dropped her head into her hands, trying to absorb. "You're seriously suggesting that Kaipo is an owl?" she asked. "Like, feathers, big eyes, puking up fur-encapsulated mouse bones, the whole bit?"

"Why is *this* the part that you're struggling with? You're talking to a bat. You saw a mo'o. Watched Pele transform to smoke. It is what it is. Kaipo is there to make sure you are protected and can bring you prosperity if properly addressed and regarded."

Anna lifted her head. "What do you mean, 'properly addressed and regarded'?"

"You want the *whole* thing? You're not gonna pass out or something, yeah?" Ilikea said.

Anna took a bracing breath, pulled herself to her feet, and dusted off her butt. She wiggled her toes in her shoes to ground herself before looking at the trail again. It didn't feel like she was going to faint. "You talk and explain. I'll walk."

"Right on, we go. Let's start with the basics. Back in the good ol' days when the death threat of the kapu system kept folks in line"— Anna's steps faltered. The kapu system? That was in, like, *ancient* Hawai'i. Not the 1980s ancient, but, like, the 1780s *ancient*. How old was this bat?—"families used to take care of their 'aumākua. They'd leave offerings and gifts to please their family protectors, and the guardians would take care of the family in return."

Anna tugged her hair band in quick, tight *snap, snap, snaps*. She knew that she was a descendant of the kānaka maoli, but some of the old consequences for breaking rules—like a high chief's shadow touched you so now you must die—seemed a tad extreme. Granted, it wasn't much different than other cultures, and Tūtū was a fan of reminding her that the purpose of that one was to make sure folks gave the ali'i the proper amount of space. Besides, some states still had the death penalty. *Snap.*

"Tūtū always offered Kaipo fresh fish when he came to visit," Anna remembered. "I've even seen her offering him 'awa once or twice. Pretty weird to offer that drink to a kid my age. I thought it was like alcohol, but when I asked her about it, Tūtū just 'pah'd' me aside and told me not to worry. But why'd Pele take him?"

"To teach you a lesson. If you don't believe in Pele, why should you get the protection and guidance of an 'aumakua? She decided to remedy that unbalance by sending 'Io down to get Kaipo and bring him to her."

It was starting to make sense now. Kaipo was an 'aumakua. Her family's 'aumakua. Anna's mind whirled, remembering him saving her from the pig, guiding her on adventures, teaching her about the jungle. "Wait, he was teaching *you*?"

"Yeah. What, you think, I'm just a bat that talks? Pah. I made the leap to 'aumakua, now I gotta get back to my family. Protect them. Kaipo was training me, helping me get to . . . what would you call it . . . graduation. Now . . . well . . ." Ilikea's voice went silent again.

"Oh, so now it's all my fault that you're just a bat? No way. Nuh-uh. You could have helped back there, too, even without the training." No wonder Ilikea was staying with her. She needed to find her teacher. Poor Kaipo, having to teach this crabby bat.

Anna wrinkled her nose. Kaipo's voice drifted through her head: *Don't judge till you've walked in their shoes.* That used to make her laugh because Kaipo never wore any shoes—and he'd smile at her giggles. Anna sighed. He must have known using humor would get her to remember.

Hang in there, Kaipo. We're coming. Anna started to walk again, but much more slowly this time since Ilikea was still just hanging stubbornly.

Ilikea fluttered past her, staying at around her height. Finally the bat spoke.

"*Fine.* I was scared, okay?" Ilikea said. "Ugh. I hate this touchy-feely stuff." She took a deep breath that made her float up then lower a bit, then said in one big rush, "I don't know what I'm doing. I'm supposed to somehow take care of you, and you keep freaking almost dying. And then what? No Kaipo forever? I . . . it's just . . . a lot." Ilikea fluttered over to a branch in front of her and hung upside down, wings hanging limply. Anna stopped and waited. "Sorry my advice sucks," Ilikea finished.

Whoa, an apology?

"Hey," Anna said, feeling like she needed to extend a truce card, too. "Thanks for catching the scale back there in the Pele chaos. I thought for sure it'd melt through your toes."

"It wouldn't do that because you gave it to me."

"Huh?"

"You gave it to me. So I could grab it. You weren't giving it to Pele, so she couldn't take it."

"How'd you know that?"

"I know a little bit about a lot of stuff," she said with a shrug.

"What about 'Io then? Oh, lemme guess, I hadn't made up my mind yet about belief so the scale wasn't sure if it should stay or go?"

"Well, you just turned *that* all sorts of insightful. I thought you were lucky you didn't lose any fingers, and the scale never felt it was in danger enough to have to melt."

"Could have fooled me. I felt there was plenty of danger."

Ilikea snorted. "Seriously. I thought you were a goner for sure!"

"Thanks for that vote of confidence," Anna said, but she found herself smiling. Ilikea was right. They'd made it through. They'd survived. They still had the scale. "But really, do you know how the scale works?"

"Nope," Ilikea admitted. "Not a clue. But I bet we'll figure it out."

A breeze swirled around them, and she knew Makani was feeling all the warm fuzzies, too.

"All right, from here on out, togetherness, yeah?"

Ilikea nodded. Anna headed up the trail again, anticipation buzzing under her skin. Something was right there. Right on the edge of her brain. She'd been too distracted earlier with the 'aumakua talk to pay much attention to it, but now that they were moving again, it came flooding back with the sound of the wind in the trees.

"Hold up." Everything clicked into place. The constantly rustling brush, the feeling of being watched, the huge snout, the memory from childhood of the boar Kaipo had saved her from. Holy pork rinds. Tūtū had told her so many stories about the shapeshifter, Kamapua'a. How did she not think of it sooner?

Anna had always felt bad for the guy. Mo'olelo claimed Kamapua'a's dad disowned him because, well, dude was born a pig. Some of the time, anyway. He was a kupua—a magical being—and was able to be a human, a little pig, a giant pig, many pigs, basically anything to do with a pig, plus things like a fish and a couple of plants. That's gotta mess with a kid. Anna could understand why he got his reputation as a trickster. He was probably just trying to get his dad's attention. But instead of getting his dad's attention, he'd gotten someone else's.

'Ula hadn't been searching for her long-lost *dog*.

She'd been searching for her ex-boyfriend. Those two had a history.

"Something 'Ula, I mean Pele, said just hit me," Anna choked out.

"Oh yeah, she gave you her recipe for kalua pig?"

"No . . . oh!" Anna snort laughed. "You did not just . . ." Ilikea grinned and wiggled her batty eyebrows, the white tuft of fur over her ear waving. "That's twisted! No, but kind of, yeah. I don't want to cook a pig, but I do want to find one. Brace yourself."

Ilikea suspended herself between two 'ōhi'a branches just ahead and made her wings wide like they were saying "ta-da."

"Funny." Anna gave one last smile then tried to make her face super serious for what she was about to say. "Are you ready for this? We're going to find Pele's ex—Kamapua'a."

Excitement rioted through her limbs at the prospect of searching for the legend—who she was pretty sure she had spotted a couple of times. Anna lengthened her stride. Tūtū wanted her to be the keeper of the mo'olelo, right? Well, telling a story to a mo'o was probably a good start. Maybe finding someone from the stories would be a solid next step? Was that even possible? Her steps faltered.

"Hold up, though," Ilikea said. "You just drop that we're searching for Kamapua'a and then start walking like it's no biggie. Um, hello! Why? What? How? All the questions!"

"'Ula—Pele—said she was looking for a dog and wanted the scale to find something she lost in the water. I remember Tūtū had mentioned a legend about Pele chasing Kamapua'a into the ocean and him turning into our state fish, the humuhumunukunukuapua'a."

Anna turned to Ilikea. "Here's the thought. What if the legend is back? What better place to hide than in plain sight? Pele thinks she knows everything going on here in her jungle, but who'd know better how to evade her than her ex who'd been with her for centuries. I think she's been looking for him. "

"Huh. Not bad—"

"AND," Anna cut back in, getting really excited as the idea grew and bubbled, "who better to know how to get on the goddess's good side! Ilikea, this could be our in. He could tell us how to get Kaipo back."

"I thought we had a plan?"

"What?"

"Well, we talked about hula and hōlua."

Anna paused. She'd forgotten they'd discussed that. That seemed like forever ago, and it had only been a few hours.

"Okay, fair point, but who's going to teach me the hula?"

Ilikea opened her mouth to respond but nothing came out.

"Just hear me out. I'm sick of wandering up, looking for Pele, hoping I'll figure it out. Let's get organized. Come at her with an actual plan that won't result in instant bat and girl kebabs."

"Bat-girl kebabs?"

Anna motioned to Ilikea. "Bat." Then pointed back at herself. "Girl."

"Got it. For a second, I thought we were talking about superhero movies or something."

"Right, 'cause that makes sense."

"Do you know how to find your legendary porcine prince?" Ilikea asked, her wings picking up speed.

"Ummm, no. Actually, I was hoping maybe you had an idea on that."

"Yessss!" Ilikea pumped a tiny fist. Anna tilted her head, confused.

"Ready for this?" Ilikea asked.

"Sure," Anna said, not sure at all what she was setting herself up for.

"To the bat cave!" Ilikea shouted with one hand pointed to the sky and the other wing crossed on her chest. Then she dissolved into giggles, and Makani worked to keep her afloat.

"You were waiting for that, weren't you?"

Ilikea finished up her laugh fest and flew ahead, making motions like she was wiping tears from her eyes. "Pretty much. But for real, follow me. Bats know everything."

"Right," Anna said, rolling her eyes. "Just promise me there aren't any mo'o in this one?"

"Promise."

"Kay, lead the way."

Bat Cave

The mouth of the cave stretched low and wide across a shallow clearing. It appeared to be an opening to another lava tube that breached the surface. If they had approached from the other direction, they might have stood on top of it and never known a massive hole was right below their feet. Cool air blew out of the gap, giving the impression that it was breathing. Ilikea pushed against the draft of air, aided by Makani. Anna approached slowly, goose bumps prickling her arms as she passed from the mottled sunshine to the shade of the cave. She had to crouch to enter the dark space. The dripping of water instantly reminded her of the lava tube.

"Are you sure about this?" she asked, trying to see anything in the blackness.

"Anna, come on, have I ever steered you wrong?"

Anna shot a shocked look at the bat.

"Kidding! Sheesh, tough crowd. What happened to forgive and forget, huh? I totally saved your butt back there with Pele."

"Mm-hmm. Let's see how this goes, and then we'll talk about forgetting."

"You're in my home, show some respect."

Anna paused on the threshold, unsure if Ilikea wanted her to take off her shoes in the cave, too, or something.

"Nah, nah, nah. Come in, relax. This is just where I hang, not really my house." Ilikea flew back into Anna's face. "Get it? Hang? Ha! Follow me."

Anna shook her head but couldn't hold back the grin at the cringey pun.

"Kay, try be real quiet, yeah? No need freak them all out."

Anna kept her mouth shut and focused on not hitting her head on the low lava ceiling. There was a steady wind pushing her hair back as it moved out of the cave, and the only sounds were the dripping and her shuffling footsteps. It smelled damp and earthy, with a tang Anna didn't recognize.

"Hold on, Ili. I need to grab my—" Anna started to reach for her headlamp when Ilikea suddenly let out a whoop that echoed off the walls. Anna's hands flew up to her ears as a raucous cheer went up in the cave and a dim purple light glowed ahead. Ilikea took off toward the light, Makani helping her through the space.

"—headlamp," Anna finished. With a sigh, she followed Ilikea. Hunching down more as the ceiling sloped toward the rear of the cave, Anna followed the light. The noise grew.

She finally rounded a corner she hadn't seen in the dark. The scene in front of her was absolutely batty.

Like, really legitimately batty.

What looked like hundreds of tiny, furry mammals were flying around the space. They were zigging and zagging, up and down, left and right. They kept rhythm to something Anna couldn't quite make out. It sounded like a loud hum, but if she concentrated, she could make out different tones. Were they singing? The purple glow seemed to be little lights all around the cave. Anna approached the closest one to inspect it. It was a seedpod that was hollowed out with a little purple flame inside. It reeked! Anna coughed and stepped back, the heel of her foot sinking into something.

Looking down, Anna realized she was standing on a dirt pile. Shaking off her foot, she moved a little deeper into the room.

"Ilikea," she whispered, trying to make out her companion's white tuft in all the chaos. "Ili," she tried again. Nothing. "Makani?"

They swooped down instantly, enshrouding her in warmth.

"Do you see Ilikea?" Anna asked.

Anna felt them glide down her right hand and tug her index finger out to the side, effectively having her point toward a little alcove with a few bats hanging inside. Anna moved in that direction. Sure enough, Ilikea's white fur patch was visible as she approached. Anna nodded as Ilikea looked her way.

"Bojo, Momi, this is the girl I was talking about," Ilikea said to two bats next to her.

"Nice to meet you," Anna said, smiling. Ilikea cracked up.

"Ahhhh, just too easy sometimes. They're bats! They can't understand you. They're not special like me." She winked.

Anna frowned.

"Don't go getting all nuha. I'm getting the info. Just hang tight. Ha! Another hanging joke. Okay, you can't hang. Just stand there."

Something warm dripped onto Anna's arm. She looked up. Bats were flying over her.

Oh.

My.

Gross!

A bat just peed on her! Or pooped. She wasn't sure, but it didn't matter. Both were disgusting. She swallowed her squeal and wiped her arm on the nearby cave wall, only to pull away quickly when she felt how wet the wall was. Okay. *Don't freak, don't freak, don't freak.* Ilikea was working on getting information. Hopefully. She looked down at the ground as she stepped away from the wall and into another dirt pile.

Only, she realized it *wasn't* dirt. She shook off her foot and stepped away from that pile toward a rock before returning her eyes to the bombardiers above her.

Continuing to dodge falling feces, she spoke up. "Um, Ilikea?"

"What?"

"Mind if I wait outside?"

"Just shush. Give me a minute."

Anna bit the inside of her cheek and darted another poop bomb. "Makani," she whispered. "Can you make a little wind above me to keep the crap away?"

Makani started up a little fan action that protected Anna as Ilikea finished up discussions. She stared at the girl bat in wonder, realizing that Kaipo, too, was an animal who could talk to other animals despite his human appearance. So much of what she thought she knew about her best friend was a cover-up. His house, for example. There were always reasons why they stayed at Tūtū's or in the yard:

Tūtū had better food at her house.

His house was a mess.

His pet mouse had escaped again (he knew Anna was freaked out by their tails).

A likely story. An owl having a pet mouse. A small laugh escaped her lips. Was he having fun messing with her, making up those excuses? He was pretty good at it. She hadn't suspected a thing. Anna wasn't the least bit mad. How could she be when obviously he knew her better than she knew herself? Maybe she hadn't been ready to know.

Some friend she was. Was he lonely having to pretend all the time? Having to hide that part of himself? Anna chewed her lip. How exhausting it must have been to constantly have to be something he wasn't. To only let Anna know a portion of who he really was. Well, that was over now. Now she knew, and he could be whatever he wanted to be around her. Though she wasn't sure how going swimming would work. Maybe he really did prefer the human form.

"Okey dokey, you ready?" the bat finally said, separating from the others and flying toward the exit.

Anna watched her step, following carefully after Ilikea. She stayed quiet, not wanting to disturb the strange humming and choreography around her.

They emerged, blinking into the daylight, and Anna sucked in the fresh air. That tang she smelled must have been all the guano! Her gag reflex activated, salivary glands working overtime to pump saliva into her mouth and try to purge the overwhelming poo odor.

Ilikea was doing spins and loop the loops in the air ahead of Anna, completely oblivious. "Wasn't that just AWESOME?! Gah, I love that place. Coolest club ever."

"Club? Like, a nightclub dancing place?" Anna had zero insight into clubs. Pretty sure those would wait till college. But in the shows she watched, people always went dancing at night.

"Think about it, for flap's sake. For bats, it's a day club!" She circled in the air. "BootsnCatsnBootsnCats . . . ," Ilikea repeated over and over while Makani bounced and jiggled her around to the beat. Must be nice to be so close and trust that they won't let you fall. Anna shook her head, erasing thoughts of Ridley dropping her like a steaming bag of bat poop.

"Okay, glad you enjoyed yourself. Did you get the info? Had any of them seen Kamapua'a?"

At that, Ilikea stopped her twirling and flew down to Anna. "You would not *believe* it. Well, no, maybe you would. It'd stretch your imagination a bit. But, I mean, given what you've seen over the past few hours, you'd have to be a complete—"

"Ilikea!" Anna cut in.

"What? Yeesh. So loud with the yelling all the time. Anyway, it seems as if you were right. The crew have spotted the Porcine Prince prancing about this side of the island. His latest resting place—"

"Wait, like, he died?"

"No, like, he sleeps. His latest sleep spot is over toward Hilo a bit more, but a couple of the bats noticed him heading this way yesterday, and rumor is he is somewhere much closer right now. Probably drawn in by the eruption, trying to figure out who ticked off his ex."

Anna pumped her fist, energy zinging through her. One step closer! Finally, it felt like they were on the right path again. Kaipo would be so proud of her for this idea. It had to work. She wouldn't worry about the fact that she was trying to find a massive legend whose tusks were known for churning up lava, whose tricks upset villages for eons, and whose affairs with Pele caused some of the most epic breakup drama in Hawaiian history. "Great! Let's go."

Ilikea flew ahead, singing to herself. Words faintly floating back to Anna on the breeze, "BootsnBatsnBootsnBats . . ."

As she followed Ilikea through the brush, Anna went over what she was going to do. She had seen Pele. Pele wanted her scale to go find Kamapuaʻa in the ocean. Anna held on to the scale, preventing Pele from finding him. Hopefully that would be enough reason for him to help her. Uncle Tiny talked about double-reverse-kōkua, constantly helping other people because you know you've been helped somewhere along the way, too. Keeping the good vibes going. It was a good system. Maybe he'd agree.

Ridley used to be a fan of that system. She and Anna had helped each other out so many times in the past, it was impossible to tell who owed who a favor last. Thinking through the pictures she had on her phone, Anna knew she had some okay ones with Ilikea in the lava tube, and Makani making her hair fly when they emerged. But if she could get a picture of Kamapuaʻa? Whoa, that'd be epic. Hennley would totally have to admit that a boar the size of a bear was terrifying, and if Anna was posing next to it? She'd be the fiercest kid at school.

But . . .

Was that still what she wanted? Anna chewed her lip, thinking about it as they walked. Why should Hennley, of all people, deserve to see proof of these *literally* unbelievable beings? Why should Anna be busting her butt over her approval? There were clearly bigger things in life to worry about than having the right shoes or saying the exact right thing all the time. Just look at Ilikea. She said the wrong thing most of the time, but they were figuring each other out.

It was too bad Anna couldn't just ignore Hennley completely. She had too much history with Ridley that she wasn't willing to let go of quite yet. She missed her old friend who was sucked to Hennley like a moth to Anna's headlamp.

Anna almost stopped in her tracks. She had never stopped to consider what it was about Hennley that drew Ridley in (and Anna, too, if she were being honest). Why did Hennley seem so special? She appeared *strong*. Powerful. Anna thought back to Pele, formerly known as 'Ula. That same powerful attitude immediately sucked Anna into her vortex. Maybe in middle school, it had done the same for Ridley.

Anna pondered this as they moved together through the jungle. Eventually, Ilikea stopped at a big tree with silvery green leaves waving in the breeze. Clusters of white flowers broke up the greenery, and greenish-brown golf-ball-size nuts hung from the branches. Anna couldn't help but marvel at how beautiful it all was.

"Right, so I'll just wait over here for you," Ilikea said, fluttering close to Anna's ear. "Scream if you die so I know not to keep waiting."

With that helpful encouragement, she flew off to a nearby māmane tree and hung upside down near the yellow blossoms, wings crossed.

Anna studied the kukui tree Ilikea had led her to, not seeing any signs of a pig or person.

"Hello?" she called out. Makani tugged at her pack, so Anna

swung it around. Guavas! She had spotted the big boar picking guavas. Maybe she could use these as an offering. She pulled them out of her side pocket. Looking around, she saw a ti plant. Anna tugged at loose strands that had fallen out of her braid. In hula, eons ago, she'd learned that offerings were traditionally wrapped in ti leaves. But what if this ti plant was sacred or something? She should have paid more attention to Kaipo when learning about which plants she could pick stuff from and what makes certain kupua mad. Better not risk it.

"Kamapua'a? I come bearing guavas." Anna approached, entering the shade of the tree. A flat stone the size of a skateboard lay near the trunk. Anna lined the three ripe guavas neatly in a row on the stone. Then she backed away slowly.

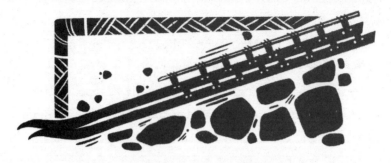

This Little Piggy

Anna glanced down at the ground while backing up. The roots and plants under the tree's canopy were tripping hazards, and it'd be embarrassing to fall on her 'ēlemu in front of a legend. As she watched her footing, she realized something had changed. Sunlight danced on her arms, warming her skin. Her own shadow was clearly visible on the ground. Startled by the sudden shift, she looked up.

The kukui tree was gone.

In its place stood a boy about her age, maybe a bit older. Dark brown skin, wide nose, high cheekbones, and a small smirk as he bit into one of her guavas. He tossed a second in his other hand and stepped toward Anna.

"Mahalo no nā kuawa. E lawe mai i ka moa i kekahi hui 'ana," he said, chewing and grinning. His Hawaiian flowed over Anna like a turbulent stream. The boy's gruff, slightly scratchy voice sounded like he had just woken up or hadn't talked a lot recently.

This was the legendary Kamapua'a?

"Um, hi. Just so you know, I didn't catch what you said," Anna said.

He blinked, and his smile widened, a guava seed stuck between his two top teeth.

"You have a . . ." Anna bared her own teeth and ran her tongue in the spot the seed was in his mouth, trying to get him to do the same.

He just tilted his head.

She pointed. "Right there, there's a seed."

His lips closed, his brows furrowed. She could see his tongue working behind his lips for a bit, and then he grinned again extra big, exposing even his gums.

"Yeah, you got it." Anna gave a thumbs-up, not sure what he understood.

"So, hi, I'm Lei," Anna said, awkwardly holding out her hand.

Then it hit her. She had called herself Lei! She didn't know how that came out of her mouth, but somehow it fit like a cozy warm hoodie on a cool Volcano day. A smile stretched her lips. Tūtū'd be psyched to hear her now. Realizing she'd been standing there looking like a fool, lost in thought, with her hand out, her smile faded.

The boy wasn't taking her hand, so she dropped it. Most of the people she met in Hawai'i were Tūtū's friends. The "aloha" greeting would be followed with a honi, a kiss on the cheek and a warm hug. Out here in the rainforest by herself, she instantly reverted to a handshake. Leaning in for a cheek kiss with the legend was a bit more than she could handle right now.

He popped the rest of the guava into his mouth, then spoke. "Whatchoo doin' out here?" he asked in accented English. A bit of guava flew out of his mouth as he talked. Anna wiped a chunk off her cheek, grimacing.

"I walked here from my tūtū's house." Anna paused. She had to start easy, start small—if she immediately accused him of following her, he'd never help her find Pele. "I'm looking for my friend," Anna continued carefully. "Somebody's been making trouble in the jungle. They think they own it all. My friend was just trying to help me out, and now he's gone."

"Who's your friend? Maybe I've seen him."

Anna gave herself a mental high five. She had him interested at least. Now to try to get him on her team.

"My friend is Kaipo. Well, he's more than a friend, actually."

Kamapuaʻa's eyebrow rose.

"No! Not like that. Gross." Heat prickled along her neck, and she knew she was probably bright red. "I just mean he's more than a friend because he's my ʻaumakua. Our family's protector."

"I know what an ʻaumakua is."

"Right. Of course you do. Sorry."

The boy took a bite of the second guava and waited.

"Yeah, so anyway, I've been trying to get him back." Anna paused and watched the boy. He stood there looking completely at ease in a deep blue T-shirt and turquoise ocean with lots of little fish–print surf shorts. Just hanging out in the woods. No big deal. He chewed slowly and swallowed before speaking.

"You gonna tell me who took him, or are you keeping it a secret for fun?"

"Oh! Yeah. Um . . . Pele?" Her nervousness made her statement come out like a question, her voice going squeaky high at the end. Kamapuaʻa's eyes widened, and he grinned.

"For real?"

Anna nodded. Didn't he remember? She was pretty sure he had seen her with ʻUla earlier.

"No way! What'd you do to tick her off?"

The tips of her ears got hot. "Does it really matter? I need to find Kaipo—"

"Ooh, this story's gotta be good if you don't want to tell me."

Anna rolled her eyes and tried to brush it off. "It's so not a big deal."

"Then why don't you tell me?"

"Because it doesn't matter." Now the heat had spread from her ears to her cheeks. She really didn't want to have to relive this.

Kamapuaʻa finished that guava and made a big show of casually walking back to the stone to grab the third and final fruit. He inspected it carefully, like it was a diamond he was searching for flaws instead of a yellow orb flecked with brown scratches.

Like he had all the time in the world.

"Fine. I picked her lehua, okay?" Anna crossed her arms against her chest. The boy took a bite, then motioned with his hands for her to continue. "Ugh! Yes, I may have said something like, *'I don't believe in her and legends are stupid'* or something like that, but obviously I came to find you and don't believe that anymore, all right?"

"Ah, and there it is. But, Guava Girl, what *do* you believe?"

"I just told you."

"No, you told me what you *don't* believe, not what you do."

"Well, obviously since I don't believe that the legends are fake, I must believe that they are, I don't know, real or something."

"Isn't it obvious?"

Anna was completely flustered by this line of questioning. How could somebody even answer that question? She only knew she was running out of time. "Oh my goodness, can you just help me find Kaipo or not? I have to hurry!"

"Is she always like this?" Kamapuaʻa called out.

"Yup. Pretty much," Ilikea said, fluttering over Anna's shoulder.

"What! I am not always like *this*, whatever *this*"—she waved her arms around—"is." Anna fumed as the legend raised his eyebrow again. "Fine! You know what? Never mind. I'll do it myself. Forget I asked." She pivoted on her heel and was about to walk off when the bat and the boy broke into laughter. Anna looked back and saw Ilikea lying sloppily on his shoulder. She felt like an outsider looking in again. She imagined Hennley's crew teaming up with those two and joining in on the laughter. Ridley would be standing on the periphery, looking awkward.

Makani patted Anna's head with puffs of air, trying to make her feel better.

"Ha, ha, so funny," Anna bitterly muttered.

"Sorry! It's just been a while since I had someone to mess with," Kamapuaʻa said. Then he looked over to Ilikea, who'd pulled herself together and was fluttering near his head. "Humans, am I right?" Anna's jaw dropped as he held up his fist, and Ilikea did a little batty fist bump into it.

"So you all know one another then?" Anna asked, the words coming out sharp and prickly. "There's a 'Legendary Creatures

Conference' you all go to and hang out? Catch up on which human you've punked lately? That's *real* cool."

Anna rolled her eyes. So she wasn't part of their crew. What else was new? She didn't care. Really, she didn't. She wasn't here to make friends. She just needed them to help her get Kaipo. Clearly, she was going to be the mature one here and get them to focus. She swung her bag around and pulled out the mo'o's scale. The laughter cut off. Ilikea watched Kamapua'a to see how he'd react.

Using her big tūtū voice, she began.

"All right. Now that I have your attention, ever seen one of these before?"

Kamapua'a stared at the scale. It was cold and firm in her hands, zero vibrations detectable.

"Yeah. Pretty awesome, huh? It is a mo'o's scale."

"Hū," Kamapua'a breathed. Then he shook himself out of his surprise and assumed another look of relaxed indifference. "Pretty cool, Guavas. But so? You still haven't told me why you came looking for me."

This was it. Anna's insides got all tight and bunchy as she took a deep breath and asked her Big Ask.

"You can drop the act," she said with as much confidence as she could muster. "I know you've been following me."

Kamapua'a just stared at her.

"I've had some time to think while looking for you. Why would an all-mighty kupua spend his time following me around? I mean, sure, today's been pretty . . . different. But surely you had better things to do, like, I don't know, churning up lava or going and messing with people in Volcano or stealing chickens or something else from the stories. And then it hit me. Maybe you don't. Maybe you're bored. Maybe you've already done all those things so many times, that you'd rather see if my day was more interesting. Like I'm your own personal reality-TV show." Anna paused to read his reaction.

He made a show of lifting his hands at a snail's pace and giving her a slow clap. "Maikaʻi nō, you've got me all figured out, uh?"

It *had* been him! Anna couldn't keep the smile from her face, even though she knew he was just humoring her. Part of her knew she was on the right track, or he'd have wasted no time in telling her she was wrong.

"So you know what would be fun?" Anna continued. "Join me in this *show*. We can team up. I bet you got a kick out of watching me with ʻUla, I mean Pele, huh? Well, I was thinking that since I prevented her from getting this scale away from me, and I kept her distracted from whatever you're doing these days, you could help me find my friend."

She was proud that her voice was even all the way to the end. No squeaky question, just a statement. The sun passed behind a cloud, sending a chill down her spine.

Hopefully this was it. Her last big stop before going to find Kaipo. She just needed him to say yes.

The entire jungle seemed to suck in a collective breath as it waited to hear the legend's reply.

B-A-N-A-N-A-S

Kamapuaʻa **walked around** the space that had once been filled by a kukui nut tree. "How did you even find me?" he asked.

"Bats. Ilikea thought to ask them. It was a great idea."

Had to give credit where it was due. Out of the corner of her eye, Anna saw Ilikea swell with pride. The bat flapped up and then soared around the clearing behind the boy, clearly pleased. Anna bit her lip to keep herself from rambling to fill the heavy silence. Kamapuaʻa shot her wary glances every once in a while. Finally, he spoke again.

"Why do you think I can help you?"

Yes! He must have been at least a little interested if he was asking about the mission. This was going to work! But she had to play it cool. Not seem too eager. Make it seem like a challenge. Like she had the power. That's how Hennley would act. And she had Ridley eating out of her hand. Pele'd probably do the same thing, and this guy dated her. Something about his demeanor made Anna feel like she didn't have to be humble and fancy with him (even though he was a legend), the way she had been with the mo'o.

And maybe it was because he looked about her age and got guava seeds stuck in his teeth.

Maybe it was because they had already bickered over him joining them.

Whatever it was, Anna felt like she could be herself.

"Well, aside from the fact that you probably have a better nose than a bloodhound when it comes to tracking people." Anna looked at him for confirmation. He shrugged in acknowledgment. She continued. "Your ex-girlfriend was trying to find you. I think she was going to use my scale to look for you in the water. That means she doesn't know you're on land yet. Even if you are in *her* jungle." Anna paused here for effect.

Pig took the bait—hook, line, and sinker.

"Her jungle? Please. Like she could create all this. She wishes. It takes a special set of tools to turn her barren, boring landscape into this fertile wonderland. She doesn't even know I've been back, hanging out right under her nose. *Her jungle.* Pfft." He scoffed.

Anna bit back a grin at his frustration. "Oh, she definitely acted like she was in charge here. I thought you might be, though. So I came to find you right away. I figured that if you beat her at her own game, that'd be the sweetest payback."

"Whatchu mean, beat her at her own game?"

"She is the one running the show and calling all the shots. Let's turn the tables," Anna persuaded. "We'll team up. I'll create a spreadsheet that outlines the most efficient route to her, taking into account the circumnavigation of the perimeter of the crater and ensuring maximum velocity and minimum duration of travel time."

Kamapua'a's face was totally blank.

Anna held her serious face for one more second. "Or we could calculate the acceleration of the lava given viscosity changes over time?" She posed, leaning back with arms crossed over her chest.

Kamapua'a blinked.

Anna cracked up. "Oh." *Giggle.* "My." *Snicker.* "Goodness." *Snort.* Anna held her stomach, eyes pinched in laughter. "Sorry, it's just been *so* long since I've had someone to mess with!" she drawled. Over to Makani, she called, "Legends, am I right?" and held up her hand. A gust of breeze hit it and blew her hair back off her face. She grinned and faced Kamapua'a.

He blinked a couple of times, then started howling. "Ho, I'm gonna need ice for that burn," Kamapua'a cracked. "Well played, Guavas. I see you. Where'd you learn all that?"

"My mom's a physicist and likes to talk about work at the dinner table. When I decided Tūtū's stories about the creation of these islands weren't going to get me As, I kinda swung heavy into the science direction for a bit."

"Ho, right on. Kay, we can give this a shot. What are you thinking, for real?"

"All right, so, you know Pele probably better than anyone else." Anna's cheeks heated as she remembered some of the stories that claimed they'd dated. She didn't want to bring up any potentially sensitive subjects, so she moved on quickly. "I was hoping you'd know maybe some of her favorite songs and chants. Maybe you could teach me a hula that would please her the most?"

Kamapua'a rubbed his chin. "You dance?"

"I mean, it's been a while," Anna hedged.

"You gonna have to be good to impress Pele."

"I'm aware."

"You have another plan?"

Anna snapped her hair band on her wrist and felt her nose crinkle in doubt. "I was thinking about challenging her to a hōlua race?"

His jaw dropped, and he froze. Anna looked up at Ilikea. The bat shrugged, and her eyes darted back and forth between the two of them. Did she break him?

"I know it's a long shot—"

"Ya think?!" Kamapuaʻa interrupted with a harsh snort.

"—*but*," Anna pressed on, "I am a pretty good snowboarder, and it might be tempting enough of a challenge to get her to agree. Even if there is the tiniest sliver of a possibility that I can win, I have to take it. I have to get Kaipo back and will try anything. If you have a better idea, I'm all ears."

He shook his head, stunned. "Dang, Guavas," he said in a lower voice. "Kaipo's gotta know how lucky he is to have a friend like you."

Anna bit her lip, knowing how wrong he was. Kaipo wasn't lucky at all. It was her fault he was in this mess to begin with. But she was sure as heck gonna fix it. There was no other option. She couldn't let him down. Couldn't disappoint Tūtū.

"How does that help me, though?" he asked. "What was all that 'beat her at her own game' talk?"

"I know she's trying to find you. Sounds like she's been trying for years. Why are you hiding from her?"

Kamapuaʻa instantly shrank right in front of her eyes. Like, literally. About a foot.

"I don't want to talk about it," he said tightly. He turned and started walking away in a huff.

"Does it have to do with the time she chased you down the mountain in a fiery flame of lava, and you had to turn into a fish and escape into the ocean? And maybe you've been a tad . . . concerned . . . about how she'll take your reappearance?" Anna called after him.

He paused.

Anna continued, "I think I have a way to get you back out in the open. You could have *your* island back." Was *that* laying it on too thick? He didn't honestly think it was *his* island, did he?

His back straightened, and he grew back to just slightly bigger than her.

"What are you thinking?"

Anna rubbed one shoe in the dirt. "Here's how I see it. You've got skills at churning up the land, right? What if when I challenge her to the hōlua, you've already gone ahead and added a couple of divots or something to the course?"

"You want to cheat? Against Pele?"

"No! She'd burn me down right where I stood. BUT if the divots were the same, on her side and mine, and I didn't see them ahead of time, is it really cheating?"

"Uh, kinda?"

"Why? She's raced on a million courses. I've never raced on a single one."

"And yet you think this is a good idea because . . . ?"

Anna rolled her eyes. "I've never raced a single one *on lava rock.* I've raced plenty on snow. I just need a little help evening out the playing field by, well, roughing it up. I can handle bumps and uneven terrain. I'm great at going through the trees back home on my board, but maybe something like that on what is normally a smooth course would give her a challenge."

"Pretty sure nothing would slow her down."

"Would you please just try? And then, as we're racing, maybe you could choose that moment to traipse across the course. I'll make sure she stays focused on me. By the end of the race, whatever happens, you'll be out in the open. Just rip off the Band-Aid."

"Yeah? And what if she decides to just burn us both?"

"But what if she doesn't? Besides, is your plan so great? Stay hidden forever? You were there when she tried to take my scale. You heard that she's looking for you. She wants to find you. Aren't you a little curious as to why? Maybe she wants to apologize for her hot temper." Anna smiled at her pathetic crack, and Kamapua'a turned to face her, grinning. "Bottom line, let her race with me be the distraction you need to make your entrance a little less grand. Take a bit of her edge off. She'll be more approachable if she isn't all caught up in memories of the last time she saw you."

Kamapua'a let a burp rip that definitely sounded like something that could have come from a pig. But then he grinned, a clear indication that he was at least a *little* impressed with Anna's plan.

"How's that's for our signal?" he joked.

"Gross," Anna said, wrinkling her nose. "What in the world was Pele thinking?"

"Animal attraction, I guess."

"Ha. Right. But, um . . ." Anna instantly regretted the new question that had popped into her head and clamped her mouth shut.

"What you wanna ask?"

"Oh, nothing."

"Come on, you can't do that."

"Really, it's nothing."

"Fine, then I don't really want to help."

"No! It was just a random thought. Really, it's not a big thing at all. Let's just go." Anna tried to turn and start walking, hoping he'd follow. When she looked back, he hadn't moved. "Ugh! Fine. I was just wondering what *you* were thinking. You know. Why you'd go back to, um, a fire goddess who apparently tried to kill you multiple times."

Kamapuaʻa's grin split his face, and Anna felt like the world's biggest fool. Who cares why he liked her! They needed to go. Now. She ducked her head and started off. She'd told him her question, so he'd better follow her.

"Have you seen her smile?" he called after her.

Anna paused.

"She's got a great one. And when things were good? Hū, felt like we could rule the island together. It's worth it when we make each other happy. Besides, she keeps it interesting, never know what to expect."

Anna remembered ʻUla's smiles. They were good, but she didn't think they were anything worth teaming up with chaos personified.

Kamapuaʻa let out another big burp, shattering any sort of mood that was filling the air. "Kay, we going now?"

"Yeah, just keep your bodily functions to yourself," Anna said with a grimace that tried to hide her smile. She reached into her backpack's side pocket for her water bottle. The nice thing about hiking in Hawaiʻi was that she didn't get nearly as thirsty as she did when she hiked in Colorado.

The birds that had gone silent when Kamapuaʻa had first arrived had come back to life, and their different songs filled the air. Anna wiped her forehead against her shirt sleeve and attempted to tuck her flyaways back into her braid as she listened to their calls.

The familiar sounds of the more recently introduced cardinal and mejiro had disappeared. New voices she hadn't heard before were weaving through the recognizable rarer trills of the native Hawaiian ʻapapane and ʻamakihi. The rainforest had changed. It was subtle, and Anna wouldn't have caught it if she hadn't spent so many days in it with Kaipo.

Or if she hadn't been so determinedly focused on it now in order to avoid constantly stealing glances at Kamapuaʻa.

It was as if there were a faint veil of time being pulled back the deeper Anna went into the jungle with her companions. Anna could practically feel a thrum of something *other* in her naʻau, her gut. Wait, no, that was just her stomach grumbling. Her back was damp beneath the weight of her backpack, and she pulled out a guava, her mouth pulling into a frown at the thought of eating another sweet fruit.

Kamapuaʻa spoke up. "Eh, I have some dry aku if you're pōloli."

Anna chewed the inside of her lip. Dried aku was dried fish, so maybe *pōloli* meant hungry? She really didn't want to have to ask and embarrass herself.

"Ummmm?" Anna looked back at him. He was holding out a bag of red dried fish. *Yes! Totally figured it out.* She grinned. "Thanks!"

Anna snatched a few pieces from his hand and popped them into her mouth.

"Ohmymmmm."

She stopped walking and closed her eyes. Heaven. The fish was the perfect blend of salty toughness after only eating sweet fruit for what felt like eternity. She took her time chewing, wanting to savor the moment.

"Thank you *so* much," she said.

Kamapua'a waited, watching her in silence. He continued to casually hold the bag of aku out in offering, and Anna helped herself to a second handful. She forced herself to take this one slowly, eating only one piece at a time.

"Kay, try follow me. I want to show you something."

Kamapua'a headed up a trail that Anna had missed to the right. Ilikea took off after him, seemingly fine with this shift in leadership. For a brief moment in time, Anna felt comfortable. She was figuring out the language—'ōlelo Hawai'i, she mentally corrected. Food and water available, decent partially sunny skies, relatively clear path up the mountain. Maybe it'd be straightforward from here.

She should have known better than to hope that.

Make Die Dead

Anna ate the rest of her handful of fish, relishing the peacefulness of the jungle around her. Her thighs burned as she followed Kamapuaʻa up a steeper section of trail. There were slippery dirt sections that would be impassable in a rainstorm without a rope. They crested the hill and came to a spot where a swath of rocky black lava cleared a path through the trees. It was similar to a cleared avalanche chute in the mountains back in Colorado.

"What happened here? Did Pele just send a finger of lava through the trees?" Anna asked, pausing to take in the clearing.

"ʻAʻole, that's a kahua hōlua," Kamapuaʻa said.

"Oh! This is where Pele does her sled racing? Her hōlua racing? Is it where she raced the snow goddess Poliʻahu? I read about that one," Anna said.

"ʻAʻole." Kamapuaʻa shook his head. "She raced Poliʻahu up on the other side of Maunakea. Uh. The ʻākau—the north side," Kamapuaʻa said, appearing to struggle a bit with the cardinal orientation. He was probably more used to using ma uka, toward the mountains, or makai, toward the sea, as their primary orientations. Or landmarks, like Maunakea. "This is another massive one. Super sweet. It dumps racers into the bay, if they don't fall off first. Got some curves in this course to throw folks off balance. Hooooooeee! I've seen some good races in my time." He leaned on a nearby tree trunk, smiling, his eyes fuzzy as if he were remembering something. "People get really hurt if they get thrown off. Even seen some make."

"And mah-keh is?" Anna asked, though she had an awful feeling she knew what he meant.

"Dead. Pau. No more."

Anna swallowed. "Cool, cool. Makes sense." She looked at the lava again. "So the next time I'm on one of these, I may be basically racing for my life, yeah?"

She looked up the hill, watching heat waves ripple across the black rock. Her hand reached for the phone in her back pocket, but she stopped. Some moments were just for her. People died here. She could die in a similar way. Had any of her ancestors raced this hill? Had they been victorious? She needed to come out of this adventure alive so she could get home and ask Tūtū. She hadn't had a chance to learn that story yet. A lump formed in her throat. There were probably so many stories left to learn. If she was going to be the keeper of them all, she needed to return to her grandmother stat.

"So if you're going to challenge her to a race, you gotta know the stakes," he said. "You win, you get Kaipo. But, Guavas, what would you even offer her if you lose? She already has your 'aumakua, what else can you attract her with?"

"I don't know . . ." Anna thought about it as they walked on. They crossed the racecourse and continued into the jungle. "What does a goddess want that she doesn't already have?"

Kamapua'a looked at her for a beat, deadly serious. Anna took a step back, instinctively shying away from whatever bomb he was about to drop.

"You'd have to figure out the thing that is most valuable to you."

What more could she give?

Kamapua'a must have seen the look on her face because he quickly continued. "Like I said. Not a great idea. Hula would still be smarter. If you show her respect that way, prove you honor her, she'd give you your friend back. She's a sucker for getting her ego stroked." He watched Anna with a cocked head. "Do you know *any* hula?"

A warm breeze swirled around her. Makani knew she was a little sensitive about this subject. "I took some lessons as a kid but wasn't very good. That's why I need your help."

Anna wasn't anywhere near fluent in Hawaiian, but she knew that many of the traditional kahiko hula chants paid respect to Pele based on the number of times she heard her name repeated during Merrie Monarch, Hilo's annual international hula competition. Anna and Tūtū would watch the televised recording of the dances since she was never able to come visit in April for the actual week of competition. It was going to be Anna's graduation present to come out after high school to see it in real life. Hula hālau from around the world traveled to Hilo for a week of cultural celebration. Tūtū said the entire town smelled of flowers and maile lei that week. Tūtū preferred the traditional kahiko competition, with its chants and ipu-driven rhythms, but Anna preferred the melodies of ukulele and singing, along with the beautiful flowing mu'umu'u the women wore in the contemporary 'auana segment.

"Even if I practiced the basics and got my hela, 'ami, and 'uwehe down, I still wouldn't dare just string them together in a pathetic attempt to create a hula for Pele." Anna shuddered. "Most of her dances have been passed down for generations. Who knows what she'd do to me if I tried to make one up and she thought I was making fun or mocking her!"

"Eh, calm down. We'll figure this out," said Kamapua'a. A cool breeze rushed over Anna.

"You know a hula I could do?" Anna asked.

Kamapua'a answered with an epic brow arch. *Impressive height*, thought Anna.

"Stay here. I'll be right back," Kamapua'a said, and he disappeared into the jungle.

Anna turned to Ilikea. "While I work here on this, I need you and Makani to go check on Kaipo."

Makani trembled around her, and Anna was flooded with unease. The time that Anna had spent getting to this point in the jungle was nothing compared to what Kaipo was going through, and she knew it.

"I'll give you three days. That should be enough for you to get to Kaipo, make sure he's . . . well . . . at least tell him what I'm trying to do, and get back to me. I'll try to learn whatever hula Kamapua'a has planned in that time. If something comes up, I'll call for Makani, and they'll let you know. Three days."

"Roger dodger. Makani, we go."

Ilikea took off, and Anna's braid lifted briefly as Makani went with her. Anna's heart slammed in her chest as she raised a hand in farewell. When her friends were out of sight, she struggled to swallow a new lump in her throat as she returned to the jungle.

Try Not to Stare

Anna barely had time to register Ilikea's and Makani's absence before a rustling in the ferns next to her signaled the arrival of Kamapua'a. He stepped into the clearing, and her breath caught. Sure, she'd seen years of kāne dancing at Merrie Monarch. Men in traditional malo—loincloths with a flap covering their fronts, and sometimes a flap or just a twisted piece of fabric on the back. This was her first time seeing someone with the outfit in person, and it was striking how the light brown fabric made all of Kamapua'a's skin seem that much darker. He had a lei po'o on his head, and ferns woven on his wrists and ankles, too. His body didn't show a hint of tan lines anywhere, and his lean chest and strong sinewy arms and legs held still while she looked at him.

Then, suddenly, he bent his knees, closed his hands into fists, put them on his hips, and called out, "Ae, Aia lā 'o Pele."

In a flurry of movement, he danced around the clearing. His hands jutted into the sky, honoring the goddess, and then he was on his knees, striking the earth. His feet stomped, kicking out to the side, before he lowered again to 'uwehe and hela, chanting the lyrics in time with his movement. His motions told the story of Pele in Hawai'i, consuming the town of Puna. Of Pele rising over cliffs and flashing in the heavens. Of finding peace while living in Pele's land of change. His chest was heaving with exertion as he finished with, "He inoa no Hi'iakaikapoliopele," his arms outstretched above and in front of him, index fingers touching, one foot out in front, his toes pointed and grazing the ground. The only sound was his heavy breathing.

All at once the rainforest came to life again. The plants and animals surrounding them seeming to send up a cheer of appreciation for the show of respect. Anna picked her jaw back up off the ground. His powerful dancing made it clear that he held Pele in high honor, regardless of their twisted past.

He relaxed from his pose and cleared his throat, shaking Anna from her stupor.

"Well, clearly you're an amazing dancer. But you're an awesome god-type-legend who has been here since the dawn of time," Anna told him. "Do you honestly think I can learn that quickly enough to save Kaipo?"

"Couple of things, Guavas," he said. He leaned against a tree, arms crossed over his chest, ankles crossed, looking like he was chatting against the lockers in school. "'Ekahi—I haven't been here since the dawn of time, but yeah, I have been dancing a while. 'Elua—I'm not sure. We would need to make changes, but you can learn it if you work. It's up to you. 'Ekolu—I'm pretty sure Pele felt that hula and knows I'm back on the island. We won't have much time." He waited for Anna to make her decision, appearing just as comfortable in his malo as he did in his shirt and surf shorts.

Anna was not nearly as comfortable and had a harder time looking at him now that his dance was over. *Gah, just pull yourself together, Anna. Obviously, he doesn't care. Don't make this a thing. You've seen guys on swim team in less. No big deal. Focus on the goal. He is offering you a way to potentially save Kaipo! Unless you have a better plan, you need to stop being such a doof and work with him on this.*

Anna forced herself to meet his eyes as she answered, "Okay. Ilikea and Makani just left to look for Pele and Kaipo, so let's do this."

Kamapua'a cocked an eyebrow.

Anna winced. *When a demigod offers to teach you hula, you say, 'Thanks!'* "That came out wrong," she said. "Thanks, seriously, for the offer. You're saving my butt here. Kaipo's, too." Kamapua'a gave a nod. Anna continued, "I recognized some of the words from Merrie Monarch. It seems like a lot of opening numbers end the same way. Just say it slowly, and I'll do my best."

He took his time, teaching Anna two lines at a time. First, he had her repeat the words back to him, then he taught her the hand motions. Only when she was able to do those on her own to his satisfaction did he show her the foot placement. The hula was different for men and women. Translating his hula kahiko from kāne to wahine for her softened it a bit. Where the men would strike a bit more harshly, and use more staccato leg motion, the women were slightly more delicate, while maintaining the integrity of the story. He had Anna kneeling on the damp ground to do some of the motions. Her thighs burned as he insisted she bend lower and lower in her kāholo and hela. Even with all the snowboarding, she was not used to maintaining a crouch this low for extended periods of time. Then there was the knee-cracking hula move called duck walk (she had to squat, butt to her heels, on the balls of her toes and waddle across the grass—mega ouch).

Too bad Tūtū wasn't here to see this. Was she missing Anna yet? Meeting Pele wasn't the safest thing to do, but Tūtū would be supportive of Anna taking whatever time she needed to learn how to get Kaipo back successfully. And why wouldn't she? It all worked out in Tūtū's favor, with Anna becoming more familiar with the moʻolelo that Tūtū wanted her to learn all along.

Would she be able to dance well enough to prove to Pele that she had changed? She would certainly try. The cocky girl who had picked the lehua flower was long gone. Anna listened to everything Kamapuaʻa had to say. Her motions smoothed, coming more naturally as her muscles memorized the motions. The spongy grass under her bare feet transported her to a different place, a different mentality. It was hard to remember the logic-based, technology-filled life that awaited her in Colorado. This place was timeless. Special. Facts and folktales coexisted.

After Kamapuaʻa had corrected her a bajillion times since her rehearsal of verse two, Anna stopped and sighed.

"I was also thinking of our plan B," she said. "The hōlua competition."

"Yeah?"

"If Pele hates my hula and agrees to race, all I need is a hōlua."

Kamapuaʻa rocked back and forth on his feet, tapping his chin. "Pele's sister Poliʻahu has a sled." He clapped his hands once then pumped a fist in excitement. "I got it. If you get Pele agree to one race, tell her you wanna race on Maunakea. She'll have to ask Poliʻahu, then you can maybe borrow Poliʻahu's hōlua."

"Why would Pele need to ask Poliʻahu? She's the snow goddess, right?"

"Poliʻahu takes care of Maunakea. Pele haaates it to have to bow down, but watching her have to act humble is the best. Eh." Kamapuaʻa smacked her arm.

"Ow," Anna grumbled. It didn't *really* hurt but caught her by surprise.

"Oh sorry, forgot how weak humans are." He flashed her a sympathetic grin but was clearly too hyped on whatever idea was brewing to pause. "But you could do the course we talked about before. The one to the north side of Maunakea."

"Hey, question. I race goofy foot on my snowboard, with my left foot back. Are there straps or anything I gotta be concerned about on this sled that I'll need to adjust, or how does it work?"

"No way, snowboarders say goofy foot, too? I thought that was just a surfer thing. But no, no bindings on the hōlua. Just good old-fashioned gravity."

Well, that made things interesting. "How in the world do you get the sled to carve without straps?"

"Carve? Guavas, there is no carving. This ain't a wave or a snow hill. You just hold on and go down straight as fast as you can. No brakes. No turns."

No carving and no brakes. Anna loved speed on her snowboard, wind whipping against her exposed cheeks, spray that the board kicked up in fresh powder cooling her off as she navigated her way down a mountain. She felt like she was flying. Hōlua sounded like a barely controlled free fall. Maybe, just maybe, Pele would accept her hula apology, and she wouldn't need to offer the death race as an option. But she needed to be prepared just in case.

"You really think Poliʻahu would lend me her hōlua?" Anna said, walking to her pack to get some water. Borrowing a goddess's hōlua seemed like a huge ask.

"I'll ask. I'll check the kahua hōlua, the course, too. Pele went cover part of it in lava when she lost last time. For now, keep practicing."

Anna danced barefoot on a barren patch of lava rock so she'd be ready when she actually met with Pele at the crater. At first the warm, black stone made Anna hobble, cutting into her soft skin. By day three, she was more sure-footed and able to dance on the sometimes-rough surface, ignoring the tenderness. For the most part, the lava was the smooth, ropy pāhoehoe flow, not the jagged, broken ʻaʻā pieces. Feet aching, she always relished returning to the cool, damp jungle floor after a lava session.

For all his chill behavior, Kamapuaʻa was a strict teacher, wanting her to get each movement perfectly before letting her move to the next. Anna tried her best, but there was one particular move she just could not get—a kneeling backbend where the back of Anna's head and butt lowered to just barely graze the ground before she used her core and quad muscles to raise herself back up to upright kneeling.

"Try again," Kamapuaʻa told her when he saw her use an elbow to push herself back up.

"I've been trying!" Anna said, frustrated, tired, and sore. "I've been at this for three days!" She shakily rose to her feet. Her knees were scraped, bruised, and throbbing from kneeling on the jungle floor so much. "I am busting my butt out here trying to be good enough for a goddess, knowing dang well that she'll probably just laugh in my face and cover me with lava! She'll think I'm just a poser haole attempting to learn hula. She'll know I'm a fake. I can't do the backbend, and my movements are choppy, not graceful and fluid like they should be. Kaipo is gonna die, and it's all my fault!"

"So try again. Go back down."

"Aarrrggg, are you even listening to me? My knees are killing me! I can't go back down."

Kamapua'a frowned. Anna's chest was heaving from her outburst. She knew her eyes were probably glistening. She had an unfortunate habit of crying when she got worked up, which was why she tried to be relaxed as much as possible.

Anna turned around, giving him her back.

"Pele has Kaipo. Meanwhile, I'm stuck here in the jungle going over and over and over the same moves that I'll never get right." She fumbled for words to explain through her tears. "You just don't get it. Everything is easy for you. You're from here. You are *part* of here. I was dreaming to think I'd ever be good enough at this." Anna grimaced, shoulders hitched to her ears when she realized she had shouted that last bit.

"I think you need a break from me to work on your own," Kamapua'a said. "I'll check on Poli'ahu and the sled."

"Ya think?" Anna cried, all her exhaustion and frustration finally coming out. "No, you know what? I don't need a break from you, I need a break from Hawai'i. I need to go home and just be around people who don't think there are goddesses controlling the fates of best friends and family homes. Back where I actually understand things!" Anna took a breath, and then another, composing herself. She slowly turned back around to face Kamapua'a. "Look, I am trying my best. I'm—"

But he was gone.

Alone Time

Anna sniffled, then tried to be strong and square her shoulders. She wasn't the one potentially being tortured right now. She was the cause, not the effect. The catalyst, not the reaction. The experiment that always ended with the same result: She should be avoided. She got her best friend kidnapped. By a freaking fire goddess. Maybe Ridley should be glad she just went off with Hennley.

Anna paced around the clearing. Then she saw it. Next to the spot under the biggest hāpu'u where Kamapua'a had been leaving bowls of food for breakfast and dinner the past two days was a little package on the ground. Had Kamapua'a left it? She rushed over and picked up the leaf-wrapped gift before looking out into the trees and untying the coconut-fiber string. The large, shiny leaves fell to the grass. Anna pulled out the gift and it unfolded. A pā'ū hula.

"Oh," Anna gasped.

The skirt was beautiful, ombre red and yellow that would look like the flickering flames of an eruption as she moved.

Anna held the knee-length skirt out on either side of her, admiring the colors. She quickly pulled the skirt on over her stained jeans and up to her waist, then undid her jeans and slid them off from under the skirt. The elastic waistband hugged her, and when she gave a little trial hip sway, the skirt swung in mighty, exaggerated swoops. Anna bent into a squat, relishing the sensation of not having stiff denim fabric gathered behind her knees. She ran through the hula, moving easily and deeply, no longer inhibited by the damp jeans.

She focused on the parts of the song where she was upright, not quite ready to get down on her knees again. The skirt was like an extension of her body, reaching out and emphasizing her movements. Anna felt its tight embrace in her naʻau. It squeezed tighter and tighter, and she practiced over and over until, finally, the bud growing from the seed of truth planted in her burst into bloom, and tears started to flow. Tūtū would be . . . what word was she looking for? *Proud* seemed trite. Like a pat on the back for a good report card.

This was so much bigger. This was understanding and embracing. Welcoming new responsibilities and taking her place in the family circle with each point of her toes, each dip of her knees. Knowing that even though she wasn't perfect, she belonged there.

All of her worries and frustrations bubbled up now that she had some privacy. Was Ilikea with Kaipo now? Would she explain that Anna was trying her best, even though her best might not be good enough? Anna willed the tears away, but they were as persistent and stubborn as she was.

She broke her final pose and dried her tear-streaked cheeks.

Anna knew she was nowhere near as good as Kamapuaʻa was—that one really tricky backbend still gave her trouble. But she was starting to understand the way her body flowed through each of the movements, connecting them together to form a story. She got it now. Hula actually was just another way to tell stories, passing them from person to person, generation to generation. Another link that her tūtū had tried to instill in her that she simply didn't understand before. Pele wouldn't be impressed by her basic grasp of the purpose of hula, though.

Taking a break from practice, she headed over to her backpack for some water. She sat down gracelessly, her body exhausted from the constant moving and bending. As she drank, a glimmer caught her eye. Her backpack's zipper had opened slightly, and the scale from the moʻo was visible. Anna quickly looked around the clearing to make sure no one was watching, then she pulled it out.

It was just as beautiful as she remembered. *How do I use this thing?* Turning it over, she was completely baffled. It was still solid, similar to a thin piece of glass and slightly transparent, like looking through water and seeing the seafloor wavering below. The ferns and trees behind the scale appeared distorted, bending and shimmering. Anna stood and moved this way and that, both hands holding either side of the small, plate-size scale like a steering wheel, enjoying how it twisted reality, until she looked up toward the sun. The glowing orb was making an appearance through a rare break in the clouds, offering a surprising amount of warmth in the clearing. When Anna held the scale up toward the sun, it softened and expanded.

"What the . . ." She felt her fingertips press indentations into the scale, like pressing into cake frosting. It became almost impossible to continue holding the scale, as it began to melt down around her fingertips like it had when 'Ula touched it.

"No, no, no, no, no!" She quickly brought her hands down to reverse the effects of gravity.

As soon as her hands lowered away from the sun, the scale began to resolidify. The goopy drips moved back toward the tips of her fingers to rejoin the scale and become a static dinner-plate shape once more. Anna heaved a sigh of relief.

She continued to stare at the scale, half expecting it to melt like one of the clocks in that bizarre Salvador Dalí painting she'd seen in art class. When it stayed solid, she started moving it around—slowly this time—trying to find the exact point where it started to transform. As she raised it higher, she noticed it start to stretch and bend, from the uppermost section that was closest to where the sun was in the sky. She lowered it instantly, and it hardened back into its original shape. Lifted up, it began to stretch. Lowered, it solidified again.

Okay, so the mo'o was a water spirit, and it seems like the sun is affecting it. Could the sun hurt it and water help it? Or maybe sun gets it to react and protect itself . . . Time to experiment.

Anna lifted the scale up toward the sun again. When it began to stretch, she used one hand to gently clasp and pull at the softened edge, using the same light force that she'd use to spread frosting on a cake. Slowly, the scale feathered out wider, and Anna turned it, giving the entire circumference a moment in the sun to soften and grow. After a complete revolution, the scale had nearly tripled in size, going from the size of a plate to the size of a bicycle wheel. Anna lowered it, and it began to shrink back to the size of a plate.

"No, you don't," Anna said. She gripped both sides and held firm, trying to get it to stay big, just to see if it was possible to keep it deformed. She felt it quiver, trying to pull in on itself, and then it stopped. Almost like it surrendered. It stayed the size of a bike tire.

"Ha, ha!" Anna exclaimed, smiling proudly. Then her smile faltered and fell. *Great. Now what do I do with this? And how is this supposed to help me beat a fire goddess?*

Maybe, thought Anna, *what I need to do is try it out against an actual fire.*

Closer . . . Closer . . .

Anna sat back down next to her backpack, put the enlarged scale on the ground next to her, and rifled through the pack till she found her first aid and safety kit. She opened the Ziploc bag and pulled out the old medicine container with the childproof lid where she stored her matches and dryer lint for starting fires. *Let's re-create a bit of what Pele's gonna bring to the competition,* she thought. She looked around for wood and realized she was going to have a problem. Here in the rainforest, she was surrounded by nothing but deep greens and browns. Everything she touched was damp. She needed dry kindling and wood to start a fire. Anna put down her fire-starter kit and picked up the scale. *It'd be great if I could get this back down to plate size,* she thought as she tried pushing opposing edges toward each other. The scale quivered, then began to compress. *That's it! Whoa! It's responding.* When it was down to dinner-plate size, Anna stood and looked around the clearing.

Along the edge of the tree line, there were small branches and twigs that had fallen. Some had been there a while and were covered with moss, some were newly fallen and still brown, and some were in an in-between phase and slightly slimy to the touch. Anna picked up a couple of twigs and put them on the scale. She was eying another stick when a dim glow caught her attention.

The scale! It was glowing the way it had when 'Io had attacked. She held it with both hands and watched as the wood in the pile dried, its dark bark turning pale while the outer husks cracked and broke. The scale's glow faded. Anna bent one of the twigs. *Snap.* Completely dry! A huge grin broke out on Anna's face, and she did a celebratory shoulder shimmy as she hurried around the clearing, piling more leaves and twigs on the scale. She watched in amazement as the glow started up again and the foliage transformed. She piled them all in a little mound in the center of the clearing. As soon as the wood was removed, the scale grew as heavy as a full pail of water, and Anna dropped it in surprise.

"Oh shoot! Don't break!" she said, dropping to her knees to lift it again. But she paused. The heavy scale had landed at a sideways tilt, one edge wedged into the ground. Water seeped off the top of the scale back into the earth. Anna watched the flow of water gradually slow to a trickle before stopping altogether. She pulled the scale out of the earth, amazed to feel it back to its original, light weight. There were no visible chips or cracks in the edge, and Anna briefly closed her eyes, thanking the mo'o for having strong, magical scales, as she rocked back on her heels. *Now to start the fire.*

Anna thought back to all her camping trips with Dad as she collected some small stones. He was patient as she ran around, mostly distracted, bringing stones along with fun leaves and sticks. Anna's nose stung and eyes watered at the memory of her dad's arms around her, showing her how to strike a match for the first time.

Mom was off to the side, telling her to watch what she was doing when Anna had looked up to show her the flame.

Anna blinked back the memory and made a circle of stones Dad would be proud of, put the dried twigs in the middle, and opened her fire-starter kit. It was definitely drier in Colorado. Way more at risk of wildfires. Pretty sure Pele was starting more fires here than Anna ever would. Still, she had to be careful. She put some lint under the stacked kindling and struck a match. She carefully guarded the flame, touching it to the lint before it extinguished. Blowing gently, she coaxed it to grow, licking and consuming first the lint and then the tinder. When the blaze seemed stable, Anna added some larger pieces of dried wood to maintain the flames.

She picked the scale back up and moved away from the fire. *Let's see what this baby can do*, she thought, starting from a good distance away. She couldn't even feel the heat from the small fire from where she stood. She brought the scale in between her body and the flame like a shield. Nothing happened. *Maybe I'm too far.* One step closer. Nothing. One step closer. Nothing. Another step. The scale dimly glowed blue, as if sensing the fire and reacting with opposing water elements inherent to every moʻo.

The edges began to soften, and Anna's fingertips that were exposed to the heat burned. Anna quickly stepped back and shook out her hands. *So about three feet away is a limit for a flame this size.* Anna paused, thinking about the next step as the fire crackled and smoke rose toward the sky. *I need to figure out a way to keep my fingers behind the scale, too. Hmm, Captain America wears his shield on his arm. I wonder if I could figure out a way to make this scale into a shield so that my entire body is behind it . . .*

Anna plucked at her extra hair band on her wrist. She took a step toward the fire and saw the glow of the burn through the scale as it began to soften. Pushing her wrist into the back of the scale, she focused all of her attention on exactly what she wanted to have happen, believing that it would. *Protect me*, she thought as she took a step closer to the fire. *Keep me safe.* Anna felt her hair band get absorbed by the scale, fixing it to her wrist. *I believe.* She was able to drop her opposite hand from the front of the scale, so she was completely behind it. *I believe.* The scale stretched to her full body height, wide enough to block her completely from the flame. Anna took another step closer, and then another, completely stunned by the transformation in the scale. *Just wait till I tell Tūtū about this.*

Anna stepped closer, then looked down to gauge her distance to the flame.

Wait—she was standing IN the fire! Anna jumped back, slipped, and fell on her butt. She rolled to her hands and knees, her concentration broken. She watched as the scale shrank back down to its original size and fell off of her wrist band. Her bare foot had been in the fire! Well, not quite. She had noticed the scale had extended under her foot, providing a thin barrier so effective she hadn't even felt the heat. She pulled her foot closer to her face. There were no burn marks at all.

A noise in the canopy caught her attention. *Who's there?* Anna crawled over to the backpack and quickly stuffed the scale into it, concealing it from any prying eyes. She sat back and scanned the trees above her, holding her breath.

Ilikea broke through, fluttering back into the clearing, flopping dramatically onto the ground at her feet, one wing over her face, remaining still as death. Anna's heart stuttered, fearing the worst as she quickly scooped her up, gently holding her soft, furry body, and unfolded her wing from her face. She released her breath when she felt the bat's strong, steady heartbeat under her fingers.

"Ilikea! Are you okay? What happened? Is Makani with you?" A cool breeze blew against her forehead, and she had her answer. Anna smiled. "How'd it go? Did you find Pele?"

"'Ae," Ilikea confirmed. "She's in her hidden grove of 'ōhi'a lehua trees farther up the mountain. Kaipo is with her. He's in a cage over a fire!"

Someone's Always Watching

The blood drained from Anna's face, and she focused on not gripping Ilikea too tightly as she absorbed this horrifying news.

Ilikea continued, "The cage must be magic because it hasn't burned yet, and he is still alive. It can't feel good to be held there, though. Pele told us to tell you that you don't have much time."

"I don't have much time? Why? What's she going to do?"

The little bat shuddered while considering her answer. "You sure you wanna know?"

Anna wasn't sure at all. In fact, she was pretty sure she absolutely *didn't* want to know. But for some reason that didn't seem fair to Kaipo. She tightened her hands into fists and absorbed the pain of her nails biting into her palms. "What'll happen? I need to know."

Ilikea sighed, and Makani settled like a comforting blanket on Anna's shoulders. "Pele will give Kaipo to 'Io."

Anna waited to see if the bat would clarify. When she stayed silent, Anna asked, "I don't get it. Like, as an 'aumakua? As a bird friend?"

Ilikea wouldn't meet her eyes. "No. Like, as a meal."

The world stopped.

It was like falling off a ski lift.

It had happened to her once. She thought for sure she was going to die. But then the fall ended, and she was stuck headfirst in a snow drift. Wind knocked out of her, cold all over, blinking but not seeing anything. People had rushed to pull her out, and she was miraculously fine and even snowboarded with the rest of the team that day.

No one was here to pull her out this time.

"I don't know if you're ready or not with your hula, but we really need to get going if we want to save Kaipo."

"I'm as ready as I'll ever be. I'll grab my things."

Anna slipped her jeans on under her pāʻū, then tugged the skirt off, carefully bundling it and putting it into her backpack before deciding to put her sneakers in the backpack's smaller pocket. Her feet had toughened up considerably, and now she was able to walk barefoot with ease. She looked around her practice clearing one last time, hoping to see Kamapuaʻa's familiar form break through the shadows. Fighting with him probably wasn't the best idea. What if he thought she had a fiery temper just like a certain other female in his past that he wasn't super fond of at the moment? Would he still be willing to help, or would he decide she wasn't worth the trouble? Realizing she might be doing this without her teacher, she shuddered, dread settling cold in her stomach. Anna turned and followed Ilikea as she started into the jungle, feeling more connected to her surroundings than she ever had.

"Did Kaipo see you? Did he say anything?" Anna asked.

"He looked pretty out of it when we saw him. Not sure if he was sleeping or unconscious, but he didn't move."

"Was he . . . um . . ." Anna wasn't quite sure how to ask, or if it would be rude or not, but she wanted to know. "Was he a human or an owl?"

Ilikea looked back at Anna from her flight up ahead. "You really ready for this?"

"Yeah. I mean, I'll find out soon enough, right? And this will help us plan better for his rescue. Doesn't matter to me what he is, we just need to make sure he's safe and I can get him home," Anna said, the truth of the words spreading warmth through her chest.

"He was a pueo," said Ilikea. "Not sure if his feathers protect him from the heat, but it's probably more comfortable size-wise to spend the time in Pele's presence as a bird in a cage than a boy in a cage." Anna worked on picturing this. *A Hawaiian pueo is only about twelve to eighteen inches tall, like a puffy crow.* She had seen pueo flying over her tūtū's home a few times over the years and always got a thrill at spotting their silent, mottled-brown-and-white wings. Now she wondered if any of those sightings were actually of their 'aumakua, Kaipo.

The dense undergrowth of ferns gradually cleared as they worked their way up the mountain. Expansive lengths of unbroken lava fields made it clear that Kamapua'a had not yet had a chance to use his tusks to churn this new hard land into rich soil. 'Ōhi'a lehua trees were growing through the small cracks and crevices where the lava had folded into and under itself during its slow crawl toward the ocean. Anna found her hands going through the motions of the hula as she watched her step up the ropy slope. She couldn't help but continue to look around for Kamapua'a, too. Once or twice, she thought she'd caught a glimpse of his tall form moving through the trees skirting the flow, but then there was nothing. *Is he actually meeting with the snow goddess? And talking about me?* Anna's heart sped up at the thought. She couldn't shake the desire to see him, though, and to have one more ally back at her side when facing Pele.

Ilikea seemed unfazed by Kamapua'a's disappearance, chattering incessantly ahead of Anna. She almost seemed to be trying to take Anna's mind off the notable absence of her hula teacher, talking about how she and Makani had tried to distract Pele and take Kaipo during their reconnaissance mission but had failed.

"I flew down to her right side, close enough to feel my wingtips singeing from her heat," Ilikea said. "Kaipo didn't so much as ruffle a feather, so I couldn't tell if he knew I was there or not, but I told him your plan and that you were coming. I spent a day finding food for him. I squeezed a few smaller fruits through his cage, so if he wakes up, he'll have some food. Then I tried to distract Madam Pele with flattery by saying how beautiful her lehua blossoms are this year, while Makani"—Anna felt them whoosh around her, proud to have played a role in the mission—"swooped in on the left and tried to blow out the fire under Kaipo's cage."

"What happened?" Anna asked, hoping that if anything critically awful had actually happened to Kaipo during their scouting mission that Ilikea would have told her that news first, rather than filling her in on the play-by-play.

"Pele didn't even flinch. She simply harnessed the wind to have the fire burn brighter and hotter. Makani was not thrilled at being used and tried to resist. Pele caught on to what we were trying to do and threw sparks my way, so I called out, trying to rouse Kaipo. Makani blew the sparks out and helped me evade Pele's burning embers by blowing me farther away. Pele must have thought we were retreating, so she yelled out her warning that our time was running out. We hurried back here as fast as we could."

Hearing the story, Anna's heart pounded, knowing that she'd be a part of the next rescue attempt. A huge shadow crossed the land in front of them, followed by a loud screech. Anna looked up in time to see 'Io circling above. The giant hawk stayed high, not making any move to dive or come closer.

Anna felt a wave of power wash over her and shuddered. "Ilikea, what was that?"

"Ah, you felt it this time. You really have gotten more in touch with your roots if you can feel Pele's power. She has sent 'Io out to watch us. She is able to see us through 'Io's eyes. We are getting closer, and she is paying attention."

Anna thought about it. *Well, might as well give him something good to report.* She took a deep breath and started chanting the words to her hula that Kamapua'a had taught her. Her voice started a bit higher than she would have liked, but she soon found the right tone and stood tall with her shoulders back, gaining confidence. 'Io gave another high-pitched screech before cartwheeling off and heading back up the mountain.

"Well, fry me up and call me frenchie," Ilikea said. "Glad to see your time with Kamapua'a really paid off. You actually sounded good!"

"Yeah?" Anna beamed. She felt more in touch with the 'āina than ever before.

"It is all about intent," Ilikea said. "You're sincere in trying to help Kaipo and appease Pele. You believe that there are certain steps that must be taken to win Pele's approval. If she sees you humbling yourself in her name, she can't help but be pleased."

They were coming to a crest of a low hill, and as the horizon dropped to eye level, Anna was able to take a clear look at the open mountainside for the first time.

Aw, crud cakes. Smoke!

Blastoff!

Anna gasped. **She** lengthened her stride to find a better vantage point to see what was burning. The faint smell of smoke hit her nostrils and made her think of Tūtū's house. Was she too late? Was her family's homestead gone, buried by an angry goddess? From the top of the hill, she could see the oozing black lava with bright orange veins slowly moving down the mountainside. She was much closer to the molten rock here than she had been at Tūtū's, but still far enough away to not be in any danger. The lava was slowly burning through the jungle, but it hadn't reached Volcano Village or Tūtū's yet. The homes were safe for now, but they needed to hurry.

A short plateau allowed Anna to make up time, crossing quickly and easily before beginning the climb on the other side. Trees were much sparser there, and she kept an eye on the plume of smoke.

"Ilikea, do you think we're in any danger of needing to cross that lava flow?" Anna asked.

"Looks like it is taking a different path. If we follow this route, we should be able to skirt around it, sticking to older flows," Ilikea said as she flew ahead of her, higher up to keep an eye on everything. Makani kept a cool breeze blowing as the black expanse of old flow heated up in the sun. Anna stopped to put on her shoes and take a drink of water. She could see where the crater touched the sky. They were almost there. *I'm coming, Kaipo. Hang in there.* She put her backpack on and opened her mouth to ask Ilikea another question, but before she could, a tremor hit.

Not. Again.

"Um, problem," Anna said, moving quickly forward. Outrunning an earthquake seemed pretty unfeasible, but standing still didn't seem like the best plan, either. Ilikea flew back toward her.

"Earthquake," Anna said, voice wobbling as another larger tremor hit, throwing her off balance.

She grabbed an ʻōhiʻa lehua tree for support—those trees were stable thanks to their deep roots—then quickly let go, scared of accidentally pulling off any blossoms and not wanting to touch ANYTHING that might send a signal to Pele. The tremor ended.

Anna let out a breath. "Okay, I think it's—"

A slender fissure split the ground in front of her. Anna screamed and fell back as a curtain of lava shot out of what moments ago had been solid ground.

"Anna! Look out!" Ilikea shouted, hovering around her head.

"On it," Anna said, crab-walking quickly backward. Makani sent a steady stream of cool air in front of her, keeping the heat away from her skin.

The fissure was a thin, jagged line, running as far to her left and right as she could see. There was no way to go around it. A constant curtain of lava erupted from this crack, shooting ten feet in the air before it rained back down. Most of the molten fire fell back into the slit it came from, but not all of it. Globs of gooey semidry lava surrounded the crack, like toothpaste around the sink drain.

Anna stood and stared at the new lava force field. A wail escaped her mouth as she looked at the curtain. How in the world would she get through a wall of fiery rock?

"Pele knows you're close," Ilikea said. "I guess the good news is she wouldn't be going through this trouble if Kaipo weren't still alive." Anna stared at her. "What? Not helpful?" Ilikea asked.

She shook her head, then looked back at the flow.

"We really gotta get Kaipo to help you get better at this 'aumakua thing," Anna said. Ilikea puffed up. "Sorry. Sorry," Anna said. "Okay. Let's think." Anna's mind was blank, heart racing.

"The scale!" Ilikea said. *Of course!* Anna thought. In the heat of the moment, she'd completely forgotten.

"Hey, good idea!" she said, surprised by Ilikea's legit advice. She pulled the pack around and got the scale out. It glowed brightly, off-setting the orangey-red flames. Looking back at the fissure, it appeared to be slightly wider than it had been a moment ago.

"Uh-oh," Anna said.

"It's growing!" Ilikea said.

Anna redid her braid so nothing would get in her eyes when going through the wall of flames. Quickly, she created a plan.

"Okay, so I'll attach this scale to the hair band on my wrist." She noticed Ilikea glance her way. "I practiced a little in the meadow when you were with Kaipo."

Anna held the scale toward the flame. When it softened, she pressed her hair band on her wrist into it, grateful that it went in easily and held. With her new shield in place, Anna approached the lava carefully. Then something incredible happened: The scale started shaking. *Ooh, maybe it'll transform into a rocket ship and just blast us safely to wherever Kaipo is.* Then she realized the shaking was coming from her trembling hands and arms. Anna clamped her jaw and lifted her head. Yes, this was scary. Yes, she may end up burned to a crisp. But could she back down now? No. Her friend was on the other side, and a four-inch-, now five-inch-, almost six-inch-wide liquid fire wasn't about to keep her away. She gulped. Really, liquid fire should be enough to keep her far, far away.

Stay positive! Anna thought to herself before mentally responding, *I'm positive I should stay away!* Anna's little inside joke gave her a bit of confidence. She called out to Ilikea and Makani over the crackling and bubbling.

"Kay," she gulped, "I can hold the shield in front of me and do a running jump through the lava?"

"Anna, bad idea. Your butt and back would burn," Ilikea said.

Anna frowned. She tried again. "I could sort of hold the shield down below me to stop the lava from coming up as I jump over the fissure?" She didn't even bother voicing her bigger question: *Do you think this scale will protect me from the lava?* Time to jump in with both feet. Well, metaphorically, as her English teacher Mrs. J would say, because literally jumping in lava would be bad.

"Anna," Ilikea instructed, "I think you should put your scale shield down over the fissure to block the lava and roll over it, like a somersault over a bridge. That would keep you protected the longest and make your body as small as possible when crossing the lava, so less room for burns." Makani shot up and down Anna's body in agreement.

Anna considered Ilikea's advice. Her reasoning made sense. They'd practiced forward rolls and shoulder rolls a bunch in kung fu, but she hadn't done it with a shield before. Willing to risk the fissure growing another inch, Anna turned away from the fountain to try a practice roll.

She got into a high squat, lowered her wrist with the scale pointed down to where the fountain would be, and rolled . . .

. . . and totally failed. She didn't have enough momentum to raise to standing and lay there in what would be a death pose if she were in the middle of a fountain of lava.

"Yeahhhh, I don't think that worked," Ilikea said.

"I realize that," Anna grumbled, pushing herself up to her feet.

"You should try going faster," Ilikea said.

"Got it." Anna got back into position. Faster. She pushed harder off her left leg, propelling herself more quickly over her right arm. Her arm and shoulder felt the pain of contact with the solid rock rather than the mats of her studio, but she pulled through quickly and rose to standing. There was a wobble at the end, and she took a big step back to catch herself, which would land her directly in the fissure if that were the real deal. She needed to practice one more time. Anna glanced at the crack. It had grown to about eight inches. Time was up. She had to go now or her scale wouldn't be wide enough to span the crack.

Be the Lobster

Anna approached the fissure, stepping carefully between the oozy spots, not wanting to melt the rubber on her sneakers.

"Anna! You gotta go faster. Don't think about it. Let your momentum carry you through the roll to the other side, pop up to your feet, and get away," Ilikea said.

Anna looked at her. "Thanks," she said with a strained smile. "I think that's your most 'aumakua-y advice yet." The fissure groaned and grew again. Heart pounding, Anna mentally judged the distance and went for it.

Two quick steps brought her to the lip of the fissure. The temperature was intense. Solid rock appeared liquid under waves of roiling heat on either side of her. Simply holding the shield must have offered some sort of protection, because Anna didn't think she could stand here without it.

She lowered her shield. Ilikea hovered in front of her, ready to go, too. Anna curled to drop into a roll.

She stepped forward with her right foot, holding her right arm and the scale in front.

Tucked the chin.

Bent at the waist.

Rolled over the shoulder. An exquisite shock of pain scorched her upper back. A scream left her lips, and Ilikea flew to her back. She heard the bat grunt, then moan, and the source of pain was gone. What did Ilikea do? Makani created a protective cool barrier, then suddenly they were gone and heat enveloped her. Curling in, she finished her roll. When her feet finally found solid ground, Anna stayed low to hobble away.

"Ilikea? Makani?" She coughed. Her lungs ached. As soon as she was a decent distance away, she crumpled to her hands and knees, before turning to her side. Her back throbbed in pain. She reached around, and there—she winced, tears squeezing out of her eyes—right above her backpack, she found the source. It felt like a puffed-up blister about the size of a quarter. Her delicately probing fingers accidently pulled away some skin, and she gasped. Some lava must have hit her. It couldn't have been very big, or she'd be dead. Anna remembered Ilikea's fast action. She must have somehow removed the drop as soon as it hit. Did she move it with her wings and get hurt, too?

"Ilikea! Makani!" Anna called, straining to hear them before dissolving into a coughing fit.

The fountain's gurgling and rushing covered up any potential sound from the other side of the curtain. Rolling back to her hands and knees, Anna spat on the solid rock in an attempt to clear her mouth of the burning taste that coated it. She swung her pack around for water to help with the coughing, only to see her water bottle had melted to the pack, the side mesh totally embedded in the plastic, singe holes of various sizes marking the pack itself.

"Oh no, no, no."

She swung to the other side. There, in the pocket, was her phone. It hadn't fallen out, but it looked melted, and the screen was warped. She pulled it out and juggled the heated metal between her hands. The power button had fused into the case, and the fingerprint scanner was completely wiped. The phone was toast. And without having any service, there was no way her pictures had uploaded. They were gone. Not that it mattered anymore. She was done changing herself for approval from Hennley and her crew. Ridley wasn't here. Who cared if the girls thought her photos were cool or not? Anna loved Hawai'i in all of its unfiltered glory, even if it was trying to kill her at the moment.

The scale stopped glowing and fell off her hair band. Anna put it back in the pack. "Ilikea," she tried again. Her voice was a little clearer. "Are you okay? Makani?"

Hot air rises, Anna thought to herself. Maybe Makani got blasted by hot air rising too fast to get through. Pele must have planned for them.

Pele had won, and Anna hadn't even reached the top of the crater yet.

Anna sat down hard, then lay on her side again, her pack pulling her shoulder. Trying to hold back tears, she bit her lip, then winced. Everything felt tight and crinkly, even her lip, like the worst sunburn ever. Her eyelids felt like sandpaper against her eyeballs when she blinked. She kept them closed for a minute, letting the tears come. What was she going to do?

Her mind flew to the image of Ilikea dead, but she couldn't bear the thought for too long. Her insides were hollowed out; all the sadness bounced around in there, echoing and amplifying into slicing misery.

Anna curled up tighter, ignoring the pain, and tried her hardest to just melt into the unforgiving lava. The sound of lava fountaining tattooed a rhythm into her skull that her bruised and battered heart tried to match. It picked up its pace, beating faster and faster, not at all what Anna wanted it to do. She didn't want to move again. Didn't want to think of everyone she had let down. Didn't want to face a goddess who thought she was pathetic. A poser. Pele would never even give her a second look.

Or would she?

If Anna didn't have a chance of winning Kaipo back, would Pele still waste her time sending lava her way? Sending 'Io after the scale?

She gently blotted the tears from her tender cheeks. Maybe the fact that Pele was still attacking, still challenging, was a sign that Anna was still worth some effort. That tiny, awful bit of reasoning—because really, being worth the effort of killing and attacking is an extremely low bar to set—settled into Anna's na'au and glowed.

Anna thought of Kaipo. He was always there for her. He supported her while she tested her own wings and tried to fly. Last summer on their visit to Hilo, they went to Mokuola (her mom still called it Coconut Island, but Tūtū insisted on calling it by its Hawaiian name). There was a double platform tower there, and despite jumping off the ten-foot-high ledge for years, she hadn't yet been brave enough to try the twenty-foot leap. Kaipo never pressured her, but he always asked, "Is this your year?"

Last year, she'd decided it was.

She'd never forget how nervous she had been, climbing that stone tower, hoping her bathing suit was covering her whole butt so the kids directly below her wouldn't laugh, scraping her knee on the way up before she figured out how to go up sort of sideways. Kaipo jumped with her. She leaned a little too far forward and had her knees bent, so her chest and shins slammed on the water. The sting on impact took her breath away. She emerged from the water red and exhilarated, and Kaipo had given her a little prideful grin. He knew she could do it. It was her year.

Something heated up in her like lava. A bubbling energy pushing her forward. Giving her strength. She would *not* give up on Kaipo. Nothing would ever go back to the way it had been. Including her. She pushed herself up, her eyes feeling marginally better from the tears, but her body still ached like a boiled lobster.

Slowly, steadily, Anna stood. A look at her body showed the scale had done a remarkable job at protecting her. Her shoes, jeans, shirt, and pack seemed fairly unharmed—filthy, but intact—other than the hole on the upper back of her shirt that felt singed around the edges where the piece of molten lava had hit her. Her arms had a pinkish tinge to them. She ran her hand down her braid, bringing it around to inspect. The ends were a bit crispy and pungent, but nothing was actively burning. Self check done, there was no reason to delay the inevitable. It meant leaving Ilikea and Makani behind, wherever they were. Anna's heart stung.

"Ilikea?" she called out one last time.

The crackling of the flames almost sounded like laughter. No way. Not today. Anna squared her chin. If the goddess laughed at her, Anna would be a fool to make a biting remark back, and it took everything she had to control that impulse. She choked it down with a huge swallow. As soon as she was sure she could open her mouth without doing anything foolish, she called out again.

"Ilikea? Makani? I don't know if you can hear me, but I'm going to get Kaipo. I'll tell him all about you both, tell him how you helped me, how you got me through the flames. Ilikea, he'll know what a great 'aumakua you'll be. I'll make sure of it."

Anna waited one more beat, listening to the lava. There was no response. With a deep breath she turned ma uka, ready to meet the goddess alone.

Sing It Loud

The horizon up ahead shimmered like an oasis in the desert. A thick grove of 'ōhi'a trees rose out of the barren lava rock, completely out of place on this black canvas. Anna had been seeing groups of no more than three trees at a time trying to carve some soil out of the porous rocks for their roots to take hold. Anna looked to the side, to see if Kamapua'a had appeared in the sparse trees, but there was still no sign of him. *Him still being gone doesn't necessarily mean things went wrong. Maybe the course was just in worse shape than he expected and took even more effort to clear. Or maybe he needed to do Poli'ahu a favor in order to have her lend me her sled. I'm sure he knows what he's doing and is fine.* When she looked back toward the trees ahead, they were gone.

"What the—"

Anna scanned her surroundings. She caught a glimmer of the oasis, but it didn't form a solid image. She turned her head away again, trying to glance at it only from the corner of her eye. The trees shimmered in the distance. A lump in the lava tripped her, and she fell to her hands and knees, braid swinging around to hit her on the cheek.

"Auē! Too bad practicing hula hasn't improved your coordination," a familiar, gravelly voice said.

Anna's head snapped up. Kamapua'a strode across the lava field, loose-limbed, like he didn't have a care in the world. Anna's heart skipped a beat. He grinned as she clambered to her feet and dusted off her palms, wincing at a new scrape. At least it was shallow, not even bleeding.

Anna looked back up the volcano and saw the flash of trees again before they disappeared. *Gotta remember to ask about that*, she thought to herself. *First, let's see what he found out.*

"You're back," Anna said, trying to keep her voice cool and even. *No big deal, just a magical demigod that returned to me to help me defeat his ex-girlfriend after I yelled at him. Play it cool.* "Hey, sorry for kind of freaking out on you before. Thanks for coming back. How'd it go?" *Yeah, that sounded pretty chill.* They walked together up the volcano, Anna lengthening her stride to try to keep up with him.

"No worries. Everything worked out. Where's 'ōpe'ape'a and ka makani?" Kamapua'a asked, looking around. Anna understood who he was asking about, and it hit her like a gut punch. She wrapped her arms around her stomach. She supposed he could sense Makani's absence.

"They're gone," she struggled to say. "We got separated by a fountain of lava."

Kamapua'a's eyes widened a fraction.

"No way," he whispered. "You must be getting to her if she'd go through that trouble," Kamapua'a said.

Anna's eyes watered, remembering Ilikea said something similar before they got separated.

"Eh, come here." He opened his arms.

Anna balked. Was he joking? He gave her a head nod, waving his fingertips, coaxing her in.

"Come on, come on. It'll help. Pretend I'm your mom or tūtū or something."

He waggled his eyebrows comically. Anna let out a huff that was halfway between a laugh and a cry and fell into his arms. He wrapped them around her and just held on tight. That was it. No jokes. No funny stuff. Just support. Anna let out a shaky sigh, absorbing his strength. The swirling misery seeped out of her skin, leaving room for the spark in her na'au to grow and spread.

After a moment, Anna felt better and moved to straighten. His arms instantly dropped, and he stepped back.

"You know," Kamapua'a said solemnly, "where I come from, this means we're married now."

A smile cracked through Anna's storm cloud of emotions, and she elbowed him in the side. "Knock it off. Focus."

With a bracing breath, she stared up the mountain, preparing for the next step.

"I met with Poli'ahu," Kamapua'a said after a beat.

Anna's eyes snapped to him. "You actually saw her?" Anna asked. "Did you have to go to the top of Maunakea? Did she make it snow? Can I borrow her board? Were you able to make divots on the slope?"

Kamapua'a smirked, and she sheepishly shook her head.

"Sorry, sorry. I'm a bit freaked at the moment. I am really glad you're back," Anna said.

"I got everything done," Kamapuaʻa confirmed. "I'll stick with you to make sure you don't get lost up here, but I'll have to disappear before Pele shows. If it does come down to the race, I'll see you on the course. You just hold on to your sled and keep going, yeah? Just like we planned. Now, try pay attention so you don't hit a tree."

"Wait, did you see a bunch of them up ahead? I mean, I'm pretty sure I'm not hallucinating. I keep sorta seeing them, but then they disappear when I look for them."

"Epic! The fact that you saw them at all is maikaʻi—is good," Kamapuaʻa said excitedly with another hand clap, fist pump. "You must be on the right track, and your heart is in the right place. If you were coming to cause harm or didn't believe, no way Pele'd show her sacred hale to you. You just gotta trust you'll get there, and it'll work out."

Anna tried to see the trees again, squinting for good measure. Nothing. Other than a few heatwaves bouncing off the black lava and a few single trees here and there, nothing indicated that she was near the entrance of the home of one of the most famous of all the Hawaiian goddesses. Should she knock? Oh! She remembered back to the Merrie Monarch videos she'd watched with Tūtū that the hula hālau always presented an opening chant as a sort of offering or appeal to begin.

Unfortunately, other than the chant and hula she just learned from Kamapuaʻa, the only Hawaiian songs she learned from Tūtū were kids' songs from elementary school. She took a deep breath— *here goes nothing*—and started singing "Kāhuli aku, kāhuli mai . . ." doing the hand motions that accompanied this song about the Hawaiian tree snails, and their shells, who were rumored to sing in the rainforests. When nothing happened, she continued into "Pūpū, hinuhinu . . ." realizing this song, too, was all about finding pretty shells, except these ones were along the ocean shore. Clearly Tūtū had a shell theme in her early lessons.

There!

The shimmer was back, right in front of her. Anna walked slowly forward—arms extended in front of her to prevent her from embarrassing herself by slamming into invisible trees. Her fingers bumped into a semisolid barrier. Kind of like Jell-O-y air. Anna pushed her right hand forward and felt it enter the shimmery thickness. The air looked like a wavy mirage over sand on a hot day. She pulled it out and looked at Kamapua'a.

"Pele's outer boundary," Kamapua'a explained. "Usually it's solid and repellant so people just turn around and go another way. Seems good to me that you can at least push through. What do you wanna do?" His head was tilted, and he waited to see what she'd decide.

"It has been too long already," Anna said. "I'm going in."

"Let's goooo," Kamapua'a said with a fierce-looking grin.

Anna swallowed her nerves and extended her hand again. It broke through and pushed into the air soup. Her wrist and arm followed. She took one last look around, closed her eyes, then stepped into the unknown.

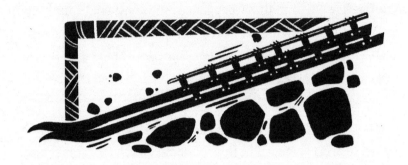

Hale o Pele

Anna **sent a** brief prayer up to Pele, repeating all of the songs that she knew, while thinking humble thoughts about never picking lehua again without asking permission. Her sincerity and positive intention pulsed in every word, and she kept her mind focused on calm, clear energy. Kamapua'a had her back, following her into the shimmering air on the volcano. He didn't seem to have any issues moving and had to keep checking himself and slowing down when he'd almost pass her.

The air was dense and clung to her legs, making it hard to move forward. It gave her the awful dreamlike sensation that she could attempt to run as fast as she could but would remain stuck in place. She pushed her arms into a swimming motion to help propel herself forward. Her eyes closed to a squint as if she were underwater. Everything blurred, like looking through a tide pool to the creatures below right after a wave had churned everything up. The jelly stuff squeezed in from all sides, making breathing a challenge. Anna took slow, deep breaths. No sense in freaking out and hyperventilating before reaching Pele.

The trees of the 'ōhi'a forest ahead were visible again, wavering and teasing through the soupy air. Her steps never faltered as she pushed forward. At last, as she thrust her fingers in front of her, she felt a break in the barrier and pulled herself through. The stench of rotten eggs slammed into her, replacing the smell of sweet fruit and damp earth she had grown used to in the jungle. The sulfuric gases rising from deep beneath the earth assaulted her nose just like the hot springs back in Colorado. Anna recognized these vents in the piles of rocks stained with the yellowish mineral Tūtū called sulfur kūkaepele—basically, Pele's poop. Anna steered clear of those odoriferous offenders, and Kamapua'a followed behind. Anna caught him looking around and peering into some of the vents, like he was checking out the redecorating an old buddy had done to their home. *Gods appreciate home makeover projects, too*, she thought to herself.

Anna kept closer to the grass-enshrouded steam vents. Smelling fresh and clear, they formed when water that made its way down into the earth would come into contact with Pele's fiery furnace and promptly hiss out into the atmosphere as steam. The deeper roots of trees recoiled from the heat of Pele's home, leaving only grasses with shallow root systems to grow in the humid air escaping the cracks.

Once they were past the gassy, vent-filled landscape, they entered a forest.

This 'ōhi'a forest was denser than any Anna had ever seen. Some of these trees were so old they had grown legs to lift their heavy trunks off the lava, up closer to the sky. A number of other plants made their homes on these lumbering giants. A hint of the spicy sandalwood fragrance came from small, whitish-pink naio blossoms.

Hāpuʻu ferns also sprouted from the enormous hosts along with a bunch of plants she couldn't name, creating a second-story forest community.

Birdsong fuller than any Anna had heard before filled the sky as winged fliers darted between the red lehua blossoms through the strained sunlight. Her eye caught a mottled-yellow-and-black bird hopping along branches and tapping the bark with its long-hooked beak. She hadn't seen one of those before and wanted to remember to tell Tūtū about it when she got home. Right. Home. *Find Pele, nicely dance hula to ask, or beg, for Kaipo back, get home in one piece. If that fails, we go sledding. I can do this.* Her footsteps were quiet as she crossed cool foliage and mosses.

She was so distracted by the birds that she hadn't noticed Kamapuaʻa disappear until a rustling in the ferns next to her brought her out of her thoughts. Anna backed up to the giant ʻōhiʻa tree and waited, watching the shaking fronds. When a large black snout emerged from the foliage, Anna was surprised by the instant recognition she felt.

"Kamapuaʻa?" she asked, pushing away from the tree and walking toward him. The massive boar fully entered the clearing and snorted once, bobbing his head. In this form, his head rose to her chest. His tusks were the size of her forearm. "Why did you go back to being a boar?" The pig made a show of taking massive snorty inhales. "Ah, got it. Easier to smell if someone is coming?" He bobbed his head again.

Anna raised a hand to touch a tusk but paused. "Do you mind?" Anna asked.

The boar tipped his head so his tusk pressed into her palm. The hard ivory was cool to the touch. And just as quickly, he removed it and shuffled to her side. She glanced at him, heat flooding her cheeks, embarrassed that she'd made a mistake. *Noted. This pig is not a pet.* He quirked his head in that familiar way and let out a low grunt. *Snap out of it, Anna. You've seen him in a malo. This is no biggie.*

Kamapuaʻa grunted again.

"Well, okay then, let's do this. And shh, make sure she doesn't see you coming."

He snorted and rolled his eyes at her.

The forest grew brighter up ahead, and the trees started to thin. They had reached the edge of the crater. Pele's home. The opposite edge of the rim danced like a distant mirage in the steam rising from the massive pit. Anna stopped at the edge of the forest to prepare.

"Kamapuaʻa, can you go find Kaipo and let him know we're here?" she asked as she took off her backpack.

She inhaled sharply when the wound on her upper back screamed at the twisting motion. Anna bit down on her cheek to distract herself from the pain. Kamapuaʻa cocked his head at her distress.

"Go. I'm good," Anna said, breathing through it. She watched as he disappeared into the forest.

Deep breath in. She took off her sneakers and put them next to her pack.

Deep breath out. Slipped the pāʻū on. Jeans pulled off, sweaty palms wiped on them one last time before they were tucked into her pack next to her sneakers. Not sure if she was being watched, Anna subtly pulled out the pearlescent blue scale that the moʻo had given her and tucked it into the waistband of her skirt, pulling her shirt over it to conceal it.

Deep breath in, down to the na'au. She removed the hair band from her braid and placed it back on her wrist. She combed her hair with her fingers, breaking off some of the singed ends, bringing it to its fullest, thickest volume. The humidity made it practically float, cascading midway down her back like a dark waterfall. Anna stood and took one last deep breath to try and calm all the bees in her stomach. It didn't work, but it was go-time, anyway.

Her pā'ū pressing against her bare legs, Anna stepped forward into the clearing and onto the crater's edge, heart pounding louder than a pahu drum at Merrie Monarch.

From her vantage point, she could look down into the pit and see that the floor of the crater wasn't solid but a moving sea of molten lava. A thin black layer of crust kept buckling and cracking, exposing red threads of the boiling rock beneath. The heat from below was enough to cause Anna to sweat, but she never wavered from her spot, searching for some sign of Pele. She extended her arms out in front of her, clammy palms facing down, slightly overlapping her left fingers with her right. Bending her trembling knees, she called out in a firm voice, "'Ae, aia lā 'o Pele!" and began her hula for the fire goddess.

Anna didn't miss a single step or word. Her hips swayed to the beat, her ombre skirt rippling like the fire and steam seething below. She made sure to crouch as low as possible when she could and extended her fingers to the sky. Then she came to the backbend movement that had eluded her in practice. It required her to get down into a kneeling position and lower her back behind her until she was as horizontal to the ground as possible. The unforgiving lava dug mercilessly into her knees, ankles, and the tender tops of her feet. She poured all her hopes and struggles over the past few days into that motion, and with her muscles aching, she successfully used her core to raise herself back up. She finished her hula with ". . . he inoa no Hiʻiakaikapoliopele."

And then she waited. Anna didn't dare to move a muscle, frozen in her finish pose, hoping for some sign from Pele.

Moments passed that felt like days.

Finally a woman appeared out of the volcanic haze at the bottom of the crater. Her dark skin glowed as if lit from within. A beautiful red dress dripped down her strong body, ending past her knees in tatters. Black hair rippled down her back almost to her waist. She elegantly made her way across the black crust before walking up the steam as if climbing a grand staircase. As she approached, Anna saw her eyes were deep black with tinges of red, like banked coals. She stared smugly at Anna; her lips quirked in one corner as she looked over the girl's frozen form.

"Ah, look who it is. The girl who openly defied me to her ʻaumakua. We meet again," Pele said as her eyes flared.

Smells like Fireworks

Anna's heart took off, beating a furious staccato in her chest that she was sure the woman could hear. She searched for any hint of the girl, 'Ula, she'd met earlier in the woods but could only see the similarity to the goddess in the paintings. *Had the artist seen her before and lived to tell the tale? If he was able to survive meeting Pele, I can, too.* Realizing she had been holding her breath, she let it out shakily and resumed breathing in a somewhat controlled fashion.

Once again, Anna promised herself that she wasn't leaving without Kaipo. She steeled her legs. Her muscles were shaking from being stuck in the bent finished pose, but she didn't dare rise before being addressed. After hearing about so many humans being engulfed in lava for upsetting the goddess over seemingly trivial things, Anna didn't want to make any wrong moves.

Anna's eyes followed Pele as she ascended to the top of the crater. She stayed silent, waiting for more direction. By the time Pele arrived at the rim of the crater, Anna was covered in sweat.

Freaking out was an understatement.

This was the big kahuna, the grand tūtū of them all. Literally the stuff legends were made of.

And then her stomach growled.

Anna winced. *Please don't cook me, please don't cook me.*

"Are you so bored in my presence that you're thinking of food?"

Pele was only a few feet away from her, standing on a cloud of steam. The temperature had risen with the steam staircase Pele climbed, and the heat from the caldera was bordering on unbearable. Instead of the smell of sulfur, Pele carried a scent completely unlike anything Anna had ever experienced. Sort of like fireworks exploding at New Year's or the Fourth of July, paired with the damp smell of deep earth.

When Pele looked at her, Anna quickly dropped her eyes, looking down at the goddess's bare feet hovering over the pit of the caldera, supported by nothing more substantial than water vapor. The tatters of her dress fluttered around her calves like Kamehameha butterflies trying to escape into the cooler mist of the forest. Anna's eyes burned with the heat, but she never broke form.

"N-no," Anna stammered.

"Well, you've called me here. What have you to say for yourself, looking all scared like a little puppy?"

Anna tried to think of all the respectful language Ilikea had taught her, imagining she was there with her. She could almost hear her saying something unhelpful like, *"Anna, you should apologize!"* or *"Anna, don't make the fire goddess mad!"* Anna kept her eyes on the ground and Ilikea's lessons in her heart when she spoke. "Please, Pele, it is not fear but humble respect for your power that keeps me still and lowers my eyes."

"Ah, pretty words for someone who doesn't believe. Who wants all to know she isn't from here."

Anna flinched. What once resonated now had bees in her belly stinging.

"I have come far, Pele," Anna said.

Time to show what I've learned. Anna harnessed the best of her classroom-presentation skills and tried to draw the goddess in with a catchy question.

"Do you know why ʻōhiʻa lehua are the first plants to grow in a lava field?" Anna asked.

Pele cocked a brow. "Of course I know. I put him there," the goddess said. "ʻŌhiʻa thought he'd refuse me. Beautiful man didn't know what was best for him. He wouldn't have been happy with that other woman, so I helped him with the decision of her or me. He's with me. Forever. In all of my forests."

"Exactly," Anna said, remembering the moʻolelo she'd been taught about the lovers that Pele had tried to separate. The other gods took pity on ʻŌhiʻa's other girlfriend, Lehua, so they turned her into a beautiful flower and put her onto his tree. Whenever people pick the flower, the lovers cry at being separated, and it rains. That was the legend that got her into this mess in the first place.

"That's why the plant is there. But, and I mean this with respect for your creation, the reason it survives, and even thrives, in this desolate environment is a little closer to home," Anna said.

After spending so much time walking across the lava, she'd had time to observe the strength and beauty of the plants defying the odds and changing the landscape. Redefining what belongs here. Pele remained silent, so Anna flexed her hands and continued, "It is their root system. They extend way down into the tiniest crevices. Their roots run deep. And so do mine." Anna paused. She hoped bringing science into a goddess's house wasn't the wrong thing to do. It blended with the mo'olelo, and Anna waited to see if Pele freaked out in a fiery rage. So far, so good. The lava lake didn't rise to swallow her whole.

Anna rubbed her palms on her pā'ū and chewed the inside of her lip. *Here it goes. One big ol' apology, served piping hot.*

"You already know I met a mo'o on my way here. I had to tell it a story to earn my scale. Yeah, you saw it's broken," Anna said, not mentioning that it now worked in an effort to avoid another game of keep-away, "but at the risk of not sounding very humble, I've got to say I was *good* at that mo'olelo. This is me. Part of who I am. My roots run deep, and I will fight for our family's 'aumakua with every cell in my body. I am sorry I acted with disrespect. Thank you for teaching me. Please, I humbly ask you to release Kaipo."

Was she laying it on too thick? It felt pretty cheese-tastic, but she was still alive, so that was a win. And she meant what she said. Her roots *did* run deep. She understood it now—the connection she hadn't felt before. Anna might not live here, she might not even look like she belonged, but that didn't change the truth. That Anna had her tūtū's tūtū's tūtū's blood flowing through her veins, and that was enough. She was enough.

And she was not leaving without her friend.

Anna stood with her hands on her hips in a traditional hula stance.

"You think that spending a few days in the forest, learning a hula, and offering an apology is enough to get your 'aumakua back?"

Pele scoffed. "'Aumākua are Hawaiian family guardians, protecting and guiding the 'ohana, and in return they are provided for and honored." Pele's eyes cracked as her temper began to flare.

"Of course! I completely agree and understand."

"You don't deserve Kaipo. Or his friendship. I saw the way you took him for granted. That isn't how friends treat each other."

Huh? They seemed to have moved past just 'aumākua issues. The smell of fireworks started overpowering the smell of the earth, and Anna saw the crust at the bottom of the crater heave and bubble. The crater began to fill, molten center rising, sloshing against the sides of the rim, way thicker than a thin liquid, more like someone blowing bubbles through a straw submerged in partially hardened glue.

"Okay, um, you are right, of course." Anna scrambled to figure out what Pele was getting at.

"We had a moment, in the jungle. Before you got greedy and selfish. Clearly you don't know how to be a true friend."

Anna's head jerked back like she'd been slapped. The words cut deeper than Pele could have known. Ridley's face flashed in Anna's mind as her eyes filled with tears. Anna blinked quickly to clear them. But wait. The goddess thought they had a *moment*?

Was it possible the goddess thought . . . no. No way. Back in the jungle, Pele didn't actually think they were going to be . . . friends? Did she?

The biggest light bulb ever went off in her brain.

Oh. My. Goddess.

Pele was *lonely*.

But she was also proud and not about to admit that she wanted a friend.

Anna deliberated how to handle this. Her mom was so good at doing the social-graces thing. Too bad Anna didn't take after her. How could she extend that olive branch while not looking at Pele with pity or anything that could result in Anna being burned to a crisp?

"Please, Pele." Anna didn't want to call her 'Ula—the name might dredge up old feelings of the *almost friendship*—but the Tūtū honorific seemed a bit much for testing this theory. She had to be approachable. Relatable. While still acting super reverent so Pele wouldn't suspect. "I have grown much these past few days and understand the error of my ways. I have a solution that may appeal to you. Would you be willing to compete in a he'e hōlua down the mountain? If I win, you would release Kaipo to me."

"You surprise me, girl." Pele's arms lowered, and the lava lake level dropped slightly. The goddess continued, "How do you know hōlua?"

"My tūtū and our ancestors have lived on your volcano for generations, and I am proud to call this island my home as well. Tūtū has told me about the Hawaiian sport, and I've read about your race down Maunakea against Poli'ahu, the snow goddess. What do you say? Do you agree to my bargain?"

Pele's eyes gleamed with interest, but she still acted standoffish. "Ha! A bargain. What could you possibly have to offer me that I don't already have?"

This had to be epic. The ultimate sacrifice to give Pele the excuse she needed to race. Sore knees, aching feet, and burning muscles were nothing to what would come next. It was time for her to lay it all down for Pele and her family's honor. There would be no going home from this if it didn't work. *I'm sorry, Tūtū, please forgive me.*

"Our home. My tūtū's and mine," Anna said. She closed her eyes as she made the offer, feeling the dread seep into her bones. Whether or not she was right about Pele, this piece hurt. "I know Tūtū and Kaipo have asked you to protect it from your lava flows time after time. If you win this race, as a direct descendant of this land, I would turn it over to you to use as you see fit. You'd be able to cover the land in one smooth sheet of lava and not have my tūtū's hale to avoid. You'd also keep our 'aumakua."

She looked Anna over again, this time unable to hold back a smile. "I could take your home anytime I choose, but you intrigue me. I am the best hōlua rider on the island and haven't had a challenger in eons. Ever since I accidentally covered my previous opponent in lava during my victory celebration, people have refused to race me."

Anna tried not to flinch at the visual of her potential death.

"Not that I consider you a proper challenger," Pele continued, getting more animated by the prospect. Anna could see glimpses of 'Ula peeking through, like the goddess was getting younger before Anna's eyes as she talked herself into it. "But a quick victory is better than no game at all. I accept."

Anna released a breath she didn't realize she'd been holding. *Okay, great. I just challenged the goddess of volcano down a mountain.* Anna tried not to hyperventilate and fall face-first into the roiling pit of lava. *At least it seems to have stopped filling.* She shook her head slightly. *Focus.*

"Can we race down a kahua hōlua on Maunakea? I have heard the story of your race against Poli'ahu there so many times. If this is to be my first and last race, I'd like it to be on that historic course. Would Poliʻahu allow you on her mountain?"

"I will make it so that she allows it. Let's go."

With that, Pele created a dense layer of steam at the edge of the crater and waited, watching Anna impatiently.

Anna stared back. She chewed her lower lip. *What was she waiting for? They had to get going to Maunakea.* The steam approached her toes. Anna looked over to Pele's feet on the steam. *Whoa, whoa, whoa, does Pele want me to get onto the cloud with her?*

"Come on, girl. Don't test my patience."

Okay, so maybe she didn't want to be *friend* friends. Frenemies seemed more the prickly goddess's type. Anna looked at the steam again. It wouldn't hold her. She'd fall right through it, go straight down to the lava lake, and that'd be it. The end. Do not pass go, do not collect the ʻaumakua. She clutched her pāʻū and closed her eyes. She'd come all this way and just made a deal with a fire goddess to race down a mountain. This was her world. She didn't just believe in it; she was a part of it. It was in her blood. Trying to think light thoughts, Anna brought her foot off the solid edge of the crater and out onto the steam.

Maunakea

hen Anna's foot didn't instantly sink through, she carefully settled her weight onto it. The steam held, so she brought her other foot off the reassuringly hard cliff onto the cloud that was held together only by Pele's will.

The steam cloud was still hot, and even her newly toughened-up feet hurt standing there. Trying to not look ungracious for the ride, she shifted from foot to foot as Pele moved beside her. She'd give anything for her sneakers that were still in her backpack, but she'd left all that behind on the floor of Pele's 'ōhi'a forest.

The steam cloud left the summit of Pele's crater, like a flying carpet in an Arabian tale but hot and ever so slightly translucent. Wisps of steam curled and coiled over the tops of Anna's feet and ankles, giving her the appearance of being shackled to the cloud. Pele stood a few feet away, still and solemn as she faced the rising hulk of Maunakea, the White Mountain. She'd climbed fourteeners in Colorado, but this mountain, just shy of fourteen thousand feet above sea level, looked massive since it trailed off into the sea at the edges. In Colorado they just flowed into the surrounding high plains. Mountains this tall in both states got snow on them in the winter. But in Hawai'i, Anna remembered Tūtū's mo'olelo that the snow was caused by Poli'ahu—the snow goddess—and her snow maidens playing winter games on their mountain home. It was the middle of summer now, and snow had long since melted off Maunakea's peak. Anna clasped her hands together behind her back, feeling the firm presence of the mo'o's scale as she went over the plan again in her mind.

As long as Pele is with me, hopefully Kaipo will be okay. She can't torture him there while she's here, can she? Anna considered that and wished her friends were with her for comfort now. Makani would be especially lovely to have nearby to help cool her cooking feet. And she missed Ilikea's well-intentioned, sometimes-questionable advice. Darkness spun in her stomach and made her knees weak, threatening to pull her under as she hoped they were okay. She refused to think Ilikea was dead. She was too grumpy to die. Not that that made any sense, but it brought Anna comfort.

Anna turned back the way she had come, searching for some tiny speck of a bat on the mountain. There was no sign of the lava-spewing fissure she had rolled through. Maybe it had drained after she passed. The eruption threatening Tūtū's home had slowed, burning some trees but remaining fairly high on the slope so far. As long as Anna could keep Pele distracted, Tūtū was safe.

They flew almost directly north, across the flanks of Maunaloa, the largest active volcano in the world though not the tallest, the landscape flying by so quickly beneath them that Anna had to close her eyes to avoid getting dizzy and feeling like she was going to fall off the cloud. Now was definitely not the time to test if the wispy cuffs would hold her ankles in place should she lose her balance.

On the other side of Maunaloa, they hit turbulence. The steam cloud shuddered and heaved. Anna's eyes flew open as she crouched lower, trying to steady herself. The jostling was too much. One big bump caused her feet to briefly leave the cloud, and she threw her arms out, instinctively grabbing for Pele to steady herself. Her hand touched Pele's dress and—

"Aaah!" she screamed. The sound of sizzling skin filled her ears as her right hand came in contact with Pele's red dress. Burning flesh, an acrid, greasy smell like bad meat on a grill, filled her nose. Anna yanked her hand back from the searing pain, but the damage was done. She dropped to her knees, the pain of steam on her legs overshadowed by the agony in her hand. She clutched her right arm to her chest and looked down at her palm. The skin was an angry red and already starting to blister in places. Anna clenched her teeth, attempting to breathe through the trauma. The turbulence ended abruptly. Still gripping her arm, she swung her eyes up to Pele. *Did she create the turbulence? Was she trying to make me fall?*

As if hearing her thoughts, Pele said, "Just checking. Guess we'll be racing after all." She gave a shrug and faced Maunakea again.

Anna blinked through tears. The wind stung her face as the steam cloud continued its fast pace to Maunakea. She remained kneeling, cradling her arm. Closing her eyes, Anna thought of Makani. She wished they were with her to buffer her from the speed so she could focus on her hand. Had they been able to figure out a way past that lava fountain by now? Were they still alive?

"Makani, help," Anna whispered, a whimper catching in her throat.

"What was that?" Pele asked.

"Nothing," Anna answered. Her breath hitched when the painful wind dissipated, and a cooling breeze enveloped her, offering relief from the stifling steam of the cloud.

Anna opened her eyes, thinking they had slowed or stopped. The island was a blur, and she quickly closed her eyes again. "Makani?" Anna whispered, barely a breath, for fear Pele would hear again, and the breeze picked up slightly before relaxing again, brushing the humid curls off her face and letting Anna know that she wasn't alone with the goddess any longer. Anna stifled a sob of relief. *Thank goodness.* That only left Ilikea. Was she all right? Anna wanted to ask but couldn't risk Pele hearing.

Anna looked down at her hand, pointing at it with her other hand, hoping Makani would get the hint. Makani turned cool, swirling around the throbbing, inflamed skin. Anna breathed a sigh of relief and held still with her eyes closed, concentrating on what came next. She'd have to race with only one good hand. It was dangerous enough to compete in hōlua when a racer was in the best shape of their life. Attempting to hold on to a narrow wooden sled with only one hand while sliding down a rocky mountain at more than fifty miles per hour was a death wish.

Minutes, or maybe hours, passed. With no vision or senses other than a gentle breeze, Anna had no idea how much time had gone by since she first stepped on the cloud.

Finally, Pele said a curt, "We've arrived."

The breeze stopped, and Anna's ears instantly plugged. Apparently, Makani had been keeping the change in altitude from her as they climbed in elevation. Anna yawned to pop her ears, the way she did when taking off on a plane. The air was much cooler this high up, but Anna refused to show Pele any weakness.

The cloud began dissolving, and Anna sank through onto the barren, rocky terrain of Maunakea. The bottoms of her feet felt sunburned after standing on that steam cloud, and she hobbled a bit on the old rock, which tweaked the sore on her back, which caused her to bend over and brace herself on her upper thighs, which hurt her burned palm and nearly caused her knees to buckle.

She was a wreck. Tears spilled over, and Anna quickly brushed them away, determined to stay strong. She could crumble later, once she was back home. Right now, she took a minute to straighten and force the pain way down deep inside.

Blinking through wet lashes, Anna surveyed the mountain. The lava here was a mix of brick red and darker gray. It was much older than the latest flows evident in Volcano and had lost most of its glossy black sheen. A service road was visible, leading to a smattering of large, spherical observatories that dotted the ridge in the distance.

They were on an undeveloped mound, and the juxtaposition between the legendary goddess surveying her volcanic domain and scientists in their structures searching the heavens was not lost on Anna. Astronomers from around the world flocked to this tall mountaintop in the middle of the Pacific Ocean to study the night sky because of the perfect viewing conditions. Recent protests on Maunakea to prevent additional telescopes from being built had made nationwide news. Some people were outraged at the proposed desecration of the special place.

Standing there with Pele, Anna felt the sacred power of this volcano and understood just how far she'd come. There was a time when she would have loved for scientists to have the coolest telescopes ever to unlock secrets of the universe. Now, she realized she didn't need to know more about the space up there if it came at the cost of hurting the 'āina—the land—right here. Anna felt a pulsing in her na'au and knew it was time to become Leilani.

There's Two of Them

Pele walked back and forth on the peak of Maunakea. Anna waited, watching, trying to control her speeding pulse.

The fire goddess turned to her and said, "I've raced every kahua hōlua on this mauna. It is all the same to me. Are you sure you want Pu'u Pua'a?"

Anna looked around, still holding her aching hand against her. Makani had formed a cool glove over the burn, soothing it for the time being. Pu'u Pua'a was the site of the legendary race between Pele and Poli'ahu in Hāmākua. Anna gazed off to the north, but the blanket of clouds below them made it impossible to see if there was a course there.

"Yeah, that's the one," Anna confirmed.

Pele's slow answering smile was terrifying as she said, "So be it."

She crouched low to the ground, the tattered hem of her dress trailing down the slope like fresh lava over the scarred old rocks. Her hair began to lift, as if held up by static electricity or a breeze that Anna couldn't feel. She put her fingertips on the earth, then dug them down deeper and deeper until her palms were submerged.

Anna could hear her chanting low under her breath, and the mountain began to tremble. A crevasse appeared between Pele's palms, and she glanced up at Anna, never breaking her chant. Her eyes no longer had any hints of black, the molten red having swallowed the last remnants of embers. Pele was pure goddess now, her human disguise melting away, cracks in her skin glowing as her ancient power trembled and was unleashed on this slumbering mountain, a dormant volcano. The crevasse grew in size, and Anna, petrified, stood watching as lava began to slowly gurgle up from its new fissure.

Suddenly, the temperature plummeted. Anna hugged her arms and looked around for the source of the change. A cloud formed around the mountain, enshrouding them in a cool mist. Light snow began to fall, and a beautiful, serene woman stepped out of the cloud. Poli'ahu! Pele smiled, and Anna suddenly understood.

Pele had never actually wanted to send a new flow of lava down the mountain.

She wanted to get the snow goddess's attention so they could race.

Clearly Pele wasn't one to ask nicely. Asking would leave her open to being refused. To being vulnerable. To being shut down. Anna could see that now. Why would anyone who'd been kicked out and abandoned at various times risk that? Nope, Pele just came in strong and terrorized the mountain in a way that Poli'ahu had no choice but to respond. Hennley would have totally been on board with that logic, and Anna could see a certain sense in it. Don't ask for approval. Demand it.

But at the same time, it sure wouldn't make her any friends, only followers or foes. The newly arrived goddess's expression made it obvious she wasn't in the "friend" camp.

Poli'ahu was ageless, her face appearing to be that of a young woman but showing glimpses of a glowing timelessness as the veneer of her human disguise was paper-thin. Her gossamer white dress, which appeared fragile enough to be made of snowflakes, trailed along the ground behind her, leaving a fresh blanket of snow in her wake so it wasn't clear where the dress ended and snow began. She kept her white hair pulled back into a tight bun behind her head. Her startling ice-blue eyes stood out against her dark face as she swept over the scene, quickly dismissing Anna and settling on Pele, who pulled her hands out of the earth and stood to face her.

"To what do we owe this *honor?* I haven't seen you on my mauna in ages," Poli'ahu said.

Her words seemed to say one thing, but her tone—whoa. She could give Anna's dad master lessons on passive-aggressiveness. If Anna asked how she was doing, she bet the goddess would say, "I'm *fine*," just like her dad did when he was hungry and something upset him, leaving Anna and her mom to interpret all the layers of not-so-fine-ness simmering below the surface. The lava coming out of the crevasse had cooled and hardened now that Poli'ahu was there. Anna didn't want to be anywhere near these two when their words became more heated.

Anna backed away a bit. "Makani?" she whispered. The breeze whispered up her arm, then went back to cooling her hand. "If these two start really battling it out, we're gonna need to get out of here. I'll have to think of another way to get Kaipo. We can hide in an observatory and figure out a plan C." Makani swirled around her waist, but Anna slumped. *Who am I kidding? If these two goddesses start fighting, the observatories are toast, too.* She'd give anything to be back on Tūtū's lānai, watching rain fall instead of standing on a mountain while ancient goddesses had a battle of words and elements, but she needed to stay strong for Kaipo. It was her fault they were all in this mess. One thing was for certain: Anna would never doubt any of Tūtū's stories again. With a great deal of luck, she would be going home with a few new ones of her own.

"Poli'ahu, how wonderful to see you. Thank you for your kind welcome," Pele replied. "Let me fix this little scratch." She kneeled, pushed her fingertips back into the earth, and pulled the crack back together, sealing it around the new slice of solidified lava. Pele rose again, the goddess in her subdued, glowing eyes banked to black coals once more.

"This little visitor has challenged me to a sled race," she said, nodding in Anna's direction, "and I thought that would be the most fun I've had in a while. She asked that we race on Maunakea for her first and likely last race. We will be off of your hill in but a moment."

The snow had stopped falling and was already melting off the sun-warmed stones. "We'd love for you to join us. Sled races are always more fun with worthy competition, and you'd at least be able to keep up with me for a little while."

"I'm not interested in your games, Pele. My snow maidens are resting till winter. Have your little race and then leave my mountain." Poli'ahu turned to Anna. "Kaikamahine, do you have a sled?"

"Me?" Anna asked, unsure of the term.

"Yes, kaikamahine. Girl."

"No, Madam Poli'ahu," Anna replied with her eyes lowered.

"You certainly can't race Pele without your own sled. Don't trust anything she tells you. Here, you can use mine." Poli'ahu handed Anna a sled that materialized out of the cloud behind her. "And, Leilani," she said before turning away, "good luck and stay to the left."

Poli'ahu knew her name! Kamapua'a must have had time to talk to her about the plan. Hopefully they were able to ready the course. Anna held the sled, tracing her fingers along the ancient wooden planks and wondering at the stories the koa wood could tell. The sled was as narrow as a skateboard. The crosspieces she'd be lying or standing on were raised only four inches off the ground by two parallel runners— twelve-foot-long, thin pieces of wood that acted like ice-skate blades over the course. They were made slick by rubbing them with kukui nut oil. The front of each runner curved upward so it wouldn't dig into the ground. The runners were fastened to the crosspieces and handrails with cord made of coconut fibers—no nails or screws were used. This was actually happening. She was going to race a fire goddess down a mountain on a snow goddess's sled.

The clouds cleared, and the summer sun shone brightly. She knew this was it. Her hula was just the beginning. This was the true test.

Pele spoke, as if reading her mind. "Are you ready?" Pele looked about to burst, trying to hold up the I'm-a-respectable-serious-goddess façade. She'd probably be as giddy as a kid in Colorado at the top of a snow hill with a sled if she thought it wouldn't have Anna thinking less of her.

Anna looked down the face of the mountain, gripping the sled that held her fate.

"Let's race."

Hōlua

Pele re-formed the cloud of steam and stepped onto it. Anna followed suit, awkwardly holding the long sled next to her with her good hand, careful not to touch the sled with her injured palm. They floated down the mountain to the start of the sledding course, the kahua hōlua. The course was a smooth swath of dark trail about the width of her street back home, falling down the mountainside, bordered on both sides by upland forest. Anna looked closely at the surface and saw the larger chunks of 'a'ā lava rock buried beneath smaller stones that filled the cracks. Tiny pebbles and dirt had been packed down on top of the smaller stones, giving the course a smooth appearance. Kamapua'a had indeed come through and put a layer of long pili grass over the dirt to finish the kahua hōlua. Anna glanced upward. The sun was shining clearly now, bringing out the oils in the pili grass that would cause the sleds to fly even faster. Anna was hot in her stained shirt and hula skirt.

The thin layer of snow that had fallen at the top of the mountain didn't reach this lower elevation. Anna kept her eyes focused down on the hard course. She waited for Pele's instructions, careful not to say or do anything to inspire the goddess's ire or cause her to end the bargain. In Colorado when Anna had snowboarded, she was bundled in snow pants, jacket, mittens, and a helmet. Barely an inch of skin would be exposed to the cold. Falling hurt but wasn't too damaging with all those layers.

Here, with so much exposed skin and the rough, unforgiving stone lying right beneath the thin layer of compacted dirt, Anna knew she wouldn't be walking away from this race if something went wrong. Especially not if she reached the speeds that would probably be needed to beat the goddess. As awful as it sounded, Anna couldn't help but be a little glad that she likely wouldn't be alive to watch Pele take Tūtū's home or see what would become of Kaipo if she messed this up.

Pele had one foot on her hōlua, prepared to stand on it as she surfed down the mountain. *All right!* Anna felt a spark of hope build to a glow. She could do this. Snowboarding Colorado's snowy slopes as Anna would come in handy for Leilani on this Hawaiian mountain.

"We will start on my count of 'ekolu. Whoever goes the farthest without falling or whoever reaches the ocean first is the winner. Any questions?"

"No, Pele," Anna said, staring down the solid slope.

"Mākaukau?" Pele asked.

"'Ae," Anna answered, ready as she'd ever be.

"'Ekahi." Pele's countdown began. Anna put her sled on the ground, matching Pele's stance with her left foot on the slender board, near the back. Anna tested the board's responsiveness by flexing her foot forward and back to see how it rocked with her weight.

"'Elua." Pele's second count rang out, and Anna copied the goddess's crouch, preparing to push off with her right foot the instant Pele hit number three. *Okay, Anna. Breathe. Focus on the win.*

"'EKOLU!" Pele cried, and both racers pushed off with all their might, taking their stances on their hōlua. Anna's right foot was forward, the way she was comfortable on her snowboard back home, too. The hōlua was narrower than the snowboard, and the slightest amount of leaning off-center influenced the direction of the sled. Definitely no carving here. Anna wobbled a bit and almost fell as she learned how sensitive the sled was, and out of the corner of her eye, she saw Pele take the lead.

"Not like where you're from, is it, girl?" Pele called out as she flew past.

"I'm just getting warmed up," Anna shot back. "And I'm from here, too!" she shouted at Pele's back before clamping her mouth shut.

Now was not the time to aggravate the goddess with her own competitive spark. Anna's heart pounded in her throat as she dropped to a knee to get her sled under control. She grabbed both handrails without thinking, cursing loudly as a blister on her right hand popped and agony ripped through it. Warm liquid oozed through her closed fist, but she held firm to the raised handrail, forcing herself to concentrate and ignore the fresh waves of pain as they washed over her. When the sled was steady, she slowly rose to standing, maintaining her balance.

Then she saw the divot. Kamapua'a had done a great job making it look like a natural trench had formed the full width of the course. Loosening her joints, she prepared to ride out the bump the way she handled all the imperfections of snow and terrain of the slopes. She just needed to make it through and hope it'd throw the goddess off her game. But wait. What the . . . ?

Anna watched out of the corner of her eye as fresh molten lava oozed up to fill the trench on Pele's side. By the time they reached the trench, Pele sailed smoothly across, and Anna felt the bumps from going over her own rough side in her joints. It barely slowed her, but it was enough to give Pele the lead.

Come on, I didn't come all this way to lose. Anna bent her knees, crouching to lower her center of gravity. She felt the increased stabilization and became more aerodynamic. *Hula lessons are totally paying off*, she thought as she welcomed the dull burn in her thighs.

An unexpected bump rattled her focus and threw Anna off balance. She strained her core and her legs to stay centered, but it was too much to recover from. *Oh no, this is it!* She raised her arms up around her head to brace herself for a sudden and brutal impact with the ground when suddenly a strong wind surrounded her, forcing her upright again. Makani!

"That was way too close. Thanks for the save!" Anna quietly said as she attempted to calm her mind. Anna felt a reassuring bracing breeze at her back, helping her speed down the slide.

Poli'ahu's board slid effortlessly down the mountain as though the rails were coated in ice. Maybe they were. Anna wouldn't put anything past these goddesses at this point. She absorbed the bumps and moved her body to account for the holes in the slide. Inch by inch, she grew closer to Pele's tattered hem, flying wildly behind her. She was doing this! She kept her eyes on the course. Anna just had to manage to stay upright long enough to reach the ocean first or for Pele to fall off.

Moment by moment, millimeter by millimeter, Anna caught her. And then it happened. The nose of Anna's sled passed the nose of Pele's. And then Anna's right foot was ahead of the goddess's. Then her body. She'd done it; she was officially in the lead, fair and square. Now this race needed to end before Pele ended it herself. Anna forced herself to remain chill and focused. Her steel gaze fixed ahead.

What Anna needed was a well-timed distraction. *Where is Kamapua'a?*

Don't Let Go

Anna and Pele flew down the mountain on their hōlua. Anna was maintaining her lead, and it grew with every passing moment. The earth trembled, and Anna knew Pele's control was about to snap. She gritted her teeth and looked between the course ahead of her and the ocean, a gleaming promise of blue too far away to offer any real sanctuary.

Anna's sled pulled a full length in front of the goddess, then another and another. The ground shifted, and rocks began to jump. Anna balanced on her hōlua, feeling nearly weightless with speed. She put on her race face and got in the zone, using the muscle memory that came almost naturally over the years of balancing on her snowboard. Ridley would never believe that this was what her training on the slopes back home had led to.

With one final shudder, ground lost its battle to remain solid in the face of the angry goddess. Anna watched in horror as the course began to steam. Hair-thin cracks of lava seeped to the surface. Sweat ran in rivulets down her back. She whipped her head around and saw Pele coming after her, still on her own sled, her eyes a fiery red.

Anna looked ahead again. Her hōlua was slowing as she attempted to avoid the danger zones.

Suddenly, up ahead where the ground was still untouched by Pele's anger, a massive wild boar popped out of the trees and ran onto the course. It paused in the middle of the lane and faced Anna and Pele. Puffs of dirt billowed from the ground as it snorted and snuffed. Anna's breath left her in a whoosh.

Kamapuaʻa had arrived.

Anna looked back at Pele. For a split second, she swore that she saw a glimmer of the young girl she'd almost befriended in the woods. The goddess's face glowed with youthful surprise and something that looked a lot like hope.

And then she hit a bump.

Pele let loose a string of Hawaiian cuss words that caused the hair on Anna's arms to stand up. Anna watched as Pele lost her balance and started to wobble. Her sled lifted off one rail, then the other as the goddess threw a leg out to try to balance herself. She overcompensated and started to topple. With a quick shift backward of her weight, she managed to stay upright. The fire goddess's contortions must have looked something like Anna's attempts at hula when she was little. Pele's arms windmilled, then she stilled and shot a smile of success at Kamapuaʻa.

Then she hit the next bump.

And this one was big. Time slowed, and Anna's eyes widened as Pele flipped up and off her sled. Oh no, no, no, no, no. This was *not* going to improve the attitude of a goddess who loathed humiliation. Anna kept her sled going as her heart attempted to claw its way out of her chest. If the retaliation for picking a flower was the kidnapping of an 'aumakua, what would Pele do when she epically crashed in front of her ex? Anna looked to Kamapua'a for some sort of sign. He watched Pele as she flew through the air, concern drawing his piggy mouth in a tight line.

Absently, Anna realized that she was the only one left in the race. She'd done the impossible and won.

But would she live to tell the tale?

Almost as soon as she'd thought it, Pele came crashing down next to Anna in a wreck that shook the earth. Time revved back up, and now it was Anna's turn to windmill her arms as she desperately tried to ride out the earthquake.

The fire goddess's embarrassment quickly morphed into simmering rage. Anna could feel the wound on her back from the lava fountain ache with awareness. The vengeful goddess was staring daggers at her. Every muscle in Anna's body was strung taut, working to keep her on the hōlua. Anna awkwardly lowered to her knees on the board and chanced a look up the mountain. What she saw was terrifying enough to nearly stop her racing heart. *Oh, Tūtū. What have I done?*

The mountain was on fire. Pele had swapped out her traditional wooden sled for a hōlua of lava and had sent fresh fingers of fire racing ahead of her toward Anna. The goddess's hair was waving wildly around her head, and her skin glowed crimson as she surfed her wave of lava in Anna's direction.

"Makani! What do I do?" She kept her knees bent as the hōlua slowed further. The ground below her was starting to shimmer, the pili grass catching on fire in little bursts. The small grass layer burned through quickly, like tinder at a campfire, and the lava rock beneath was beginning to liquify. The thin racing rails of Poliʻahu's sled that were in contact with the ground began to smolder. She was going about as fast as she would be if she were snowboarding through trees but couldn't keep this up much longer if the hōlua burned.

Whoa.

An idea slammed into her with the force of shore break tumbling her into the sand.

Her snowboard. What if . . . ? Was it possible . . . ? Could the scale be turned into a snowboard? Well . . . a lava board?

A spark hit her hand, and Anna hissed. No time to waste.

Anna pulled her scale out from behind her skirt with her good hand. It glowed brightly as Anna held it between her knees and worked frantically to stretch and shape it into a snowboard using only one hand, not wanting to risk more pain on her blistered palm. She balanced the roughly shaped board on the burning hōlua and stepped onto it.

Anna would have to leave Poliʻahu's burning sled stuck in its tracks since its rails burned. It had almost slowed to a stop. She had to move! She used her uninjured hand to push both her hair bands into the malleable scale, one ahead of the other. *Yes! It totally worked!* She held both hair bands open using both hands, causing her blistered palm to sing in pain at the tugging sensation. Anna jammed her sunburned feet into the tight bindings, and they tingled in relief as they stuck to the cool scale. She did a bunny hop off the hōlua, then a couple more to gain some momentum to begin her ride down the mountain on a course that had become a river of lava.

Anna's mind whirred. Even though she'd technically won when

Pele fell off her sled, her na'au told her this wasn't over yet. And she couldn't just lava-board away. She needed to rescue Kaipo. She cut sideways, leaning back on her heels, taking it slowly to avoid splashing lava, and brought herself to a stop with some help from Makani.

Makani helped steer the snowboard as Anna took a second to totally freak out. What in the world was she supposed to do *now*? Anna wanted to yell, *"This is SO not how you make friends and get your boyfriend back!"*

Forget the race, this was survival. She crouched down, balancing on the moving board, and took her feet out of the bindings so she could carefully turn around to face Pele.

Facing backward while speeding down a hill caused her hair to whip wildly around her face, neck, and shoulders, so she pulled a hair band out of the scale and hurriedly gathered her hair into a sloppy bun. Then she took in the scene above her.

Flames of lava licked down the mountain as if there were a river of gasoline running down the course. The mo'o's scale continued to glow. Anna remembered how good it felt on her sunburned feet, so she placed her burned, cracked palm on the surface. The relief was so incredible that Anna couldn't hold back her sob. All of the heat and throbbing seemed to fade into the surface of the scale, which glowed even brighter. Anna looked back up toward Pele.

Taller flames were gaining on her.

Fast.

Great, time to whip up a plan C. She pulled at the tail of the snowboard-shaped scale and stretched it. *Let's see what this baby can do.*

The scale expanded upward and outward, becoming a wide L shape, protecting Anna's body from the flames that had caught up to her and had begun to kiss her knees. Anna got even lower, lying on her stomach on the scale as the flames continued past her.

"Makani," Anna said, "go ahead and stop us." She ducked behind the scale, using it as a shield. Makani slowed the sled to a stop. The snowboard was surrounded.

Anna scrambled onto her knees to avoid getting burned, sweat dripping down her back, her mind racing.

Anna panted. "Makani, can you lift me at all?"

She felt a pressure underneath as her legs lifted briefly off the scale before dropping back down. A cool breeze trembled around her. "It's okay. It's not your fault. Thanks for trying. Just stay as cool as you can and keep blowing the flames away from me," Anna said, bracing to face a ticked-off goddess.

Fire licked the edges of the scale. Anna turned sideways and pulled the front nosepiece, stretching it upward so she was sitting in a lowercase U. But the fire could still reach her front and back. Rocking to the side, she twisted the bottom of the scale so that it lifted off the lava, and she pulled the edge up to close in the front. With some careful maneuvering that caused her back wound to erupt in pain and drip down her spine, she managed to do the same to the edge behind her. Now she was protected by a bathtub-shaped scale as flames pressed in on all sides.

"I'm not sure if this scale will be able to protect me from multiple angles," she told Makani, panting through the pain in her back.

"If this is it, if I"—Anna stumbled over the word—"die, I need you to find Ilikea and let her know. If she's still alive. Have her warn my tūtū. Maybe she can escape and go live in Colorado with Mom and Dad. Let her know that I tried my best, and that I believe."

Makani's strong breezes weren't enough to keep the heat from the encroaching fire at bay, and Anna could feel herself quickly overheating. Sweat poured off her forehead as she stared at the scale. *I believe.*

The scale glowed and continued to grow. It reached the full height of kneeling Anna, then expanded over and around her, forming a translucent blue bubble that encased Anna and cut her off from the flames and approaching lava, with Makani tucked safely inside. Fire hissed and jumped at the scale's protective sphere but couldn't get in.

Anna and Makani waited, watching as a furious goddess approached. Now that her wave of lava had consumed the mountainside and spread around Anna's scale, Pele stalked across the burning lava field, her bare feet causing sizzling embers to erupt with every step. Eyes glowing like red coals, Pele leveled a glare at Anna. She had beat the goddess, and now Anna hoped to live long enough to tell Tūtū.

Sparks shot from Pele's fingertips as she clenched and unclenched her hands, her hair crackling with electricity that shot toward the sky like lightning. Anna shifted her body to face the approaching storm, and when the scale's protective bubble moved with her, she slowly climbed to her feet, meeting Pele's wrath head-on. She felt Makani swirl around her legs, giving her comfort that she wasn't alone. Pele raised one hand in her direction, throwing flames at the thin, blue orb. Anna heard a low growl as the fire harmlessly fizzled out. She wasn't sure if it came from the gathering thunderclouds overhead or from Pele's throat. The scale was protecting her, but it was getting softer and starting to melt over Anna's arm. *Crap! If this turns to ooze again . . . No, I'm not going there,* Anna thought.

It was time to end this.

"Pele!" Anna wanted to shout. *"I won that race. Kaipo is mine, and you're a sucky sore loser!"* But then this would never end. And her tūtū would never forgive her for being so disrespectful. Tūtū always stressed that she should be ha'aha'a. Even if Pele had the temper of a toddler.

Anna swallowed her pride and anger and sucked up to the goddess.

"Pele, thank you for racing me," Anna said, hoping Pele couldn't tell she was gritting her teeth. "It was truly an honor to race such a skilled athlete as yourself. I humbly ask that you remember our bargain. All I seek is my family's 'aumakua." She took a breath, checking to see what Pele was doing. The goddess stared, eyes slitted. Anna continued, hoping to push it over the edge. "I understand that I was wrong and beg that you give me another chance to prove my family's worth."

The orb-shaped scale continued to soften as flames licked along the base, searching for a way through. Makani snaked in, out, and around her ankles as they waited.

Pele smiled a horrifying smile and her eyes flamed. Terror shot through Anna as the goddess stalked closer.

"No, I don't think I will," Pele said, sealing Anna's fate.

What's in a Name?

A **shudder in the** trees coincided with a crash of thunder above. The skies opened, and rain poured down as Kamapuaʻa appeared from the forest. In human form, he walked out onto the quickly cooling lava field, through rapidly growing rivulets of rainwater.

"Pele, uphold your bargain," Kamapuaʻa commanded, sounding much bigger and scarier than he ever had during Anna's time with him in the jungle. He was pure magic, a kupua, his powers commanding the storm that swirled around them. "Leilani has done what you've asked."

A jolt went through Anna at her name.

She braced her legs and steeled herself. This was her fight. Shape-shifting demigod, no matter how intimidating right now, would have to step aside and work on his relationship issues with his angry ex later. The orb-scale brightened, as if sensing Anna's renewed energy. She had to stay crafty, though. She couldn't really fight fire with fire here.

"Pele!" Anna called. "We are on Poliʻahu's mountain, and you just burned her hōlua. Do you really want to upset her further by killing me? Remember, she favored me enough to loan her favorite sled."

Anna smiled. It was a gamble, but Anna hoped the reminder of being on her sister's mountain would be enough for Pele to make a graceful exit with her pride intact. Anna could do this. The orb reacted to her confidence, expanding and putting out the hot tongues of fire that pressed against its shell.

The closest flames to Pele didn't react to the rain and continued to dance around the goddess's legs, blending with the ends of her tattered dress. Anna chewed the inside of her lip and thought through a plan D in case the temperamental goddess decided to make the entire mountain explode, anyway.

"Oh yes, my dear sister's favor means *everything*."

Pele's dripping sarcasm reminded Anna of Ilikea's attitude when they first met, and of Hennley's back at school. She thought back to the light bulb moment earlier at the crater; the idea that maybe this goddess was more human than Anna could have realized and loneliness was at the root of her temper. Maybe her fear of being left again caused her to lash out first.

"You know, I was wondering if maybe you'd want to give this race another shot next year? I come back every summer to visit, and this was kinda fun"—in a sick, I'm-about-to-die-a-fiery-death way. "Without Kaipo or Kamapua'a involved. And, you know, without the lava-trying-to-kill-me piece."

Pele slowly lowered her hands, extinguishing the flames at her fingertips. *Oh, thank goddess*, Anna thought. Pele paused for a moment, as if evaluating her options, then spoke again.

"You'd want to race again?" She slit her eyes. "You're lying."

"Are you kidding me? I don't lie. Besides"—Anna knew this would be a major stretch, but if her na'au was right, she had a lot more in common with the guarded goddess than she'd care to admit—"*friends don't lie.*"

It was a gamble to use the word. She knew it was too soon, but she needed to make a point. To hint at potential. Possibility.

Pele's face blurred, skipping over ages like she wasn't sure how to present herself. Finally 'Ula settled in, her wide, dark eyes peeking out from a cloud of dark hair. "I know what you're doing, you know."

Anna made her eyes big and innocent.

"Could you be any more ridiculous? Friends. Please. You're just being all nice to get Kaipo back and save your house."

"I mean, you're not totally wrong." Anna felt like she owed 'Ula as much honesty as possible. "But think about it. A yearly race could be kinda cool. If you promise not to kill me. No lying."

'Ula hesitated. It was obvious that girl had some major trust and power issues. Anna couldn't blame her—getting kicked out of her family and living all alone in a volcano with no one other than a massive hawk for company? That kind of life for a couple of centuries was enough to make anyone a little fiery.

So Anna waited. She could practically hear Kaipo whispering in her ear, *"Patience, she'll come around."* It took everything she had to stand still and quiet on her scale as the rain continued to pour down, dripping down the orb. Anna counted the drips, and when she lost count she thought of her parents. How her dad would be impressed with her riding and her mom would be proud but also ticked that she didn't have a helmet and almost burned to death.

Thought about Ridley and how she was definitely going to be texting her again as soon as she had a phone that worked. No human girl could keep her from her bestie. And maybe if this worked out with Pele, Anna could try it back home. Maybe Hennley just needed a bit of friendly competition to show her there is more than one way to exist. More than one way to be friends. Anna wanted to push her hair out of her face, to wipe the sweat off her brow, to check her healing hand, but she worried that 'Ula would startle and they'd be back at square one.

Slowly, like the emerging of a hermit crab from its shell, 'Ula smiled. It grew and filled her whole face, and Anna could see why Kamapua'a would want to make her happy. Anna cautiously relaxed her shoulders and offered a soft grin in return. The girls stared at each other for a bit more, testing the tentative truce.

Finally, with a quick nod of her head that sent a cascade of raindrops toward Anna, 'Ula spoke. "I'd like that. You really did race well today, Leilani."

Hearing her Hawaiian name coming from 'Ula's lips was a shock to her core.

"Thank you," said Lei.

The goddess continued, "I think I could have caught up if *somebody*"—she spun and glared at Kamapua'a, who'd gone back to looking about Lei's age—"didn't surprise me. I'll have 'Io drop Kaipo off at your tūtū's place. And I'll find you next year." And with that ominous promise, she walked toward the forest.

'Ula stopped in front of her ex, who let loose a loud burp and grinned. "Ugh, you're such a pig," the goddess said. He smiled even wider, and her wind-chimey giggle floated to Lei. "I'll be expecting a visit from you soon, now that you're back on land. You know where to find me. It's been too long, Kamapua'a."

Lei saw his eyes flare at 'Ula's use of his name. A steam cloud grew around 'Ula as the flames around her legs finally became vulnerable to the rainwater running down the mountain. The steam enveloped the goddess, and when it dissipated, 'Ula was nowhere to be seen. Lei waited a few heartbeats more, staring at the spot where 'Ula had stood. *Is it really over?*

Pride, happiness, and something else, something harder to name, enfolded her. A sense of oneness, of belonging, of two halves becoming whole.

She smiled and felt a wave of power flow through her, shooting through her arms and legs, down to the scale she stood on. *I believe.* The scale trembled and glowed even brighter, stretching and strengthening as she stood tall and felt her role in this land fall into place.

Everything swirled through her mind: the lehua, the sinkhole, the hawk; Ilikea and Makani; the jungle, the birds, the mo'o; meeting Kamapua'a; racing Pele on Poli'ahu's board. It would have seemed completely outrageous if Tūtū had told her about all of this three days ago.

But today?

Now?

Now it was a part of her history. It would be woven in with all the other stories that her family had passed down over the years. Were there other stories Tūtū had held back from sharing, worried that Lei would have laughed? A jittery eagerness filled her at the thought. She needed to get back home. To talk to Tūtū. To hear everything she knew and to tell her about what happened today. She was the keeper of the moʻolelo. Sheʻd make sure their familyʻs stories were remembered.

The fires around her subsided, sizzling out in the rain. The blue bubble shrank back to dinner-plate size and released the second hair band. Lei pulled the elastic band off her foot and onto her wrist with a familiar snap. She cautiously toed the lava next to the scale, making sure it had cooled enough to step on. The rain had chilled it perfectly. Stepping aside, she picked up the scale and held it on her injured palm, sighing again at the instant relief. The torrent of rain slowed to a drizzle and then stopped.

Lei looked up the mountain where she last saw Poliʻahuʻs sled. The lava had engulfed it, leaving a long skinny bump in the middle of the smooth, ropy river. A perfect landmark for her familyʻs newest moʻolelo. But what would Poliʻahu think?

A rattling noise startled her. She looked around, saw Kamapuaʻa staring at her, and realized the noise was her teeth chattering. Now that the immediate threat of death disappeared, the adrenaline completely drained out of her body, leaving her weak and shaking. Makani turned warm, cocooning her like a blanket. Lei took a step toward Kamapuaʻa, but her knees buckled, and she collapsed onto the new field of hardened lava.

He walked over and squatted next to her, looking toward the forest, too.

"Hū, you totally rocked that, Lei," he said holding a fist out for a bump.

"I-Ilikea would s-say I s-sledded that," she said, bumping her knuckles against his on her good hand.

Makani bounced on her shoulders, remembering Ilikea's joke from earlier.

Kamapuaʻa chuckled. "I can't believe you didn't die."

He was back to acting like the boy she had met in the jungle, but Lei would never forget the power he'd unleashed.

She crossed her legs under her tattered and torn pāʻū. There were a couple of singe marks where embers had gotten her before the shield grew up the sides. Reminders of just how close she had been to death. *No wonder the bottom of Pele's dress is so ragged if she has adventures like this all the time.* Lei cradled the scale in her right hand as the trembling subsided. Her palm began to heal at a remarkable rate, and the pain had reduced to a dull throb.

"Thanks a lot, um, mahalo nui loa," she said, heat blooming in her cheeks at her use of Hawaiian, still stumbling on her tongue but getting smoother. "I wasn't sure the moʻo's scale—" Lei began, but Kamapuaʻa interrupted.

"Hey, when did you figure out how to use it?"

"I didn't know for sure how well it'd work," Lei admitted hesitantly, watching her fingers play with the frayed hem of her pāʻū. "I practiced when you left." She glanced in his direction again. "Thank you. Really. And now you have your in," Lei finished, patting down her skirt.

Kamapuaʻa smiled. "Maybe I'll give her a little space but just work my way closer slowly. And loudly. That way, there are no surprises, and she can make the call if and when she wants to see me. But no more hiding." He nudged Lei with his elbow and grinned again. "Thanks for that."

He stood and looked around as if sensing something coming. Lei looked around, too, and tried to rise. He offered her his hand, and she took it, pulling herself unsteadily to her feet.

"Here." He held out the little bag of dried aku. "Take it."

"Aku! Thank you so much!" Lei gratefully took the bag of food, balancing it on the scale. She hungrily popped a few pieces of the fish into her mouth, chewing slowly as her mouth flooded with saliva.

"I need to get going, but I'll see you later. Makani, help her home, yeah?" Kamapua'a said.

Makani swirled around them both. Kamapua'a gave one last grin, before turning and heading back into the forest.

Makani nudged Lei's shoulder, shaking her from her dried-fish happiness daze. It was like Makani was trying to remind her of something.

Lei's smile fell. Ilikea. She wasn't here.

Chutes and Ladders

Makani blew a cold breeze on Lei's face.

"Ilikea? Is she . . ." Her voice cracked.

Makani swirled around her and tugged at her bun. "What? What does that mean?" Makani tugged her hair again, twisting Lei's head.

A cloud formed in front of the forest, blurring the trees from view. Her stomach dropped. Did Pele change her mind? Was she coming back? Lei clutched her scale, heart pounding, confused as the temperature began to drop.

Poli'ahu emerged from the mist. Lei let out a surprised *pah* of visible breath in the plummeting temperature. The goddess looked as ethereal as ever, blanketing the fresh lava flow with pristine white snow.

"Oh shoot." Lei winced.

She quickly dipped into an awkward bow, tightening her shoulders against her back pain, determined to honor the goddess.

"Poli'ahu. I'm so sorry, but your sled is, well . . ." Lei stayed lowered but waved her arm in the direction of the lava mound.

"Thank you so much for letting me borrow it." The words seemed so insignificant in light of all that Poliʻahu's sled had helped her accomplish. It was more like something you'd say to a friend who let you borrow a pen in class. "Mahalo nui loa," she tried again, the words flowing a little better than they had earlier.

"You may stand, Lei. I am glad you proved to be a worthy rider. It has been a long time since Pele has been successfully challenged. I saw that you were also prepared for her anger. That was very wise of you."

Lei straightened and smiled, feeling her cheeks burn from the praise, unsure of how best to respond to the snow goddess.

"I wondered," said Poliʻahu, "have you also planned how to get home?"

"Not really. I couldn't really plan anything past facing Pele."

"I am able to hasten your journey." Poliʻahu flicked her wrist and created a snow chute down the mountain, curving south through the forest as far as Lei's eyes could see. "If you sit on your moʻo scale, the chute will carry you down the mountain safely."

"Mahalo, mahalo, mahalo!" Lei said emphatically while looking down the long path. "Walking over your mountain slope is no joke, and without my backpack and shoes, I just want to get home as fast as possible."

She realized she was rambling. She turned to look back for Poliʻahu, but the goddess was gone. She was alone with Makani. Her brain felt tired and bruised from the whiplash of shooting from exhaustion to sorrow to gratitude and now back to exhaustion with sorrow seeping in at the edges.

Lei held the bag of fish under her arm as she examined the scale.

She needed to stretch it, but there was no heat source. Lei pulled at one side, shocked when it easily conformed to her movement.

"What the—?" She stretched the scale into a big hubcap she could sit on. Maybe believing was all she really needed.

On the verge of collapse, Lei tucked the bag of fish into the wide waistband of her pāʻū.

"Makani, let's get home and see Kaipo. We'll have to tell him about Ilikea." Her voice cracked on her friend's name. "Hold me steady a minute, kay?" Lei asked and gratefully smiled at the almost instant pressure of wind she felt against her chest and knees. She got settled into the saucer, crossing her legs and tucking her skirt in around her. "Okay, we go," she said at last, quoting Ilikea.

They took the snow chute down the ropy barren slope, down through the high ʻōhiʻa forest, down into the familiar hāpuʻu and guava-filled jungle on the edge of Tūtū's yard. Lei's eyes welled with tears as she took in the cozy house she'd come so close to losing. She uncrossed her legs and shakily stood. The scale shrank back down, and she tucked it into her skirt.

Reenergized, barely noticing the ache in her feet, she stepped over the machete she'd dropped in the grass what felt like a lifetime ago. The sound of familiar birds—cardinals, mejiro, and more—singing in the trees and the smell of yellow ginger that framed her tūtū's house brought tears to her eyes, and she wanted to drop to her knees and kiss the ground—

or run around the yard frolicking and screaming with joy—

or sink in a bathtub full of hot water and stay there till her fingers and toes shriveled up and the water went cold.

But first, more than anything in the world, she wanted, no, *needed* to find Tūtū and Kaipo. To see them with her own eyes and hug them with her own arms. Her heart throbbed like it would jump out of her skin to get to them.

"Tūtū! Kaipo!" Lei called out, making her way across the grass. She quickly hosed off her filthy feet, skipped up the steps to the lānai, dried off on the mat, and opened the screen door. Her bare feet made no sound on the dark wood or the lauhala mat. No one in the kitchen or living room.

Lei listened. Murmurs drifted out of the back room, and she headed down the hall. Her throat tightened as the voices became distinct and familiar. She paused for a minute, facing the old family photos, trying to pull herself together. Her eyes drifted past her dad's happy face, catching on the boy in the number two spot in the canoe, his right hand on Dad's shoulder, the other pumping the air in a fist. Lei blinked. That smile. Could it be . . . ?

His hair was different, shaved around the bottom and slicked back on top. How had she never recognized him before? She looked over to the picture of Tūtū as a tween, her long hair big and poofy, parted down the middle. And there, just behind her and another girl. Lei leaned in closer, her eyes darting between this boy and the one in her dad's picture. His hair was longer, down to his chin, and he had sunglasses on, but his smile was the same. And there he was on the beach, and at a luʻau, and outside a house with all her kūpuna. In every single picture. Again and again. Kaipo. Warmth spread through her veins. He'd been here all along.

Lei passed the photo of her and Kaipo from last summer and

looked in the bedroom. Her heart swelled until it felt like it would burst as she soaked in the scene before they noticed her. The bees in her belly were calm. Nothing tingled. Just a sense of peace and rightness. She was *home*.

Tūtū was in a chair by the bed. And there was Kaipo! Alive and, well, human shaped. He lay on her futon, blankets halfway up his chest. Lei stepped into the room.

Tūtū looked toward the door, saw Lei, and gasped. The empty bowl she'd been holding clattered to the floor as she rushed toward Lei, arms outstretched, eyes glistening. Lei burst into exhausted tears and noisy sobs as her grandma's warm arms came around her and held her tightly. Tūtū rocked her from side to side, and Lei let it all out. Finally, Tūtū pulled away, her eyes shining.

"Pah," Tūtū said with a smile. She cradled Lei's head in her palms and wiped away her tears with her thumbs. "You gonna get my sweater all wet." Tūtū kissed her on her forehead. "My brave girl. You did it. You okay?"

Lei nodded, unable to speak.

Tūtū nodded. "Of course you are. You're a Kamaʻehu." Her eyes gleamed. "I bet you stay hungry. I'll go heat up food. You two catch up. Leilani, good to have you home," Tūtū said. At the use of her full name, Lei found her voice.

"Oh." She knew this would make Tūtū happy. "I prefer Lei."

Lei felt her lips twitch as she met Tūtū's eyes.

"Oh yeah?" Tūtū cocked her head, and Lei was reminded of Kamapuaʻa.

"Yeah," Lei said, letting the grin break through.

Tūtū smiled back. "Okay-den." Tūtū picked up the bowl from the ground. "Good to have you home, Lei."

"Oh, and Tūtū," Lei called out as her grandma left the room. Tūtū peeked her head back in. "I've got some great moʻolelo to tell you."

Tūtū chuckled. "I bet. I gonna be in the kitchen. Come out when you ready."

Lei listened to the retreating footsteps, then turned to face her former bestie who now knew that she knew that he could turn into an owl.

Totally. Awkward.

She hurried to the bedside and did a scan, searching for any obvious injuries. He looked rough. His upper arms and shoulders were wrapped in gauze, so she couldn't see how bad his wounds were. His skin was paler than usual, and dark circles bruised the skin under his eyes. No missing eyes or ears or anything that major, but there was something different about him. Lei frowned. She studied him some more but couldn't put her finger on what was wrong.

Kaipo broke the silence, his voice soft and a bit scratchy. "Are you gonna tell me what's bugging you, or do I have to guess?"

All Pau

Lei's eyes shot to Kaipo's face. He met them steadily and she smiled, remembering he'd said the same words when she was madly chopping at the jungle with the machete. What had she been so mad about, anyway? Not fitting in? Pah. She could fit in anywhere. Just wait till she showed off the scar that lava was gonna leave and explained to her classmates how she got it! If only she'd kept that piece of lava . . . Not like she could take it off the island. According to mo'olelo, Pele would curse you if you took her rocks. She definitely did not want to go through *that* again.

Focus. Talk to Kaipo. Apologize. The bees were starting to wake up in her stomach.

"I'm so glad you're here," Lei said at last. Understatement of the year. "Are you okay?"

Kaipo lifted a shoulder in a half-hearted shrug, then winced and lowered it. "I'll live, thanks to you."

Um, nope, that was just absurd. "Are you even serious right now? You were taken because of me! I never should have picked that flower or questioned Pele. I—" Lei broke off when Kaipo touched her hand.

"It is done," he said, before moving his hand back onto the bed.

Lei bit her lip. She had thought a lot about what would come next on her trip home. Her heart splintered at the thought, but she knew it was only fair to Kaipo. She squared her shoulders and focused on her fingers, twisting her dirty pāʻū. "I want you to know I completely support whatever you want. I know you're our ʻaumakua—"

"Lei—" said Kaipo.

"No, don't interrupt. Let me just say this. I know you're our ʻaumakua, and even more, you're my best friend. But if you don't want to be—"

Kaipo broke in again. "*Lei—*" But Lei wasn't having it. She plowed ahead, eager to get this over with and have him understand that he was free.

"—I will totally understand. I met Poliʻahu, and she's nice. I don't know how ʻaumakua assignment works, but I can maybe talk to Poliʻahu and see about finding you a family that won't be as much trouble—"

"Please—" Kaipo interrupted again.

"Just consider it, Kaipo. You're hurt. You're tired. You'll never know just how sorry I am. Let's get your strength back, and we can talk. I just wanted to let you know that I completely understand whatever decision you need to make." *No matter how much it hurts,* she silently added.

An idea struck her. "Oh! Do you want to go to your ʻaumakua home? I don't even know what or where that is. Do you have a nest or something? Don't worry, I'm solid and won't flip if you need to change into a pueo and fly. I've seen some stuff recently, so . . ."

"Lei, stop. I'm just glad you're home safe. You stood up to Pele and walked away in one piece," Kaipo said. His sincerity rang through his words.

Lei reached out to hold his hand again and lowered herself into the chair next to him. She slouched down to rest her neck on the high back.

"Gah!" she cried, leaning forward quickly. The lava-induced wound on her back left a wet mark on the chair back behind her. Showering was going to *suuuuuuck*.

"What's wrong?" Kaipo asked.

A knock from the front door interrupted them, and Lei held her finger to her lips. Pele wouldn't make a house call, would she? And if she did, she wouldn't knock, right? Lei listened as her grandma's footsteps padded toward the screen door. The voices were too quiet to hear distinctly, but there was something about the new voice that was familiar. Suddenly, Lei knew where she'd heard that voice before, and her eyes widened to the size of saucers.

"Ilikea!" Lei cried.

She rushed to the front door but then skidded to a stop, completely crushed. A strange girl with brown, wavy hair, a white plumeria behind her ear, and smaller dark eyes stood in the doorway. Not Ilikea at all. Her head spun from the mood shift. Going from elation to utter disappointment in two-point-four seconds was hard to manage. She bit back tears as she turned to head back to Kaipo.

"Lei!" the girl said.

Her heart stopped. *No. Way.* Lei slowly turned around and looked at the girl on the porch, whose smile was so big she could see her gums.

"Ilikea?" she asked, wanting with her whole heart for it to be true.

"Oh, flap, sorry. Meant Anna," the Ilikea-voiced girl said.

"No, no, Lei is good. Lei is great. But how—"

"It's Ilikea! I'm an 'aumakua now. Poli'ahu found me and let me graduate early because I helped you through the fountain! I brought your backpack." The girl held the bag out in front of her.

Lei flew across the floor and embraced her friend, smashing the bag between their stomachs.

"I'm so glad you're okay," Lei said into her shirt. Something was poking her collarbone. She stepped back, and noticed Ilikea wore the pendant of a bat. "Oh! Cool necklace. It's what your 'aumakua shape is. Wait a minute!" Lei's eyes went wide as her mind made a connection. "Come with me." She grabbed Ilikea's arm and dragged her through the hallway, back to the room with Kaipo.

"Kaipo!" Ilikea exclaimed.

"Ilikea? How—" Kaipo started, but Lei cut him off.

"Kaipo," Lei said, dread creeping into her stomach, "where is your necklace?" Her eyes were glued to his chest. That's what was different! He was missing his owl pendant!

Kaipo's hand flew to where the pendant used to lie out of habit, as if searching for a safety blanket. Finding nothing, his hand dropped to his stomach, his eyes closed.

"Yeah, she took it from me, then sent me here." Lei had to strain to hear his words, they were so soft and low.

Kaipo breathed in sharply. Letting it all out, he opened his eyes and met her gaze dead-on.

"Pele stripped me of my powers. She was upset that she'd lost the race. When she couldn't kill you, she decided this was the next best thing. I'm no longer an 'aumakua. I'm a human. I can no longer protect your family."

Wait, what?!

Was that even possible?

Lei's knees gave out, and she collapsed into the chair.

"Kaipo." Ilikea spoke up in a hushed tone. "No. I cannot believe . . ." She paced down the bedroom floor, then stopped and looked directly at Kaipo as if she had made a decision. "I'm an 'aumakua now," Ilikea said. "I'll protect both of our families."

Lei looked at Ilikea. She looked so sure of herself, shoulders back, head high, face stern, that she could almost believe she was completely up for this. But then she noticed her trembling hands and knew the girl was just as scared as she was.

"How'd you become an 'aumakua without me? I thought we still had training to do?" Kaipo said.

Lei was grateful for the distraction. She was reeling from this new information. She cost Kaipo his 'aumakua-ness? *How am I going to fix this? It's connected to the necklace, so maybe we just need to find the necklace. Think, Lei.*

The voices washed over her as Ilikea told Kaipo the stories of their adventure. When they got to the lava fissure that opened, Lei listened, curious about what had happened to her friends.

". . . Lei screamed," Ilikea was saying. "I flew faster than ever before to help. It had already burned through her shirt and was getting her skin, but I pried it off. I used my wings, but then they got burned too badly for me to fly. I think I probably passed out for a bit, because the next thing I knew the lava fountain was done, there was just a crack in the ground. Makani had pushed me far enough away that I didn't get burned by the falling lava spit." Lei's head perked up at the mention of the wind.

"Makani was amazing," Lei said as a breeze filtered in through the window. She smiled, knowing Makani had come. "Makani heard me call them when I barely whispered their name. Pele tried to shake me off her steam cloud, and I burned my hand. Wait! My hand. It's better! I could fix my back, too!" She pulled the scale out of her skirt. Kaipo's eyes got huge.

"Lei—" Kaipo said. "You really do have a moʻoʻs scale," he said, voice filled with awe.

"Like I said, I've seen some things," Lei said, handing the scale to him.

Kaipo handled it like it would shatter any moment. Turning it this way and that, he admired the color and shine.

"Okay," Lei said. "I'm going to turn around. I have no idea what my back looks like, but judging from the ooze factor, it probably isn't great. Can you just oh-so-very-incredibly-gently place the face of the scale on my back? If it starts to glow, don't freak out. That means it's doing its job."

She lowered herself to the floor beside the bed so Kaipo could reach her easily and flinched as Ilikea and Kaipo both gasped. "Oh, just get it over with," she said. Lei waited, hearing shuffling movements as Kaipo shifted closer.

"See if you can just heal it enough so that it isn't a complete disaster that'll worry Tūtū. I kinda want to have a scar, so don't fix it completely," she said with a smile.

"You want a scar?" Kaipo asked, sounding confused.

"I totally earned it," Lei said.

"Okay, I'll see what I can do," Kaipo said. And then the most incredible cool sensation washed over her. She was able to focus.

"So," Lei started, "by my calculations I should have about two and a half weeks left here before I go back to Colorado." Her brain flitted to Ridley. She was eager to go home and try to patch things up with her friend. Hey, if she could win over Pele, she could probably see some good in Hennley.

"Mm-hmm," Kaipo hummed, working on her back.

"You've been watching over me all these years," Lei said. "Now it is my turn to look out for you."

"I can help!" Ilikea offered. Lei gave her a grateful smile.

"We need to figure out how to find Kaipo's necklace and get him his powers back before I leave," Lei said.

"Lei!" Tūtū's voice called out from the kitchen.

"Wait, what?" Kaipo said, removing the scale from her back and handing it to her. "You just got home. I'm fine. We survived Pele. Let's just let it go."

No way in the world was Lei about to just let this go. But she also knew that she needed to think this through. Do some research. Learn some new moʻolelo that might touch on what happens to demoted ʻaumākua.

"You sleep for now," she said, rising and stretching her neck from side to side. She felt light-years better. "Rest up tonight. Heal as best you can." She and Ilikea headed to the door, Makani blowing on her healed back.

"I'm in," Ilikea whispered, grabbing her wrist. She brought her head toward Lei's ear. "We'll figure something out."

"Lei!" Tūtū called again. "Let Kaipo sleep. Come eat."

"Coming, Tūtū," Lei called. "Awesome," she whispered to Ilikea. "Want to stay for dinner?"

"Oh, I can't stay any longer," Ilikea said, her voice returning to normal volume as they headed into the living room and to the door. "I have to go home. Oh! You have to come over sometime. In addition to helping Kaipo, I have a task for you. My, let's see, great-great-great-and-some-more-greats-granddaughter is turning twelve, and hoooeeee, I think you could teach her a thing or two."

"Me?" Lei asked. "What could I possibly teach?"

"Well," Ilikea said with a smile. "She's having a little trouble believing."

ACHNOWLEDGMENTS

The fact that this book is in your hands is due to the efforts of many incredible people.

In chronological order, thank you to:

My parents, for raising me to know my roots, even if I didn't really appreciate them until I moved away. I get it now.

My younger sister, who thinks I'll be good at whatever I decide to do and pushes me to live up to that expectation.

Hawai'i, for being the absolute best place to grow up. You have the best food, the best weather, and the best people, IMHO.

All my teachers along the way and teachers in general. This extends to coaches, librarians, mentors, everyone who helps guide and mold youth. You are so important. For this book I specifically recalled third and fourth grade at Waiakeawaena (Kumu Lee, who taught me so many Hawaiian songs and stories, and Mr. Koochi, who taught me about Pele and Poli'ahu's race) and Ms. Luna at Waikea Inter, who helped me manage my ADHD before I knew I had it.

My husband, for supporting me in my chaos and focus. For taking over so much of the other stuff so I can hole up in the office and write. For being excited for my milestones and for encouraging me to just go for it. You are the absolute best.

My kids, who are probably tired of hearing me explain how awesome our culture is. I wrote this for you.

SCBWI RMC and my SCBWI RMC critique partners, Anna and Meg, and everyone who helped get those early drafts in working order!

Tom "Pohaku" Stone, who graciously shared his ʻike of hōlua with me and helped me with the location and details of the race.

Uncle Steve, for Volcano questions. Master Beau, for kung fu questions.

The wonderful ranger at Hawaiʻi Volcanoes National Park who spoke with me about various flows, fissures, and hōlua on that side of the island to help me plot out Anna's path.

MGwaves, I love you all and so value all of your advice, critiques, camaraderie, tears, and laughter. You make my days better. Couldn't do this without each and every one of you.

Sabrina, Jenny, and Maureen, to have your support, excitement, and love going over this edit letter during our retreat was seriously a writerly dream come true. Can't wait for our future creations.

My SCBWI RMC Rooster's Scholarship that made it possible for me to apply for the Michelle Begley Mentor Program. I scored Andrea Wang as a mentor. Andrea, thank you so much for all of your help and encouragement!

WNDB's Mentorship Program paired me with Alan Gratz as a mentor (with Anushi! What a joy it has been going through this with you). Thanks for helping me use the Force to figure things out!

#APIpit for providing a platform for Asian and Pacific Islanders and for giving us a #PI hashtag! Never before had I felt so visible.

Patrice Caldwell. You are a fierce, organized, fast-talking force of nature, and I'm so thrilled that you're my agent. Joanna Volpe, thank you for stepping in and calling me in the woods to discuss what to expect on "THE CALL." I appreciate the entire New Leaf team and their willingness to meet with me early on to answer my questions. Trinica, you rock. Seriously.

Elizabeth Lee, editor extraordinaire. Thank you for seeing the promise that *Lei* had and for helping me get her to the finish line. Your insight is fabulous and I appreciate your willingness to advocate for me and listen to my ideas.

Mary Claire Cruz, Phung Nguyen Quang and Huynh Kim Lien of KAA Illustration, and Shar "Punky Aloha" Tuiasoa. Your design, illustrations, and artistic visions are incredible, and I couldn't be more thrilled with the cover and interior designs. Thank you so much for all your hard work and stunning creativity.

Pōmaika'i Iaea for being an authenticity reader to help make sure I'm accurately representing our mo'olelo, 'ōlelo, and 'āina.

The entire team at Penguin Random House, including Caroline Press, Shara Hardeson, Rebecca Behrens, Vivian Kirklin, and the best marketing and sales team an author could ever hope for, thank you for your thoughtful guidance in bringing this book into the world in the best possible way.

Most importantly, thank *you*, dear reader! Thanks for picking up this book, going on this journey, and inviting Lei and Hawaiian mythology into your life.